PUSHKIN
VERTIGO

THOSE
WHO
PERISH

EMMA VISKIC is an award-winning Australian crime writer. Her critically acclaimed debut *Resurrection Bay* was shortlisted for two CWA Daggers and won five Australian awards, including the Ned Kelly Award for Best Debut. Its sequels, *And Fire Came Down* and *Darkness For Light*, also won Davitt Awards. Emma studied Australian sign language (Auslan) in order to write the Caleb Zelic thrillers, of which *Those Who Perish* is the fourth.

PRAISE FOR THE CALEB ZELIC THRILLERS

'As compelling and intriguing as ever – Viskic's best yet. Caleb Zelic is one of the great, flawed heroes of crime fiction'

Chris Hammer, author of *Scrublands*

'Outstanding, gripping and violent... a hero who is original and appealing'

Guardian

'More than lives up to its hype... Fierce, fast-moving, violent... it is as exciting a debut as fellow Australian Jane Harper's *The Dry*, and I can think of no higher praise'

Daily Mail

'Trailing literary prizes in its wake... superbly characterized... well above most contemporary crime fiction'

***Financial Times*, Books of the Year**

'Combines nuanced characters and thoughtful plotting'

Publishers Weekly **(starred review)**

'Clever, brilliantly observed... Viskic just keeps getting better. Caleb Zelic is the perfect character to explore Melbourne's diverse culture and all aspects of its society, high and low, ugly and beautiful'

Adrian McKinty, author of *The Chain*

'Tense and atmospheric, a stripped-down crime thriller that delivers twists until the last page'

Garry Disher, author of *Peace*

'Has everything you want in a thriller – it's tight, tense, atmospheric and twisty'

Christian White, author of *The Nowhere Child*

'Caleb Zelic lives in a genre of his own: the perfect outsider in an uncaring world. Inventive, loyal, tormented and whip-smart, he stands at the moral centre of a twisting tale of corruption'

Jock Serong, author of *The Rules of Backyard Cricket*

'Terrific... Grabs you by the throat and never slackens its hold'

Christos Tsiolkas, author of *The Slap*

'Outstanding... Pacy, violent but with a big thundering heart, it looks set to be one of the debuts of the year and marks Emma Viskic out as a serious contender on the crime scene'

Eva Dolan, author of *Long Way Home*

'Adds to a bumper year for quality Australian crime fiction... The dialogue is excellent... [it] zooms along'

Sunday Express

'Emma Viskic is a terrific, gutsy writer with great insight into the murkiness of both criminal and heroic motivations'

Emily Maguire, author of *An Isolated Incident*

'Accomplished, original and utterly riveting, so much so that I read it in pretty much one sitting'

Raven Crime Reads

EMMA VISKIC

THOSE WHO PERISH

PUSHKIN VERTIGO

THE CALEB ZELIC THRILLERS

Resurrection Bay
And Fire Came Down
Darkness for Light
Those Who Perish

Pushkin Press
71–75 Shelton Street
London WC2H 9JQ

Those Who Perish was first published in Australia by Echo, 2022
First published by Pushkin Press in 2022

9 8 7 6 5 4 3 2 1

ISBN 13: 978-1-78227-632-6

Offset by Tetragon, London
Printed and bound by CPI Group (UK) Ltd, Croydon CR0 4YY

www.pushkinpress.com

For Campbell

Those who perish could have been saved,
but they did not receive the love of the truth.
2 THESSALONIANS 2:10

1.

Caleb's car finally died on the outskirts of Resurrection Bay. After a last shuddering jolt, the Commodore cruised to a stop in the middle of the empty highway, windscreen-wipers at half-mast, headlights dimming.

Shit, not now. He'd broken every road rule and speed limit, but it had still taken three endless hours to get here. Six-twenty a.m. Twenty minutes late already.

He threw open the door. Ran. Down the darkened side street towards the bay, rain misting his face and arms. He'd been asleep on the couch when the text came, TV still on, mind fogged with dreams. Blocked number, no name or greeting.

—*Anton in danger. Res bay foreshore 6 am*

He'd bolted from his flat before fully awake, typing questions as he went. No reply.

At the Bay Road shops now, chest heaving, the foreshore park opposite. No cars, just Marty McKenzie's dump truck abandoned as usual near the pub. Caleb sprinted across the road.

The rain had stopped. A pale wash on the horizon, daylight peeling back the shadows. Empty boardwalk and wide-open lawn, mounds of struggling garden beds. Everything still, except the beacon out on Muttonbird Island flashing its warning. No standover men beating Ant with iron bars, no drug dealers demanding payment. Cops couldn't have scared them off – he'd passed both patrol cars attending a pile-up

1

outside town. Ant would be here somewhere, hiding.

Lot of ground to cover, the reserve stretched all the way to the marina in the distance. He zigzagged across the grass, looking behind the pavilion and broad red gums, breath rasping in his throat. His brother had to be here. Couldn't bear it if he wasn't. Nearly a month now, desperately clinging to hope.

Through the playground to the orange dump truck, its squat shape glowing faintly in the nearby streetlight. Empty, not even Marty passed out drunk on the front seat.

A flash in the corner of Caleb's eye as he turned from it. Something moving? He wiped the water dripping from his hair. Scanned the inky landscape. Up near the toilet block, someone was crouched in a garden bed, waving. Dark hoodie pulled up, familiar hunch to his shoulders – Ant. Relief dissolved the bones in Caleb's legs. Not dead. Not lying blue-lipped in an alleyway, needle still in his arm. But was he high or hiding? Couldn't have chosen a worse place for it either way, a few straggling bushes in the middle of a sloping lawn. Once the sun was a little higher he'd be exposed like an overgrown garden gnome.

Caleb hesitated; Ant would never forgive him if he ruined a deal. Then again, Ant was never going to forgive him, anyway. He started across the grass.

Ant waved urgently, then switched to Auslan, hands a pale blur as he signed, 'No! Get out of here. Run!' Expression hidden, but fear showing in each sharp motion.

Caleb stopped. Checked behind him. 'Who,' he signed. 'Where?'
'Toilet block. He's –'

Beside Caleb, a flicker of movement in the truck. He whipped towards it. The window had cracked. Small hole in the pane, as if someone had thrown a stone.

A spray of light.

2

Glass flying. Disintegrating. Window gone, a gaping crater in the passenger seat.

Brain and body frozen.

Gun.

He threw himself to the ground. Jesus, fuck. Exposed out here, keep moving.

On his hands and knees, scrabbling across the muddy grass to the shelter of the truck. Over the kerb and onto the road. Sitting with his back pressed hard against the tray, heart pounding. Had to be a rifle – the toilet block was too far for a handgun. Barrel poking through the lattice-work blocks at the top. Nearly killed him. Had no idea they'd been shooting.

Hearing aids. In his hip pocket where he'd shoved them, running out the door. Didn't give him much sound, but at least he'd hear a rifle shot. He dug for them, fumbling at his wet jeans, fingers numb with fear and cold. Forget it – couldn't avoid a bullet once it'd been fired.

Oh God, Ant. Sheltering in that scrappy garden bed.

Caleb shuffled around. Scooted backwards, keeping the dumper tray between him and the toilet block. Ant was still there, peering towards the truck, tensed as though about to run. Eyes black in a stark white face. Easier to see him now, colour bleeding into the grey as the world lightened. He slumped back when he saw Caleb.

'You hurt?' Caleb asked. Hands surprisingly steady as he signed.

Ant shook his head.

No point asking if he'd called the cops. OK, think it through. The sniper obviously thought he was Ant, so just stay put until help showed up. Miserable Sunday morning, but a town of three thousand. Someone would eventually come out to walk their dog or wonder if those rifle shots were too close to be from a fox-hunting farmer.

Except the sniper wouldn't be dazzled by the streetlights much longer. Only minutes until daylight separated the shape of Ant's body from those bushes. Seconds.

Ant was clearly thinking the same thing. He lowered his hands into a runner's position again, arms trembling. Nothing but open park all around him. Wouldn't make it.

'Stop!' Caleb said it out loud, tried to yell. Ant's head snapped towards him. 'Wait,' Caleb signed. 'I'll distract him. With the truck.' Making it up as he went, anything to stop Ant from dashing into the line of fire. 'Meet me behind the supermarket. The carpark.'

Before Ant could reply, Caleb was up and running. Hunched low, he reached the driver's side. Cracked open the door – keys in the ignition like he'd expected, but too bright, the high windscreen capturing the lightening sky. Dog hair and takeaway boxes, a shining layer of glass across the seats. He slid in, head first. Eased himself into a crouch behind the wheel.

The truck shuddered to life as soon as he turned the key. Slow lurch forward, hauling hard right towards the shops. A jolt. Cracks streaked across the windscreen. Bent lower, arms and knees wedged. Come on, come on, turn, you fucker. Percussive thumps, hard pebbles raining down, icy wind in his hair. Windscreen half gone, sagging inwards. There, the top of a wrought-iron veranda. Truck's nose pointing to the newsagents, arse to the foreshore. He risked sitting up. Into reverse, eyes on the side mirror, the blocky form of the public toilets. Gradually gaining speed. Splintering light – the mirror shattered. And the other one. Just have to guess. Faster now, must be close. Shit, seatbelt. Yanking on it, one hand on the wheel, tugging hard. Clipped. Jarring stop, head smacking against the seat.

Stillness. Metallic taste of blood and fear. Get out, move.

He shoved hard at the door, keys in hand, half fell from the cabin. Scrambled to his feet, muscles braced.

The back of the truck had punched into the building, collapsing stall walls. Dust and gushing water, tumbled grey blocks. The acrid smell of stale piss. Iron entrance gate flung wide. No sniper, no gun. OK, breathe. Wouldn't have to attack an armed man with a couple of keys and a rego tag.

Around to the far side of the truck – bare swathe of lawn to the boardwalk. The garden bed where Ant had hidden only shrubs and silver-green saltbush.

Over. Nearly over. Just had to bring Ant home.

Caleb headed for their meeting point in the carpark, breaking into a jog as he crossed the road, bright crystals of glass showering from him as he ran. Past the shops. Up the pedestrian walkway, out into the asphalt lot. It was empty.

2.

Caleb went to the house on Waratah Street in the faint hope Ant might be waiting there. The family home, only Ant living there these days – at least, he had been until six months ago. A solid two-storey with blunt lines, every brick had been laid by their father, the rest done with help from Caleb and Ant. Up and down ladders for months, wielding saws and hammers. Comforting pride in the end result, despite Ivan Zelic's never-good-enough standards.

A tussle with the door, the key sticking, finally got it open. Stale air greeted him. No damp footprints on the terracotta tiles. Already knowing it was pointless, he made his way down the hallway. Vacant rooms to either side. Furniture long-gone, sold by Ant in the bad years. Into the small sunroom overlooking the garden; Ant's favourite place, once their mother's. Dust motes hung in the air. Blinds still raised on the long wall of windows, letting in the wintery light. Cold. No sign anyone had been here since he'd done his usual check last week. A watery droplet of blood ran down his hand, spattered on the floorboards. Shivering now. Clothes sodden and caked with mud, scratches gouging his arms. He lowered himself to the couch, hugged his body.

At least he knew Ant was alive, that was something. That was a lot. Weeks not knowing, trying every trick and contact he'd developed in his ten years as a fraud investigator. Ant had kept in sporadic contact for the first few months, replying to his

6

messages occasionally, to Kat's more often. Then nothing. Phone untraceable, emails unopened and, most terrifying of all, bank account drained.

Caleb's fault. After a long sunlit period when Anton had been clean and happy, he'd come along and fucked it all up. Involved Ant in a case, driven him to using again. Driven him to more than that, judging by this morning. What the hell was Ant involved in? A sniper. Could only hope they weren't an expert, just someone with a grudge and a weapon to hand. Had to be a few guns around, despite Australia's strict laws – dusty rifles not given up in the '96 amnesty, or hunters and farmers with permits. But the shooter hadn't hesitated to pull the trigger.

Anton in danger. A fair chance whoever had sent that text was dodgy, but Caleb would deal with anyone right now. He typed a short message.

—Ant gone. Need help finding. Will pay

An almost instant response, but it was Kat, not the informant.

—*Koori grapevine says your car's parked in the middle of the highway ??*

He smiled. A very Kat-like text, the digital version of a raised eyebrow. Wondering why he was in the Bay given that just last night he'd complained about being stuck working in Melbourne. She'd be in her parents' kitchen only a few blocks away, drinking Irish Breakfast tea. Four weeks since she'd moved in with them. Not a perfect arrangement, but a temporary one, and for the very best of reasons.

A sudden realisation of exactly how dangerous that stunt with the truck had been. What had he been thinking? Should have smashed into the shops instead, set off the burglar alarms. Got people running.

Some delicacy needed in crafting his reply. Keeping things from Kat had nearly cost him their marriage, but not alarming her was a very high priority these days. His priority: Kat tended to get a little shitty when he was over-protective.

—Arranging a tow. Explain everything soon x

He messaged his mechanic to make the words true. Hauled himself to his feet. Go to Kat and wrap his arms around her, hold tight to the happiness. Then get to work, fix what he'd broken.

———————

Kat's ancient VW Beetle was parked on the road instead of in her parents' driveway. A danger to all who passed, with an eye-catching mural of entwined bodies one of her friends had painted, every panel covered, no crack untouched. Soon to be replaced by a car with airbags and ABS braking, maybe even a less pervert-attracting artwork. Very soon, if Caleb had anything to do with it – which he didn't, but it was nice to dream.

The roadside parking was explained as he reached the driveway. Both parents and all three of her sisters were here. Damn, forgotten it was Sunday. Family Day, the whole mob gathered to solve the world's problems over a pancake breakfast. He liked Kat's family, even its more terrifying members like her mother, but a crowd was difficult at the best of times. Tired and distracted, he would struggle to lip-read everyone except Kat. A lone, confused gubba in a room full of Kooris who had good reason to doubt him.

He fished his aids from his pocket. They only gave him muffled sound, not enough to make a phone call or hear a footstep, but invaluable in helping fill the gaps that lip-reading left. Quick scan for damage: no cracks on the pale casings, tubes unfogged. Good news for his bank account – the most expensive ones he'd had. Smallest too, almost undetectable beneath his brown hair. He hooked them over his ears, tensed as he inserted the receivers, waiting for the tinnitus that had been tormenting him lately. The wail slid into his brain but stayed muted.

Brushing his hair in place, he headed for the back of the house. Blurred noise hit him as he opened the kitchen door. People eating and drinking, flipping pancakes, Kat's middle sister fishing Lego from one of the twin's mouth. An overflow of kids into the adjoining living room.

Kat was a point of calmness in the bustle. Drinking tea at the end of the table, dark hair hanging in loose curls, eyes still clouded with sleep, the tattooed eagle's wing that flowed down her arm resting on the high mound of her stomach. A white-bellied sea eagle, her totem animal.

Warmth spread through him. Five days since he'd seen her, every one of them too long.

She blinked when she noticed him, lowered her mug. The rumble of noise died away as heads turned towards him. Adults first, then the kids. Open mouths and slow, up-and-down looks. And he was suddenly very aware of his muddied clothes and scratched arms, the wet-dog odour rising from his jeans. A wiser son-in-law would have stopped to shower and find clean clothes before fronting up to his wife's family. Particularly one who'd deservedly come close to being an ex-son-in-law not that long ago.

Kat caught his attention with a wave, touched a finger to her cheek. 'You've got a little something on your face.'

After showering, he retreated to Kat's room. Some fast footwork needed to dodge his three sisters-in-law, but he arrived uninterrogated. A cosy space, filled with odds and ends from Kat's old house. She'd set up a makeshift studio for her stay, the desk stacked with sketchpads and modelling clay, old tea tins sprouting pencils. Plans for a new sculpture were pinned to the corkboard above it. A self-portrait: Kat standing, head raised to an unseen sky, her stomach rounded. The first time she'd captured this pregnancy. Always a thrill to see her work, but this was cause for celebration. Another big tick for her decision to spend the last few months of her pregnancy under the watchful eye of her doctor mother. A gut-wrench when she'd suggested it – poised to move back in together after their separation – but he couldn't argue with the results. Excitement lit Kat's eyes instead of the old terror, even with the looming date of the final ultrasound. But he missed her.

The overhead light switched on and off as he was pulling on clean jeans. Kat was in the doorway. Still in her pyjamas, an oversized T-shirt with an Aboriginal flag on the front, the yellow sun in the middle stretched tight across her stomach. Shorter every time he saw it, a lot of long brown leg showing below the hem.

She crossed to the bed, lobbed him a box of bandaids on the way. 'Stop you scaring the boorais.'

'Thanks.' She'd come to check on him while he'd showered, her gaze a fair bit more medical than he'd hoped for, but understandable – the bathroom mirror had shown the glint of crystals scattered through his dark hair. A lot more blood than seemed reasonable for a few minor scratches.

He slapped on bandaids a few shades too dark for his olive skin, but a perfect match for Kat's, soon to be a match for their child's. Only eight weeks to go. Heart-stuttering joy at the thought. Long past the bleak milestones of their first two losses, rushing breathlessly towards their future.

'Basic first aid amuses you?' Kat asked. She was cross-legged on the bed, pillow propped at her back.

'I see joy in all things.'

'It's what I've always loved about you.' An expression so dry she risked dehydration. Using Auslan now they were alone; a natural signer, with her expressive face and open emotions. She'd learned the language for him, something his parents hadn't done. Had immediately understood its importance. The daughter of a culture still fighting against the efforts of colonisers to eradicate its language.

He hunted through his overnight bag for a clean top. Down to his last one – two, if he included the T-shirt 'resting' on the back of the chair. Constantly between things at the moment: half his time working in the city, the other half here with Kat. But only another week or so till he could shift here and await the birth. Where they'd live afterwards was less certain. His cramped flat sold, the lease on Kat's place ended, nothing she'd seen online tempting her enough to make the trip up to Melbourne for a walk-through. A good feeling about the shortlist he'd given her last week, though. All three houses inspected by him, their glossy flyers only moderately exaggerating their charms.

When he turned, she was watching him, the tattooed eagle's wing resting easily on her stomach. No hint of sleepiness in her blue eyes now. Impressive, how clearly she could communicate without moving. Currently saying, 'Don't make me drag it out of you.'

He went to sit beside her. 'It's Ant. He's all right,' he added quickly as she tensed. 'But something's happened.' He gave a clinical rundown of the morning's events, possibly neglecting to mention how close the bullets had come.

Kat stilled as he went through it, inhaled sharply when he got to the part about the truck.

'It's OK,' he told her. 'I was careful.'

'Careful? At what exact point were you careful?'

11

'I used the seatbelt.' Wanting to snatch the signs from the air as soon as he'd formed them.

'Jesus, Cal. I thought you'd stopped doing that kind of thing.'

He had. He really had. But he'd reverted to past form this morning. Couldn't blame her for being alarmed; she'd designed those intricate tattooed feathers to cover her scars. His fault. His mistakes.

'I have,' he said. 'Promise. It's just – I panicked. It's Ant.' He'd used Ant's childhood sign name by accident, instead of the usual simple 'A': one hand chasing the other like scurrying insects. Bestowed on Ant by Caleb's classmates from the School for the Deaf. Reference to his spoken name, but mainly for the way he'd followed them around on their rare visits, asking ceaseless questions. It'd been fucking annoying at the time.

Kat's face softened. 'I know.' Warm fingers pressed his. 'He is OK, isn't he?'

'Well, probably using.'

'I mean, he's not hurt?'

The same fear had nestled in his guts, but he'd gone back to wipe his prints from the truck after Ant's no-show, given the area a thorough search. 'Don't think so. I'll go and see his mates today, he's probably run off to one of them. Though God knows why when I was right there.'

'He's ashamed. He's looked up to you since he was a kid and he's stuffed up in a big way. Again.'

'We're a long way past those days.'

'Oh, babe.' The words slipped from her lips.

'What?'

She changed to sign. 'Your relationship's frozen at the age you were when your mum died.'

So teenagers, then; that couldn't be good. Possibly something to examine with his therapist when he found the time to make another appointment. And when Kat wasn't within arm's reach, sleep-tousled and warm, smelling faintly of cinnamon.

'Very insightful.' He touched her arm, smooth silk beneath his hand. 'I've missed you.'

Clear blue eyes held his. 'My insight?'

'Among other things.'

'My other things have missed you, too.' She leaned in for his kiss, their lips just brushing before she broke away, looked at the door. Good idea, should definitely be locking that. But Kat's head slumped. She called, 'Hang on,' to someone on the other side. Turned to him. 'You're wanted for questioning.'

A flash of alarm. 'Cops?'

'Tiddas. Apparently there's been a shootout on Bay Road. They're wondering if their brother-in-law knows anything about it.' She stood. 'I'll distract them while you adjust your, ah, expectations.' At the door, she turned back. 'Sorry, I forgot. Mick wants a word. Rang while you were in the shower, said he'd texted but you hadn't replied.'

Kat's favourite cousin, barman at the roughest pub in town, easily able to quell trouble between bikies and bar-room brawlers. Mick's own wild days were long gone, but he was very protective of his family. A chat about 'responsibility' had struck terror into Caleb's seventeen-year-old heart when he and Kat had first started dating, in part because Mick lived right across the road from the Zelic family home. Not impossible he'd observed Caleb's dishevelled appearance this morning and made the connection to the shooting.

'An angry word?'

Kat's smile was serene. 'Who can tell?' With a blown kiss, she was gone.

Lucky. Very lucky. They'd come so close to divorce he could still feel its shadow. But somehow she'd forgiven him the pain he'd caused, all her years of loneliness. And if sometimes the thought surfaced that she'd be better off without him, he shoved it back down.

He found dry shoes and his grey woollen jacket, headed for the kitchen. Stopped at the bookshelf next to the door. The real estate flyers were lying where he'd left them for Kat last week, untouched.

3.

He arranged to meet Mick at the foreshore shops so he could check out the police response. Unlikely the sniper would have left any clues, but adrenaline could make people do stupid things. Or so he'd been told.

The street ran in a lazy curve along the bay, mismatched buildings with wide verandas. A few bluestone originals among the charmless renos of the past sixty years. Busy for a Sunday. People standing in small groups, clutching fresh bread and takeaway coffees, the word 'teenagers' on a lot of lips. Caleb wound his way through them, one eye on the park across the road. The wind had picked up, fluttering the blue-and-white tape stretched between lampposts and trees. Looked like the police didn't ascribe to the theory about teenagers letting off steam – a uniformed cop blocking access to the boardwalk, another near the shops. The town's most senior officer, Sergeant Ramsden, was talking to a woman near the toilets, dump truck still wedged into the wall behind him.

Ant's hiding place in the garden looked even more exposed in full daylight. They'd been lucky, with low visibility and wind on their side. Caleb had spent the past hour researching snipers, now knew far more about calibres and kill rates than was comfortable. Scant relief that it apparently took time to choose a position and adjust the rifle, or that most shooters were hobbyists with a limited range – once in place, a skilled marksman could hit a target a kilometre away. Some, much further.

Caleb stopped opposite Sergeant Ramsden, assuming an interested-bystander expression. The cop didn't have his notebook out, but there was a lot of gesticulating from the woman, someone with a story to tell. Witness to the shooting? God, he hoped not. Even the mildest interaction between Ant and the cops was bound to end badly, a legacy of the dark days after their mother's death when he'd slid from a heavy grass habit into heroin, financed with a string of clumsy B and Es. An over-the-top response from the cops had ended with him doing a six-month stint. Nineteen years old; sitting hunched in the cafeteria-like visiting room, eyes more sunken every time Caleb visited.

A heavy hand clasped Caleb's shoulder, then Mick came around to face him. Barrel-chested, with dark brown skin, a touch of grey to his stubbled head. The prison tatt *FUCK COPS* across his knuckles was on full display as he gripped the legs of his two-year-old daughter perched on his shoulders. Eldest two daughters trailing behind, footy uniforms spattered with mud. Always reassuring to see Mick in parenting action, a man who'd become a great father despite much worse odds than Caleb.

'Cal, mate. Thanks for meetin'.' Unrushed words as easy to read as usual. Mick nodded towards the action in the park. 'Big day for the gunyan. They found a blackfella to blame yet?'

'Only been at it a few hours.'

'True. So, you sticken around a few days? Got a job if you're interested. Standard rates and so on.'

Not a tell-off; couldn't deny he wasn't relieved. More work down here would be good, too. His one-man business in Melbourne was booming, finally recovered from all the fuck-ups of his ex-business partner, Frankie, but he needed to be with Kat, not three and a half hours away in Melbourne.

'Yeah, I am. This to do with the pub?'

'Nah, footy club. Got a tricky problem.'

Talia unwrapped her plump arms from around Mick's head and held them out to Caleb, the legacy of some bonding time over a bottle of bubble mix on his last visit.

He smiled, went to take her.

Mick swung her down. 'Sorry to break up the love fest, but you two'll have to play later.'

A few words between Mick and his older girls, money exchanged, and they whisked their sister off towards the supermarket. Unusual for Mick to send his children away.

'This job,' Caleb said, 'I won't touch it if it's dangerous.'

'Should friggen hope not. But no, just sensitive – someone's nicked Norm.'

A second to realise Mick wasn't talking about a person, but Norman Numbat, the local footy club's mascot. The human-sized suit was supposed to look like the cute marsupial but was halfway between a Tassie devil and a coked-up squirrel. Trust Mick to take a prank like that to heart. Long retired from the team, but still a keen supporter and coach of the under-fourteens.

'A manky one-eyed numbat suit? You'd be wanting the full force of the law for that, wouldn't you?'

'Considered it. Reckon we need something more discreet.'

Across the road, Ramsden had his notebook out, sandy head lowered as he wrote. Not the brightest of men, but not a complete fuckwit. And he knew Ant's long history, had been party to some of it.

Caleb turned back, found Mick waiting patiently. 'Why the need for discretion?'

'Been posting pics of Norm online, made to look like club members. Doin' drugs and stuff. Right in the middle of the fundraising drive, too. Fudging publicity nightmare.'

Caleb paused. Mick had been on an anti-swearing kick driven by his kids, all of whom had proved willing to throw him on the mercies of their mother, but this took it to a new level. 'It's OK, I can handle the big boy words.'

'What? Oh, yeah. Do it without thinken now.' The *FUCK* on Mick's knuckles wriggled as he scratched his bristled scalp. 'Goes down a treat at the pub, I can tell ya.' He swiped through his phone, handed it to Caleb. 'This sorta thing.'

Three badly framed snaps of a large numbat posing with booze, white power, a blow-up doll. Each with a different person's face roughly photoshopped onto it. All familiar, including Caleb's mechanic, Greg Darmon, supposedly smearing a jar of something over an intimate part of his body. Caleb zoomed in. Well, he was never going to look at peanut butter the same way again.

Quick check of the park. Ramsden was striding towards the uniformed cop on the boardwalk. The obvious direction for Ant to have run. Was there CCTV along there now? Hope the hell not.

Mick had stopped talking, dark eyebrows raised.

Could tell him, ask him to be on the lookout for Ant. No fear of Mick talking to the authorities. Father and aunts members of the Stolen Generations; children ripped from their homes in the name of assimilation. Put into care, fostered out, adopted. Broken.

'Possible Ant connection,' Caleb said.

'Bit of a worry. Keep an eye out for ya?'

'Thanks. That'd be great.' He returned Mick's phone. 'Any messages with the photos? Demands?'

'Nah, but they're maken people nervous. Rumours flyen they're true. And now with young Robbo's accident, the sugar's really hit the fan.'

Accident? OK, full attention on Mick now, had to know what he was getting involved in. 'What accident?'

'Big smash out on the highway this morning. Young player got hurt. Don't worry, nothin' to do with the club. Already spoken to Robbo's dad – clear-cut accident, according to the cops. So you'll do it, yeah? Club's just hanging in there financially. People start leaving, it'll fold.'

The Numbats were renowned for their ability to snatch defeat from the jaws of victory, but the town took pride in them. A great leveller: lawyers, the unemployed, tradies, business owners, a good third of the team Koori. Even the occasional player who went on to play pro.

'I dunno, Mick. Isn't the entire town going to hate me – the black part especially – if I rock up asking about their sex lives and drug habits?'

'Sure.' Mick seemed at ease with the prospect. 'Come on, cuz. Family favour.'

Family, the one F word Mick was still happy to use; no defence against it.

'Good on ya,' Mick said before he'd replied. 'I'll send you the pics. Jarrah can give you everything else you need.'

Caleb tried to control his grimace. 'Jarrah?'

'Team captain.'

Of course he was. Jarrah fucking Davies, Kat's some-time artistic collaborator and one-time boyfriend. Good-looking, talented, pillar of the Koori community – and definitely still yearning for Kat. Bastard didn't even have the decency to be unlikeable.

'Thought you'd be pleased.' Mick nodded up the hill towards the oval. 'Trainen starts in ten. You can meet him there.'

'Great. I'll –' Caleb stopped. People were gathering near the esplanade, an ambulance driving slowly across the park towards them, lights flashing. Movement in the bay, a runabout lifting on the swell. Private boat, but a couple of cops on board. Leaning over the edge, poles in hand, dragging something limp and heavy through the water. A body.

The air left Caleb's lungs.

No. Not Ant. Couldn't be Ant.

He ran.

4.

A thin-necked constable was standing guard near the boardwalk: aggressive stance, scrawny arms folded across his chest. Caleb shoved his way to the front of the crowd near him, got a narrow-eyed stare. The cops in the boat were trying to thread straps under the body as it shifted in the waves. Dark hair? Hoodie? Couldn't see, had to get closer. The constable flung an arm out to stop him. No time to argue with an aggro baby-cop. A double-back through the onlookers to the far side of the waiting ambulance, almost running as he reached the timber walkway. He stopped. The cops had secured the body, were gradually hauling it up. Lolling head and arms, beige jacket. Middle-aged man.

Not Ant.

Swooping dizziness, unable to catch his breath in the slipstream of fear.

Someone suddenly in front of him, thick-set body, thinning sandy hair – Sergeant Ramsden. Hadn't even realised the cop was nearby. Already speaking, freckled skin flushed red. '…you…here…?'

'Um, what?'

'… you … here… this …?'

Get it together, pretend he was a regular citizen, not someone held together by fast unravelling threads. Ramsden knew exactly how well he could lip-read, would realise something was wrong.

'You're a bit fast,' Caleb told him. 'Can you slow down?'

Ramsden lost some of his bluster. Happy to go the odd biff on a drunk or troublemaker, but his old-school country manners kicked in when he was uncomfortable. Probably a ten-second amnesty, with his temper running this hot.

'This. Is. A. Crime. Scene,' the cop said. 'What are. You doing. Here?'

Crime scene – the cops on the boat had made that call quickly. Had the guy been shot? Natural reaction to look at a body being pulled into a boat, so Caleb let himself. Still not Ant. Just a balding middle-aged man. Face marked by something, maybe a gunshot wound. Caleb looked away, swallowed; two strikes against him if he vomited on Ramsden's ugly black shoes.

'Sorry,' Caleb told him. 'Didn't realise. Just wanted to ask you about –' Shit, what was the injured footy player's name? Bob, Rob, Robbo. 'Robbo's car accident. I'm doing some work for the Numbats.'

Ramsden didn't bother holding back the sigh. 'It was an accident, Caleb, nothing more. Oncoming truck blew a tyre. Don't go stirring up trouble.'

'No trouble.' He paused. Had to balance the need for information against drawing attention to Ant. Or to himself; the cops might manage to get his DNA from that biohazard of a truck. Then again, if it came to DNA samples he was in trouble anyway. 'What happened here?' he asked Ramsden. 'The guy shot?'

'I can't comment on an ongoing investigation.'

Which meant yes: Ramsden didn't have the city-cop talent for blanket denial. The sniper had killed someone. Might still be after Ant.

Caleb kept his expression neutral. 'OK, I'll let you get on with it.'

Ramsden put a hand out to stop him leaving. 'Do you have any knowledge of this morning's events, Mr Zelic?'

'No.' Back to surnames, never a good sign with Ramsden. Not a close relationship, but they'd developed something approaching trust after Caleb had worked a case in town last year. The one that had sent Ant spiralling.

Ramsden was giving him the cop stare. Good attempt, but no hearie in the world could out-silence him. Nearly thirty years honing that particular skill, ever since the meningitis had destroyed his hearing when he was five.

The sergeant finally spoke. 'A man matching your description was seen running from here around the time of the shooting.' His hand brushed towards the path. 'Care to explain that?'

Ant or the sniper? Heading west towards the marina, going by Ramsden's involuntary gesture. Shut it down fast – better to risk the cops suspecting his involvement, than them going off to look for the shooter and accidentally finding Ant. Storming in, guns raised.

Subtle glance at the light poles as he pointed along the boardwalk: no CCTV. 'Running that way? Dark hoodie?'

'So you admit it was you?'

'Sure. Went that way for my morning run. Don't know about the timing, though – didn't see anything unusual.'

'You didn't hear gunfire?'

'Ah, no.' Caleb pointed to his ear.

Ramsden's gaze didn't waver. 'Drop by the station later, we'll be needing a statement. Bring your phone.'

'Sure.' Caleb turned, steady pace, the brisk walk of a man at work. In the ambulance's windscreen a reflection of the policeman standing still, watching him.

Mick was waiting just past the vehicle. No kids, keys in hand, ready to swing into action. Caleb gave a slight headshake as he passed, got a nod in return.

A physical effort not to go straight to the marina to look for

Ant, but he'd done enough damage in the past sixty seconds. Too many losses in his life to take any more chances, too much blood on his hands.

He turned right, headed up the hill towards the footy oval.

———

The Numbats' clubhouse had been built by the council in a flush of town pride after the club's 1982 grand final win. Neglected ever since. Particularly shabby at the moment, with a couple of windows boarded up and sagging gutters. No hope of money from the council these days; budget cuts had been brutal over the past couple of years.

Caleb ducked under the white railing onto the oval. Uneven surface, with patches of bare dirt, but it had a great view, overlooking the town and broad sweep of the bay. Down in the park, the man's body had been laid on the walkway, covered with a blue plastic sheet. Ramsden was still there, sandy head just visible on the far side of the ambulance. The cop was out of luck if he wanted to check Caleb's movements via his phone – only a warrant and a lot of patience could do that. GPS and bluetooth were permanently disengaged on all devices, including his hearing aids, a lesson hard-learned on his last job with Frankie. Better not think about that – Frankie was gone.

Two rows of men were practising their hand-balling in the middle of the field. Teens to forties, most of them with a lot more enthusiasm than skill. The Mighty Fighting Numbats to their supporters, the Numbnuts to everyone else. Jarrah was at the end of the line, effortlessly returning his young teammate's wild passes. Having a laugh while he did it, teeth bright. Couldn't trust a man who smiled that much. Or one who looked suspiciously like one of his own bronze sculptures.

Not jealous. Ridiculous to be jealous. A brief relationship from the dark days before Caleb got his shit together enough to reconcile with Kat. Didn't matter that Jarrah gazed longingly at her and found excuses to be close, brought her little pastry treats whenever they worked together; Kat showed zero signs of returning his affections. But Caleb could still hate the man.

Jarrah caught sight of him, fumbled the ball. Quickly scooped it up and punted it to his teammate, jogged over. 'Cal.' Quick handshake, firm grip. 'Uncle Mick called. Great you can help out. What d'you need?'

Mick wasn't wasting any time. He'd already sent Caleb the complete spread of Numbat mascot photos: six people targeted, a mix of board members and players, including Jarrah.

'Contact list for all the members, to start with. What's your take on it? Rival team?'

'Rival? Mate, we're bottom of the ladder. But it's upsetting people. Lot of talk about the photos being true.'

'Upsetting you?' Didn't seemed like it; still smiling inanely.

'Just how lazy mine was. I mean, drunk Abo? Got worse in kindy. You might want a word with the coach, though. He got a second pic last night, same as the first.'

Caleb mentally reviewed the photos. 'Ross Greene? Snorting white powder off a footy?'

'Yep. That's what started the rumours – likes a pick-me-up every now and then.'

The only person to be targeted twice, too. Could be the quickest solve in history – these things usually came down to money or revenge. 'He here?'

'Yeah. Come and I'll introduce you.'

Caleb followed Jarrah towards the boundary line, where a red-faced man was yelling at players. Familiar face, if not name – assistant coach when Ant had been in the under-sixteens. A bullish man whose playing career had been cut short by injury, and who inflicted his bitterness about it on the world. If Greene's attitude towards his own physical limitations was anything to go by, he was going to be a complete prick about making accommodations for someone else's.

Jarrah lifted a hand to get Caleb's attention. 'Wanted to ask about Kat. She OK?'

He stiffened. 'Yes.'

'Really?' Jarrah frowned. 'Just, she hasn't taken me up on working at my studio.'

'She's good.' She was, wasn't she? Nervous about next Friday's ultrasound, but relaxed enough to be working on that self-portrait. The lack of decision about the house was out of character, though. She'd gone through the flyers as soon as he'd mentioned them, made plans to see all three houses in person. But without much enthusiasm. Might be worth raising the topic at dinner tonight, a reservation already wrangled at her favourite restaurant.

He looked away as Jarrah began speaking again, kept his eyes averted until they reached the coach. Ross Greene didn't seem thrilled at having his yelling interrupted, but he stopped long enough for Jarrah to explain Caleb's presence.

'We met?' Greene asked. 'Look familiar.' His gaze went past Caleb. 'Catch the ball! I said, catch it!' Demonstrating the concept.

'Don't think so,' Caleb said. 'The photos of you seem personal. Anyone upset with you?'

'I –' Greene's words were lost as he turned to follow the ball.

'Sorry, what?'

An irritated glance. 'No.'

'What about work? Any problems there?'

The coach's head swivelled towards the players.

Caleb held back a sigh. 'Can you face me when you speak, I'm lip-reading.'

Greene turned back, clicking his fingers in triumph. 'Knew I knew you – Anton Zelic's brother, right? Deaf and dumb.'

Dumb. The old playground taunt. Thrown at him along with the punches until he'd learned how to fight back. Jarrah gave him a look of stomach-churning sympathy. A sickening realisation that one day his own child would witness a moment like this, see him with new eyes. So practise some role-modelling; see how Daddy gently corrects the silly man.

'Just deaf,' he told the coach.

'What?'

'Just deaf. Dumb's a slur.'

'Right.' Greene nudged Jarrah's ribs. 'Not dumb, but plenty touchy, hey? Wouldn't let it worry you, mate. You sound normal.'

See how Daddy forms a fist and smashes it into the fucker's mouth.

Jarrah shifted uncomfortably, went to speak.

'Thanks, Jarrah,' Caleb said. 'I'll let you get back to training. You can email me that info.' He waited until Jarrah had jogged slowly away, then looked at the coach. 'Your work?'

'Between jobs.'

Unemployed. 'Anyone with a grudge against you? Ex-wife? Neighbour?'

'Can't think of anyone.'

'Really?' Because he could name at least one person standing on this footy field.

'It's me who should be pissed off. Bloody photos are ruining the fundraising drive. Due a pay rise, but the treasurer reckons the club's skint.'

Interesting. Maybe not a personal attack, but a cover for fraud?

'Who's the treasurer?'

'That –' Turning away again.

A lifetime lip-reading, endless childhood drills with his father, state-of-the-art hearing aids, all of it for nothing if some arsehole kept turning his head. 'Could you face me?'

Greene heaved a sigh. 'Look, mate, I'm working here, and this is getting old quickly.'

'Treasurer?'

'Peanut butter guy, council bloke.'

Also known as Greg Darmon, the mechanic who was hopefully fixing Caleb's car right now. Very convenient, one of the advantages of a small town – or disadvantages, depending on your point of view. Like a sprawling family that knew and remembered all your secrets and failures: your childhood fights and brief stint stealing cars. Your inability to be the son you were supposed to be.

The coach was facing away again, but Caleb let him. Down on Bay Road, Sergeant Ramsden was getting into a patrol car, leaving the crime scene.

5.

Caleb walked to the far side of the harbour looking for Ant. The working end of the bay. Boatsheds and chain-link fences, stained concrete instead of timber boards. A toothcomb of piers jutted into the sea, moored fishing boats bobbing up and down on the choppy waters. Only a few buildings open, workers inside scrubbing hulls and fixing engines, the rest padlocked from the outside. Nowhere Ant could be hiding. No CCTV except for a couple of cameras aimed at the commercial trawlers.

When he reached the sandstone bluff, he turned back. No chance Ramsden or the other cops could spot him here, but he still couldn't risk flashing Ant's photo about indiscriminately. So think about why, not where. Ant knew every inch of this town; if he'd run this way, it'd been for a reason. If not to hide, to escape? By boat? Unlikely he'd jumped in a tinnie – as a kid, he'd vomited on every boat trip, rollercoaster and twisting car ride with almost comforting reliability – but he might have caught the ferry. A local service out to Muttonbird Island, an old quarantine station in the mouth of the bay, now home to a few hardy farmers. The Zelics had gone on a failed camping trip there when Caleb was nine or ten, Ant seven. An entire week of rain. Not much memory of it except the muddy campsite and their mother's quiet misery, their father's refusal to cut the trip short. Not a place where Ant would voluntarily spend time, but Caleb was out of other ideas.

According to the faded sign on the pier, the ferry ran every few hours. More of a guide than a promise, the midday service fifteen minutes late and counting. Caleb waited for it on the end of the pier, along with four unroadworthy-looking vehicles. Hands in his jacket pockets, collar up. Thudding vibrations beneath his feet as waves smacked the upright posts.

Hard not to think about Frankie on a day like this, in a place like this. Three months since she'd died, her blood leaching into the silvered boards, staining them black. Business partner, friend, betrayer. An ex-cop who'd plucked him from his dead-end job as an insurance investigator and honed his skills. The person he blamed most for Kat's scars, apart from himself. Yet he'd fallen for Frankie's lies again, almost died because he'd forgotten the most important lesson she'd taught him: people rarely change. Wouldn't forget it now. Carved into his heart, scar tissue tight.

At half past twelve the ferry finally arrived, nosing into the pier with a surprisingly gentle thud. Room for seven or eight cars, with a couple of bolted-down benches for pedestrians. Not much more than a floating metal platform with a lowerable ramp at each end, it didn't look up to the thirty-minute trip to the island.

Caleb waited for the vehicles to board, then went to speak to the ferry operator selling tickets by the ramp. *World's Best Dad* according to his lidless coffee cup; Max Dallman, according to the timetable. A shaggy-haired man a few years older than Caleb, with the squint-lines of someone who spent a lot of time outdoors. He shook his head before Caleb got halfway through his vague story about a missing person. 'Sorry, mate, but I see people all day and I'm a bit shit with faces. Doubt I'd recognise him.'

Never ceased to amaze Caleb when people said that. How did they function? He pulled out his phone anyway, found the photo of Ant, happy and smiling. Six months ago, just before Caleb brought the world crashing down on him.

'Might be thinner,' Caleb said, showing Max the screen. 'He's – He's been sick.'

The ferryman's squint lines deepened as he peered at it: not the instant dismissal Caleb had expected.

Hope sparked. 'You've seen him.'

'Maybe. Someone like him, anyway. Took him back to the island a few hours ago. Thought he was gunna die on me.'

Shot. Bleeding out in an unknown location. 'He was hurt?'

'Seasick. Puked two seconds into the trip. Dunno how there was anything left – spewed on the way over, too.'

Definitely not a case of mistaken identity. More than a lead: an end. Could have Ant safely home within hours. 'He came over from the island?'

'Yeah. Six a.m. and I'm hosing carrot chunks off the deck.' Max shook his scruffy head. 'Always carrot. Doesn't make sense.'

Ant spending last night on the island didn't make much sense either – wilfully incapable of pitching a tent. Caleb grabbed his wallet from his back pocket. 'How much for a return trip?'

'Sorry, mate, but you'll have to wait if you're on foot. Sea's up and I've hosed off enough puke for one day.'

No fear of that. The meningitis had chewed through his inner ear, leaving him impervious to motion sickness. One of its best gifts, running a close second to his capacity to sleep through anything.

'I don't get seasick.'

'That's what they all say.'

Caleb pulled out a wad of notes: interview and bribe money, always to hand. 'He's my brother. He's in trouble.'

The ferryman regarded him mournfully before plucking a twenty from his hand. 'Just try and do it over the edge, will ya?'

6.

The sun struggled from behind the clouds, briefly illuminating a wind-punished coastline, as the ferry approached the island. Rocks and scrubby bush, stunted trees. Steep hills rising beyond, a patchwork of bald grazing land and native forest. The bay was smaller than Caleb remembered, a neat semicircle ringed by white limestone sand.

They docked at the longest of three piers. Good choice. The other two looked like salvage jobs, their warped boards low to the water, but still in use – tinnies and fibreglass runabouts moored alongside. Caleb followed the disembarking vehicles down the ferry's lowered ramp, flinched as the wind ripped across his aids, setting off a high wail in his ears. Shit, not now. He'd suffered the occasional bout of tinnitus before, but the past few months it'd sunk its teeth in, shrieking for hours. A tone too high-pitched for him to physically hear, an irony not lost on him. Neurological glitch, according to his audiologist, his brain trying too hard to make sense of auditory feedback. Exacerbated by stress, tiredness, too much noise, not enough noise, the alignment of the stars; cured only by removing his aids. Tempted to rip them out right now but he'd need them to lip-read strangers. Moderate his own voice, too. Always a good idea not to whisper at people in a monotone if he wanted to go about his business unnoticed.

He paused as he reached the quayside. A lone dirt road led into the hills. Shop on the left, a dozen or so houses clad with fibro and rusting corrugated iron. Probably twice that many again scattered throughout the island. Now he was here, he could see a few minor problems. Like how to find Ant in sixty square kilometres of bushland and farms without an address or car. Maybe the shop, an old timber shed with bleached lettering on its siding that advertised holiday lets along with food, grog, fuel, ammo. Half a dozen rust-eaten vehicles were parked nearby, only a few with rego plates. No road rules here. No electricity, town water, sewerage; no police. The last one a possible insight into why Ant had run here when a solid family home lay just across the water.

A stocky man in a beanie was outside the shop, manoeuvring a 44-gallon drum across the dusty forecourt.

Caleb approached, photo ready. 'Hi. I'm looking for this guy. You seen him around?'

The barest of glances. 'One o'clock slot.'

One o'clock slot for what? Lunch? Karaoke? Context was half the trick of lip-reading, and that sentence was hanging there by itself, swinging in the wind. 'Sorry, what?'

The man set the barrel next to the bowser – another 44-gallon drum with a hand pump – straightened. Broad face, black beanie pulled low on a prominent brow. 'Wanna luck's lot.'

Damn it. A feeling Beanie wouldn't respond well to being asked to write the words down. 'Could you say that again?'

Beanie stepped towards him, arms wide. 'Got a problem, mate?'

Clear words that time. Clear attitude, too. The fast-boiling anger of an insecure man. Couldn't back down from someone like that – a lesson learned in the early years of his deafness. Formerly nice boys, friendly boys, had turned savage, circling him like sharks in chummed waters.

Caleb stared Beanie down, took his time before speaking. 'Didn't hear you. Mate.'

Beanie's eyes were dark slits. 'One. Of. Loch's. Lot. You hear that?'

'Yeah. Thanks.' Push his luck and ask for directions? Why the fuck not. 'Where would I find Loch?'

Beanie jerked his head to the left. Caleb followed the trajectory, the road cutting through the trees to a building at the top of the hill: the old quarantine hospital. He waved a hand in thanks, began walking.

———————

Bushland stopped abruptly at the hospital grounds, held back by a high brick fence and row of ancient pines. Beyond them lay open lawn and a handful of structures from clashing eras, including a hulking water tower that looked like a punishment for the 1970s. Some beauty in the hospital itself, a flat-faced limestone building the size of a small mansion, its block work softened by a century and a half of raw weather.

Kat would love it, if it'd been built somewhere else. The island was special to her and the rest of the local Koori community. She rarely mentioned the place, but it was plain she regarded the buildings and cleared land acts of desecration. Not entirely sure how she was going to respond to him being here. Or to his news about the dead man, the fact the sniper was almost certainly his killer. Caleb had been texting her updates, but her phone was off as usual while she worked. Not a great way for her to learn about the murder, but better than her hearing about it on the news or through the grapevine and thinking the victim was Ant. Caleb checked if she'd replied: no service. Which was fine, only half an hour since he'd had coverage on the pier. He looked again, but no one had built a phone tower in the past five seconds. Tucking the phone away, he headed up the driveway.

The old hospital was in better repair than he'd expected, the windows intact, new roof tiles, a sign of ongoing renovations in the paint tins stacked by the front door. Lights were on inside, a handful of cars parked out the front. Not a squat like he'd assumed. A new hotel, getting set up before the marketing campaign? If Ant was gainfully employed, it'd be a very good sign.

Movement caught Caleb's eye as he neared the front door – someone working on a gazebo in the garden. Ant. Halfway up a ladder, drill in hand, dark head bent in concentration as he fixed the wooden fretwork. At last. Like surfacing to take a breath after a too-deep dive.

Ant glanced over as Caleb approached, did a double take. His shoulders slumped, but he descended the ladder with an air of resignation. Clothes more muted than usual; jeans and a blue shirt and jacket, everything slightly too big or too small. He set the drill on a step, signed with loose flicks of his bony wrists, 'How'd you find me?'

'Skills.'

A glint in Ant's brown eyes. 'Yeah? Whose?'

Usual quick humour, but he was too thin, cheekbones jutting in a hollowed face. Dark needle marks dotted the back of his hands. There'd be more beneath those borrowed clothes, marking his legs and arms, any working veins he could find.

The stomach-drop sensation of the ferry ride over. Despite everything, Caleb had hoped he was wrong, that those days were long gone.

Ant's smile fell as he caught the examination. 'Yeah, I fucked up as badly as you thought I would. Happy?'

'I've been shitting myself, you selfish prick! You disappear for months, don't reply to messages. Then you run off again this morning. How fucking hard would it've been to let me know you're OK?'

Jaw jutting, Ant signed slowly, 'Pretty hard.'

Fuck. A how-not-to of reconciliations, nothing like the conversation he'd practised. Start again: calm hands and expression, lots of 'I' statements. 'I'm sorry. I've been worried. I *am* worried. What happened this morning? Did you know the cops found a body? Middle-aged guy, floating in the water. Think he was shot.'

'Got nothing to do with me, I was just there.'

'Why? Who was he?'

Ant's attention shifted to something behind Caleb: an open-tray ute pulling up to the hospital, a fair-haired woman at the wheel. 'I'm busy,' Ant said. 'You should go.'

'Tell me what's happening first. You're obviously in trouble, let me help.'

'Jesus. You haven't changed at all, have you? Just completely unstoppable. I don't need your help, so will you kindly fuck off.' He stalked past Caleb towards the ute.

Couldn't get any clearer than that. But if Caleb left now, a chill certainty Ant would disappear forever. Ant was a bolter – at the first sign of stress he lit up, shot up or ran off. And there was nothing in their relationship to stop him. Caleb had made sure of that.

Ant was unloading the ute, the driver out and helping, her short blonde hair lifting in the breeze. Not a big job. Only a few seconds and he'd be done and through that front door. Caleb jogged towards them.

The ute was pulling away when he reached Ant's side. Half a dozen cardboard cartons on the ground, filled with tins and bulk bags of rice and flour. Ignoring him, Ant bent to grab a closed box. The largest one there, a clear effort to lift it. Always trying to prove himself. Maybe Kat was right about the whole shame thing; it'd certainly explain Ant's overreaction earlier.

'Just give me ten minutes,' Caleb said, then broke off.

Ant had gone rigid, staring at the driveway where the package had stood, the dark stain on the gravel. Red. Wet. He dropped the box, stumbled backwards, bloodied hands held away from him. God, what was it? Caleb made himself go to the carton, gingerly open the flaps.

Orange-brown fur, sharp muzzle: a fox. Glassy-eyed and stiff. Shot, its grey entrails spilling from a wound in its side. Next to its head lay a folded sheet of paper, stirring slightly in the wind as though the animal was still breathing. He picked it up, eased apart its blood-stiff folds. Plain block letters in black ink.

I'm watching

7.

Ant was motionless, his eyes on the fox. Looking up, he met Caleb's gaze, signed shakily, 'Guess I should bury it.'

Not the response of someone taken completely by surprise. So there'd been other notes, maybe other dead animals. Killed by the same person who'd fired at Caleb and Ant this morning? Murdered a man? Farmers shot foxes all the time – an introduced species, predator of native and farm animals alike. But rarely with rifles powerful enough to punch gaping wounds through flesh and bone.

Resisting the urge to grill him, Caleb refolded the note, slipped it in his jacket pocket. Asked the most pressing question. 'Want to tell someone first?'

Like the cops. Even if Ant didn't want to talk to them, someone else here might. Should.

'Yeah,' Ant said, 'but he's busy right now, and there are a few fragile people around. I don't want them seeing it.' He edged closer to the fox's bloodied body, swallowed hard.

Caleb had seen worse, done worse. But something about dead animals ... Well, he was going to have to toughen up to deal with the dead guinea pigs and rabbits that came with parenthood. He shoved back his sleeves, hoisted the carton. The wet cardboard sagged against his forearms. Cold, like dead flesh. He suppressed a shudder. Should've left his sleeves down, burned the jacket.

They buried the fox in the shelter of the pines lining the fence, just out of sight of the hospital. Slow work, taking it in turns to chip at the root-tangled ground with a shovel Ant had borrowed. Grit from the turned earth blowing in their faces.

When they'd finished, Caleb set the shovel against a tree, faced Ant. 'This has happened before?' A glimpse of blood smearing his hands as he signed. He wiped them on his jeans.

Ant's eyes followed the movement. 'Three times. Not like that, though – the foxes were dumped on the porch at night. No box.'

Very public. And a significant change of methods if Ant was right.

'Who saw them?' Caleb asked. 'You, or someone else?'

'Everyone. Well, some people were smart enough not to look, after the first one.'

'They're connected to the guy who was killed?'

Ant hesitated. 'Started a few days after he arrived.'

So almost certainly. The delivery driver probably wasn't behind it, given her lack of anonymity. Someone had dumped that box on the ute so it would arrive in daylight, just hours after the man's murder. A man linked to a spate of threats. Linked to Ant.

This just kept getting worse. Ant would probably crack the shits if he asked too many more questions – already standing very stiffly – but he had to try.

'Same thing written on all the notes?' Caleb asked.

'No, the first couple said *Leave.*'

'What about the one before this?'

A few seconds before Ant answered. '*Final warning.*'

Not a threat: a promise delivered and executed.

Ant was looking at him, the pines casting shadows across his gaunt face, obscuring his expression. 'We can clean up in my room,' he finally said, turning for the driveway.

OK, a chance here; don't fuck it up. He jogged after Ant.

Someone had taken the boxes inside but the dried blood was still there, marking the gravel like a rust stain. Ant skirted around it to the old hospital, opened the front door. A shock of colours and textures. Paisley wallpaper and swirled purple carpet, the narrow staircase at the back of the foyer painted burnt orange. Matching orange doors to either side.

Caleb stopped just inside. 'Jesus. I thought this place was a hotel.'

'It was, back in the 70s. Failed one, anyway. It's a clinic now.'

'For STDs?'

A quick grin. 'Rehab. Only been open four months, renos are underway.'

Rehab. Ant was doing rehab. And voluntarily, not by a court order. A new shine on the day, casting the world in a warmer light. Be good to know more about the place though, run the usual checks.

'Yes, it's accredited,' Ant said before he could ask. 'And no, you don't get to vet it or do any of the other things you're dying to do. Run by the fully qualified Doctor L.O.C.K.E.' Spelling the name on his fingers.

Either the correct version of 'Loch' or just Ant's usual slapdash style. Near enough, good enough, fingerspelling the Anton Zelic way.

'Am I allowed to ask how long you've been here?'

'Three weeks.' Ant set off for the stairs.

Three weeks. Twenty-one days. And he hadn't bothered letting Caleb know he was alive, let alone getting treatment. Could kill him.

Ant's fingerspelling was vindicated when they reached the upstairs landing, the door opposite labelled *Dr Ian Locke*. A more tranquil space up here; polished timber and gentle creams and blues, the smell of turps lingering. Good sign that money was being spent on the patients first, not PR-worthy foyers, but how was Ant paying the fees? Private place like this, being renovated, had to cost more than he could earn doing odd jobs. Or even burglaries.

Some effort required not to ask. Quite a lot of effort. Caleb shoved his hands in his pockets as a precaution, followed Ant down a short hallway. A few doors were open, showing simply furnished bedrooms, the people inside fitting Ant's description of 'fragile': wan and shaky, two of them curled in their beds. Five patients in total, according to Ant's reluctant rundown, with daily visits by a nurse, cook and cleaner. The staff all islanders; good way to keep the locals happy.

Ant's room had the same soothing colours and simple furniture as the others, the narrow window giving a good view of the treetops. Neat for him, bed almost made, a couple of garish shirts slung over a hard-backed chair.

Caleb scrubbed his hands and arms clean at a small basin in the corner. Had a go at the dabs of blood on his jeans, rubbing them with a cake of soap, managed to smear them around nicely. A near heart-attack as he reached for the towel, came eye to eye with a ceramic figurine the size of his head sitting on a shelf. Half-cherub, half the stuff of nightmares, grinning maniacally while holding a four-leaf clover. Coming to suck his soul.

'What the fuck is that?'

Ant looked doubtfully at the statuette, but had a go at defending it. 'Lucky Louie. He was a present.'

From an enemy? Caleb retreated at Ant's pre-emptive scowl. Pretended to look at his serviceless-phone while Ant cleaned up and changed clothes. Overt modesty wasn't usually one of Ant's problems, but Caleb didn't want a repeat of the scene in the garden.

Ant finally flopped onto the bed, waving a hand towards Caleb's phone. 'No reception. No internet either. Have to go to the shop for that.'

'Why?'

'Tranquillity etcetera. Plus, no infrastructure.' He went to open the bedside drawer, changed his mind. 'So, short version of things – the dead man was a patient here. Peter Taylor. Came about two weeks ago. Quiet guy, birdwatcher, but sneaky as fuck. Like I said, the foxes started a few days after he arrived. They freaked everyone out, but Taylor got even quieter, creeping around like he was up to something.'

Where were the cops? They should have been swarming all over the place, digging into the dead man's life. Unless they didn't know he'd been a patient.

'Taylor got any family?' he asked Ant. 'Spouse?'

'Estranged, I reckon. Never had any visitors, and he always clammed up in that part of group therapy. Well, clammed up more.'

Group therapy sessions about families. Pretty sure an older brother would come under that topic. Excellent. Feeling really relaxed about that.

'Does Doctor Locke know Taylor's dead?' Caleb asked.

'Yeah, of course. I told him.'

'But he hasn't spoken to the cops?'

Skin tightened over the sharp bones in Ant's face. 'I knew you'd do that! He's protecting me. You know they'll jump all over me if they find out I was there.'

Might as well double-down now Ant was pissed-off. 'Why *were* you there?'

Mouth set, Ant yanked open the bedside drawer, pulled out a tobacco pouch and saucer. When had Ant switched to rollies? More to the point, when had rehab allowed smoking?

A long wait while Ant assembled the cigarette and lit it, took a few drags. Keeping it between his fingers, he signed, 'If that's your unsubtle way of asking if I was doing something dodgy, the answer's no. I was trying to work out what Taylor was up to. He turned up at the shop when I was there last night, around eight-thirty. Scared witless, asking about ferry times. Got more freaked out when he realised he'd missed the last one, ran around asking people if he could borrow a tinnie. Islanders looking at him as if he wanted their first born.' The upwards sweep of the sign flicked ash onto Caleb's chest. 'Oops.'

Caleb brushed the front of his T-shirt. 'Many people in the shop?'

'Packed. Saturday night drinks.' Making a show of it, Ant tapped a millimetre of ash onto the saucer. 'Anyway, he ended up tailing it back to the clinic, but it was obvious he was going to catch the first ferry out this morning. So I popped along too. He tried to shake me off when we got to the foreshore, but I snuck along in the shadows, doing ninja shit.' The cigarette wavered in his hand. 'And then – *bang* – he was in the water. Guess I made a noise, because the next thing I knew, bullets were flying everywhere. Think I spooked the shooter.'

Just a bit. But the killer must be confident they hadn't been ID'd – Ant would have been easy to follow back here and pick off as he wandered the grounds. Terrifyingly so.

'So you didn't see them?'

'No, I just threw myself at the nearest bush and sat there shitting myself. Thought I was hallucinating when you showed up. Regressing. Like I was ten – you coming to the rescue at the park when Jasper Halloway was about to kick my head in.' Ant frowned. 'Hang on, how'd you know I was there?'

'Anonymous text. Came around three.'

'That's weird, no one knew I was going. Or has your number.'

Possibly not a huge mystery. 'Phone's on my website. You chat to anyone at the shop?'

'Oh. Got the ferry ticket there.' Looking sheepish. 'They run a tab for patients.'

'Ninja shit.'

Ant raised a faint smile, but his knobbled shoulders were hunched again, the looseness of his storytelling gone. 'I thought it'd be safe now, you know. That Taylor had just brought the trouble with him.'

Maybe he had – the speed of events suggested it – but it looked like the trouble was here to stay.

I'm watching

An obscure message for such a gruesome delivery. Because the intended target knew what it meant, or because everyone here was in danger?

Ant's belief that the cops wouldn't link Taylor to the clinic wasn't a complete fantasy. They'd do it eventually, but if the man was a loner without family it'd come down to grunt police work of subpoenaed bank records and emails. Days for that, even weeks. Ant roaming the island in the meantime, very likely attempting more investigative work.

'You should leave,' Caleb told him.

'Can't. Got a month to go.'

'I'll find you another rehab.'

'No.'

Why did he always have to be so stubborn? Caleb grabbed every one of his instincts and made them shut the fuck up. 'How about I have a poke around, then? See if I can work out what's happening.' When Ant didn't answer, he went on. 'A few hours. Talk to some people here, the delivery woman. I can be on the five o'clock ferry.'

Had to be – he couldn't stay here without decent phone service. Over an hour now, the urge to bolt down to the quay and check messages growing stronger each second.

'With me,' Ant said. 'Not by yourself.'

'OK.'

'And not here. This is the best rehab I've ever done, I don't want you stomping around upsetting people.'

'I won't upset anyone.'

Ant took a last drag and stubbed out the butt. Exhaled a long stream of smoke at Caleb.

'Got it,' Caleb said. 'Just the islanders.'

For now. None of the other patients seemed physically capable of holding a rifle steady, but he needed to talk to Doctor Locke, find out exactly why the man hadn't spoken to the police.

'Well, come on.' Ant stood, made a hurry-gesture. 'We're not here to fuck spiders.'

8.

Ant borrowed the clinic's communal jeep, a bright yellow hard-top as rusted and dinged up as all the other vehicles on the island. The car Taylor had been driving last night, according to Ant. Now they were on the move, he seemed almost back to his normal self, keeping up a constant stream of Auslan as they careered down the hill, his hands rarely touching the wheel. Apparently the blonde delivery woman, Skye, ran the shop. Born on the island, thirty-three, bored, an arsehole husband. The wealth of information wasn't surprising; there were a lot more of their mother's genes in Ant than their father's. Five minutes with anyone, and he usually knew the names of their celebrity crush and least-favourite child.

He pulled up outside the shop, stopped a bee's dick short of a white van with a bumper sticker: *Save the planet, fuck a Greenie.* 'Keep wondering about that sticker,' he told Caleb. 'You reckon it's pro or anti environmentalism?'

Caleb released his death-grip on the seatbelt. 'Tell them you're a Greenie, find out.' He pulled out his mobile – still no cover. Have to get a satellite phone before he set foot on this island again. Blood pressure couldn't handle it.

'Told you,' Ant said. 'No service.'

'Yeah. Back in a sec.' He got out, jogged past the houses towards the pier. A couple of men stopped their work mending a front fence to stare as he passed. He nodded, got slight nods in return.

His phone buzzed as he reached the end of the pier. Two texts coming through, both replies from Kat. What was probably a troubled 'OK thanks' to his message about Taylor's murder; a much more effusive one wishing him luck finding Ant on the island. He video-called, waited as the tiny wheel of despair circled on the screen. Gave up. A text was too blunt an instrument for news about slaughtered animals and threatening notes; Kat had always held a place in her heart for Ant, even when Caleb had closed his. Doting big sister, Ant the equally besotted little brother. Caleb sent her a quick update about Ant and rehab instead, received an immediate answer.

—*That's great!! How is he? I'm so proud of him*

—Rough but OK. Need to look into few things. Patchy service, will keep checking. Home in time for our date

— *Everything OK?*

— Just making sure he's safe. Tell you everything when I get back

It took her a few seconds to reply.

—*Tell Ant I miss him. Tell Caleb to be careful x*

—I will and he will x

He found Ant waiting near a jumbled row of oversized letterboxes outside the shop. Around thirty of them, fashioned from old fridges and barrels, salvaged timber. Recurring surnames along the line. The flat-tray ute Skye had been driving was parked behind them, easily accessed through the shop's service door – and by anyone wanting to shove an extra box among the groceries. There went his hope of easily identifying the note-writer.

'Worried about Kat?' Ant asked as they crossed to the veranda.

'Cautiously alert.' A feeling he hadn't handled that conversation well, Kat's sign-off seemed tense even with that *x* at the end. Should he have said less or more?

'But everything's still on track?'

47

'Yeah.'

'That's great,' Ant's face brightened. 'Really great. How is she? Feel bad I haven't seen her.'

'She's good, sends her love.'

'What about you? You going OK with it all?'

'Yeah.'

Ant gave him a long look. 'Good conversation, thanks for sharing.' He climbed the steps to the shop's wide veranda. Skye was visible through the window, serving a customer, wearing a T-shirt and low-slung jeans despite the cold. Lanky build of a track and field runner.

Stepping out of sight, Caleb signalled for Ant to follow him. 'Does Skye know I'm deaf?'

'Up yourself much? Doubt I've mentioned you.'

Good. Skye might not be top of his suspect list but she was on it, and it was much easier to observe someone when they didn't know he could lip-read. Easier too, not to have to deal with all the You Poor Thinging.

'Don't tell her. And don't sign – I want to keep a low profile.'

'Of course,' Ant said out loud. 'I wouldn't want to hinder your exhausting need to overcompensate.' Theatrical enunciation and delivery, spreading his arms wide to an invisible audience. An easy-to-read arsehole at least. Familiarity. It had been a voices-only household in their father's presence, Ivan forever convinced that using sign was akin to giving up.

Caleb pushed past Ant to the door, and into a barn-like room. Warm; a fire blazing in a potbellied stove. Part grocery store, part café, with an ancient computer and payphone down the back. A lot of alcohol on the half-stocked shelves, along with a disturbing amount of mosquito repellent. Someone had put effort into the café section: mismatched chairs painted cheerful colours, tables made from wooden pallets, odds and ends. The kind of decor that cost big money in the city but would be genuine salvage around here.

Skye was wiping down the coffee machine as she half-listened to the customer. An angular face softened by a short, feathered haircut. The kind of fair skin that burned easily. Her slightly glazed look morphed into a genuine smile when she noticed Ant. 'Hey, fancy seeing you again.' Audible pitch and perfectly formed words: a lip-reader's dream. Caleb should carry gold stars for these occasions – real gold, wouldn't have to buy many. She turned her bright smile on him. 'And you must be the famous investigator brother Anton's been boasting about. Two peas in a pod. Caleb, right?'

Jesus Christ, so much for the low profile. Ant didn't meet his stare, studying the display of teas behind the counter with urgent interest. At least he seemed to have left out any mention of deafness; Skye hadn't done the usual checks for hearing aids or started speaking faster, slower, louder.

The middle-aged woman she'd been serving had turned to examine him. Faded brown hair and eyes, as though the bleach she smelt faintly of had stripped her colour. Two goats on the front panels of her hand-knitted cardigan, very ugly goats with tufted chin hair and watchful eyes.

He dragged his gaze from them, realised Ant was halfway through telling the women about Taylor's death. '. . . in town this morning. Shot.'

Skye's mouth opened. 'That was him? I heard about it on the radio. The poor man.' Her eyes went to the computer in the back corner. 'He was in here all the time, but I never really spoke to him.'

The ugly cardigan woman shifted. 'Another incomer, bringing trouble.' Dry lips pursed at something Skye said. 'Like you're not thinking it too. Rude man. Nearly killed me when I was turning into my driveway last night. Came flying past, no headlights.'

Just before Taylor had turned up at the shop, looking shaken. Or thereabouts. Dark by 6:30 this time of year, so a two-hour window. Could be relevant, could just be evidence of a bad driver.

'Which way was he headed?' Ant asked. 'Did you see anyone else?'

Caleb briefly closed his eyes. He'd warned Ant not to mention the notes or investigation, hadn't thought to tell him not to interrogate people.

Ugly Cardigan set her cup on the counter. 'I'll see you later, Skye.' She paused in the doorway, then made a beeline for the fence repairers across the road. Caleb gave it thirty minutes before the entire island knew they'd been asking about Taylor.

He smacked Ant's arm as Skye turned to the sink with the dirty coffee cup, then signed quickly, 'Get the computer's search history. Two weeks. *Try* to make it subtle.' Might have overemphasised 'try', his cheek smarting where he'd dragged his finger down it.

Ant displayed one of his own fingers as he said out loud, 'I'm going to check emails. Have a coffee while you wait.' He sauntered away.

More than a little suspicious of that suggestion. Still, the espresso machine looked good, and Skye had turned to him expectantly.

'Long black, thanks.'

She went about preparing it, spoke while still facing the machine.

'Sorry,' Caleb said. 'What was that?'

Another gold star awarded as she immediately turned him. 'You must be happy about your brother. He's looking good. Put on a lot of weight.'

'Really?' Jesus. Didn't bear thinking about.

'Much better.' She placed his coffee in front of him, touched his arm. 'It must be hard for you.'

'Harder for him.' Caleb picked up the cup. Could a liquid look limp? Apparently yes. Limp and anaemic, exhausted by its own existence. And surprisingly bitter, given its weakness. That bastard, Ant.

'How is it?' Skye asked.

'Yeah, um, good.'

'That bad, huh?' She slid the sugar canister towards him. 'I swear I'm doing everything the instructions tell me to. Are you here to investigate Taylor's murder?' Slipping it into the conversation without pause; nicely done.

No point in lying outright to someone that sharp, have to cover with a partial truth. 'Yeah. I don't want Ant to know, but it's obviously connected to the clinic. What do you know about the guy who runs it?'

'Doctor Locke? Seems decent. Patient, anyway. Came in here a fair bit when he first started the place, trying to get friendly with us locals. Didn't get much love in return.'

'Why?'

A small shrug. 'People don't like change around here.'

But some of them appeared to like Ant. 'Did you text me about Ant?'

'Text you?' Her bewilderment seemed genuine.

'Just chasing an unknown number. Where does the woman with the ug–' He caught himself. '– amazing goat cardigan live? Anywhere near the clinic?'

Skye smirked. 'Joyce. No, she's out near Muttonbird Cove, miles from the clinic.' Her gaze travelled across his face towards his hair; he resisted the urge to check it was covering his aids. 'I do haircuts, you know. Could do yours.' Taking a lock between her fingers. 'Nice hair, wouldn't want to take much off.'

'Um,' he said. Couldn't think how to continue.

She lowered her hand as Ant appeared, holding a wad of folded paper. 'Hey, Skye, I've been meaning to ask. We've got a fox problem up at the clinic. D'you know anyone with a rifle we could borrow?'

For fuck's sake, could he be any more obvious?

Skye seemed undisturbed. Leaning against the counter, her angular face relaxed. 'Shouldn't be too hard, half the island owns one.'

9.

'That was painful to witness,' Ant told him when they were back on the veranda. '"Oh no, a woman's touching my hair, and me a married man."' Still speaking instead of signing, possibly in support of Caleb's wish to keep a low profile, possibly to be a pain.

'I was working out if she was trying to distract me.'

'Root you, more like. You know, for an observant person you can be surprisingly thick about relationships.'

Could be his epigraph: *Here lies Caleb, keen-eyed but clueless.* The closer he was to someone, the more unfocused his gaze.

Across the road, the fence-menders had been joined by the guy in the black beanie he'd enjoyed chatting with earlier. Hard stares from all three of them. Ugly Cardigan Joyce had clearly done a first-rate job at explaining what he and Ant were up to. Excellent – nothing like stirring up resentment to make a difficult job harder.

Ant waved to the trio as he descended the steps, didn't get a response. 'Friendly bunch. The big bloke with the beanie's Arlo, Skye's husband. Did I mention she's got a husband? Bald. Hates men with good hair.' He passed Caleb the printed pages. 'Nothing interesting unless you're into Copro Cops dot com or Hot Pegging Mammas.' A sideways look. 'No judgement.'

'None at all, Ant. You must be getting bored here.' As they walked to the jeep, Caleb leafed through four pages of private information, the result of people not knowing to delete their search history on a public computer. Everything from banking and self-help sites to sewing patterns and cancer treatments. Nothing obviously linked to Taylor, but it could be worth pursuing the cancer angle. People could behave recklessly when they had nothing left to lose.

Caleb looked up as they reached the battered jeep 'Was Taylor sick?'

'Seemed healthy to me.'

Which was more than could be said for most of the patients. 'He doing rehab for drugs?'

'Dunno. Kept quiet about himself. Never seemed strung-out though, so maybe gambling or something. Locke works on all addictions.'

Killed over a gambling debt? Unlikely; hard to collect money from a dead man. He got in the passenger seat as Ant climbed behind the wheel.

'Where to?' Ant asked. 'We've got an hour.' He'd returned to signing; both a relief and a concern. Ant's driving was always an extreme sport, but the dirt road had made things extra fun on the way to the shop. Currently looking especially keen, engine on, right knee jiggling.

'Ferry doesn't leave for another two.' Caleb glanced at the dash clock. 'More than.'

'And yet we've only got an hour.'

'That's not enough. What's the rush?'

Ant shoved back his sleeve to reveal a cheap digital watch, signed, 'Fifty-nine minutes, fifty seconds. Forty-eight seconds. Forty-seven seconds.'

Once upon a time Caleb would have been tempted to grab that watch and rap it over Ant's knuckles. Once. Definitely not now. 'You know the way to Muttonbird Cove?'

Ant pulled onto the road. 'Let's find out.'

Muttonbird Cove was a lot closer than the 'miles' Skye had said it was, but it still took them forty minutes to get there. A combination of twisting roads and wrong turns down dead-end tracks. They'd passed Cardigan Joyce's place a while back, a tumbledown farmhouse opposite a quarry, nothing else along the way except sheep-dotted paddocks and stands of gumtrees. At least Ant was driving with both hands on the wheel, hugging the rocky embankment as they began the steep descent towards the sea. An abrupt cliff to their right, no safety rail to prevent the jeep tumbling to the rocks below. If Taylor had been out here doing something illicit, he'd chosen a good place – a no through road and only one nearby house, a small hut perched on top of a hill.

As they passed its driveway, Caleb caught an unexpected flash of colour on the ocean-side of the road: a boulder streaked the same bright yellow as the jeep.

'Stop here,' he told Ant, who gave him a puzzled look but pulled up just short of the boulder, eyes widening when he saw the yellow paint.

Caleb got out, grappling with the door as the wind tried to snatch it from him. Finally got it shut. A scrape along the duco matched the swipe of paint on the rock. Just past the boulder, tyre tracks veered off the road, slicing through the muddy verge, stopping just shy of the cliff's edge. Only centimetres, seconds, and the jeep would have toppled over. Accident or attack?

Around to the back of the vehicle: a lot of old damage but some newer, rust-free dents, a broken brake light. Taylor had been forced off the road. A very different kind of attack than a shooting. Rough and immediate, not calculated. An accomplice? Or just someone who'd baulked on their first attempt to kill, retreated behind the barrel of a rifle for their next?

Ant came to stand beside him. 'Why didn't they just kill him here?'

The words of a man who'd never held another person's life in his hands. Hard enough to kill someone from a distance, much harder when you could see the light fade from their eyes. Something Caleb still dreamed about, even after all the therapy; woke dry-mouthed and gasping.

He looked back along the road to the hut they'd just passed, its meagre front windows facing the crash site. Near enough for a resident to have seen headlights, maybe heard the smash. 'Let's have a chat with the neighbour.'

Checking the time, Ant nodded unenthusiastically.

The old jeep struggled with the driveway's sharp ascent, so they walked up. A slower pace than Ant's usual bound. He was shivering slightly, his forehead damp with sweat. Shouldn't he be over that stage of withdrawal? A dose or two of methadone getting him comfortably through the day? No real idea.

Caleb had only witnessed Ant's first, failed, attempt at rehab years ago. Had kept his distance after that. Stayed true to the Zelic family motto of 'pull yourself together' and refused to give money, help, love, support. Even after those stomach-twisting visits with Ant in jail, skeletal and panicked. Particularly after.

The grounds of the clinic appeared in the distance, a hard oblong cut from hazy bushland.

Caleb risked asking the question he'd been holding back. 'Rehab – do you need money for the fees?'

'No.' A short jabbing motion. Not much chance a non-signer would mistake the handshape for an 'OK' like they sometimes did.

'Must be expensive. I –'

'It's free.'

'Free? How?'

'Doctor Locke's generous.'

Unbelievably generous, some people would have said. Suspicious people who didn't take others' goodness at face value. 'There a charity involved? Or is he loaded?'

Ant raised his face to the sky, eyes closed, as though in prayer. 'I'm helping with the renos, and Locke's giving me mates rates as a favour to Etty. Healthcare professional and all that.'

Ant's ex-girlfriend. A sweet, no-nonsense woman who'd been great for him, but had held true to her promise to walk away if he started using again. One who also made random, inexplicable purchases of terrible ornaments. Like possessed good-luck figurines.

'You're back with Etty?'

'Provisionally. Rehab's part of the deal. She's the one who suggested Locke.' His tight expression loosened into a grin. 'Can't believe she gave me a second chance. Scariest moment of my life, fronting up to her house. Well, second to getting caught in the middle of a shootout.'

Outstanding news. Much easier to fight your demons when you had the support of someone you loved. And since Etty had recommended the clinic, she'd be able to provide background info on the doctor. Possibly. She'd stopped returning Caleb's calls soon after Ant's disappearance, a move that might have been self-protection but was probably anger, given his part in Ant's downfall.

'Don't hassle her,' Ant said, apparently reading his mind.

'OK.'

'I mean it. Don't talk, text, send a carrier pigeon or communicate with her in any way. It's all new. I don't want you upsetting her.'

'OK.'

The driveway flattened into an open stretch of land with a few weedy vegetable beds and a neat timber hut, a Land Rover parked beside it. No other houses in sight, just rolling hills and a wide expanse of sea. Caleb understood the need for solitude, but this was a few too many steps along the road to isolation.

'Let me do the talking,' he told Ant, got a shrug.

Before they reached the hut, a man stepped outside, closed the door firmly behind him. A fit-looking forty, with an impressive nose. The kind of hard jaw and mouth that didn't bode well for lip-reading. He nodded but didn't offer his hand.

Caleb did likewise. 'I'm Caleb, this is Ant.'

The man's mouth opened, snapped shut. Shit, was that speech? No sound, scant movement. Keep going, get the name from Ant later. If he was listening; an unfocused look to his eyes.

'We're here about a car crash,' Caleb said. 'Insurance claim. Yellow jeep smashed down on the road last night. You know anything about it?'

Open, shut. Mouth like a constipated turtle's. Damn it. Pointless turning up his aids; no amount of amplification could make sounds or mouth movements clearer.

'Could you –?' He stopped. Hearies didn't usually respond well to being asked not to mumble. 'Could you speak more clearly? I'm deaf. I'm lip-reading.'

'Mussbeapainforya.'

Caleb pulled apart the shapes then stitched them back together: *Must be a pain for you.*

'Yeah,' he said. 'Sometimes. Did you see the accident? The jeep belongs to Doctor Locke's clinic.'

'Heard it.' A pause while the man seemed to consider whether to impart any more information. 'Went down to look. Bloke nearly went over the edge. Bit shaken.'

'He say what happened?'

'Just asked me to help push him out of the mud.'

'Did you?'

'Not a total prick.'

58

Good, achievable goal that. Could learn a lot from this man.

'He must have talked,' Caleb said. 'All that adrenaline. He say what he was doing out here?'

'Witching.'

As in brooms and cauldrons? 'What was that?'

'Twitching. Bird watching.'

'Wasn't it dark? What time was it?'

'Yep. Around eight. That it?' Without waiting for an answer, he retreated to the house. Went inside.

Ant gazed at the closed door, still pale and clammy-skinned. 'Chatty guy. Reminds me of you.' Back to signing, the ease of it almost a shock after trying to read Turtle Mouth.

'Get his name?' Caleb asked.

'Yeah.' One fist on top of the other, then a flurry of fingers: G something, something, something. Laziness, not lack of skill. Ant had learned Auslan as a sponge-like toddler, was almost as fluent as Caleb.

'Again. Try for fifty per cent accuracy.'

'G.I.D.E.O.N.' Ant spelled with agonising deliberation. He turned for the driveway, moving as though his bones ached. 'So that's completely dodgy, yeah? Birdwatching at night. Someone's telling porkies. Reckon it's Gideon or Taylor?'

'Muttonbirds come in at night.' Caleb thought it through. 'Migratory, though. Might be too early for them to be back.'

Ant gave him a derisive look. 'Mr Big Expert on Birds. You can't tell the difference between a goose and a swan.'

'One goose, and it had a long neck.' Admittedly not his finest moment, but he did know about muttonbirds – one of the reasons the island was special to Kat and her community. Her ancestors had hunted them on the mainland for millennia, but they were protected here. Women's business, he suspected, though Kat had never told him and it wasn't his place to ask.

'Swing by the quarry near that cardigan woman's house,' he told Ant when they were in the jeep. 'The gate had CCTV.' Cloudy last night, but there was a slight chance the camera had captured Taylor and his attacker driving past.

'Have to get back,' Ant said. 'I'm late.'

Change of plans: return to the clinic and suss out Doctor Locke. Try to get Taylor's belongings and home address, too.

Ant fumbled as he went to put the keys in the ignition, dropped them. He picked them up and sat, head bowed, breathing shallowly as though fighting back nausea. No idea whether to acknowledge his discomfort or ignore it; no shared language for vulnerability.

Fist tightening around the keys, Ant faced him, said out loud, 'You can stop with the judgemental looks, I know I fucked up. I'm aware of it every minute of every day.'

'Not judging, concerned.'

'Bullshit. You're channelling Dad so hard I'm looking for the ouija board.'

No, Caleb wasn't going to be that kind of man. Definitely not going to be that kind of father. Just not entirely sure how.

Ant stabbed the keys in the ignition, took off in a spray of dirt.

10.

At the clinic, Ant swung the jeep in beside a weathered Jaguar. Was out and heading across the gravel before the engine stopped shuddering. Caleb scrambled to catch up. As they neared the building, a man opened the front door, as though he'd been waiting. Bland good looks and ash hair, the kind of top-quality clothes found up the back of old-fashioned department stores and kept for years. Possible owner of a Jag with dulled paintwork.

'Locke?' Caleb asked Ant, received a brief nod.

The doctor smiled gently at Ant as they reached the porch. 'Anton, there's no need to push things like this. It's important to be kind to yourself.' A warm blanket of a voice, settling comfortably on each syllable. Caleb missed Ant's short reply, but it was apparently an introduction, the doctor turning his level gaze on him. 'Ah. Caleb.'

That pause between the words; filled with knowledge. God, what secrets had Ant spilled?

'Go in,' Locke told Ant. 'I'll be with you shortly.'

Ant rushed past him into the building without a backwards glance.

Caleb went to follow, but Locke shifted to stop him, looking apologetic. Hazel eyes the exact colour as his shirt. 'I'm sorry, but we don't allow casual visitors. Visiting hours are twelve till four, Saturdays. You're very welcome to come back then.' The slightest of pauses. 'At Anton's invitation, of course.'

Stay away for nearly a week? Yeah, that wasn't going to happen. 'I need to talk to you about the shooting this morning. I'm concerned about Ant's safety. He said Taylor was a patient here.'

'Ah yes, I can see how that might trouble you. While I can't discuss patients' histories, I can assure you that Peter Taylor's death has nothing to do with the clinic.'

'So it's connected to his gambling problem? Loan sharks? Organised crime?'

'As I said, I can't discuss patients. I'm sure you understand.'

That soothing voice; an urge to rub its nap the wrong way.

'Sure,' Caleb said. 'You can just give me his home address. I'll have a look through his room here, too.'

'That would be quite unethical. Now, if you'll excuse me, I need to attend to your brother.' Locke was turning for the door.

'There was another dead fox. Came a few hours ago.'

Locke drew back, his gaze dropping to the porch's newly laid mosaic tiles. 'You saw it?'

'Ant and I buried it. We found this.' Caleb pulled the bloodstained note from his jacket. Handed it to the doctor.

No change to Locke's calm expression as he examined it; a man practised in keeping his feelings hidden. But his hands were tight as he refolded the paper. He kept hold of it. 'I'm afraid it comes with the territory. Not everyone responds well to having a rehabilitation clinic in their backyard. It's best ignored.'

Like the murder of a patient was best ignored? Locke might be protecting Ant by not going to the police; people often kept information from the cops, especially in a murder investigation. But that was usually because they were scared. Or trying to hide something.

'Why haven't you told the police Taylor was your patient?'

Locke seemed to give the question serious consideration.

'Confidentiality doesn't end with a patient's death. Only a court order can breach that trust.'

'So you won't mind if I tell them? Get them over here?'

'You should do what you think best, of course, but that could be quite detrimental to a number of people here.' Hazel eyes met Caleb's. 'Some more than others. Some with reasons you may not be aware of.' He went inside, closed the door.

What the hell did that mean? That Ant had more cause than usual to avoid the cops? Six months on the gear; could easily have a possession charge against him. And Locke could just as easily be bullshitting. The doctor seemed very confident the police weren't going to connect Taylor to the clinic, which meant there probably wasn't a money trail. Surely not another work-for-treatment deal like Ant's; an expensive place like this to run. Cash payments from a patient with a gambling problem, or something even more dubious?

A tap on Caleb's shoulder.

He started, spun around. A woman in a baggy flannelette shirt was looking up at him. Closer to seventy than sixty, silvery-white hair flowing down her back. 'Well, come on,' she said, 'bring me up to date.'

Mistaken him for someone else. He'd glimpsed her briefly inside the clinic, but they hadn't met. Possibly doddery.

'Who do you think I am?' he asked gently.

She stuck a scrawny hand from her too-long sleeve. 'Doctor Livingstone, I presume? Lara Sullivan, resident therapist.'

Quirky sense of humour and clearly not doddery. Great diction too, part of a generation that had put stock in elocution lessons. But much more likely to be a patient than therapist, given he'd last seen her lounging in one of the bedrooms near Ant's, wearing a bathrobe and eating biscuits.

He shook her offered hand. 'Caleb, Ant's brother.'

'Well, yes. So who do you think killed Peter Taylor? According to Joyce with the terrible taste in knitwear, you're investigating his murder.'

Up to speed with everything and surprisingly unconcerned about the murder of a fellow patient.

'You didn't like him?'

'I shouldn't speak ill of the dead, I suppose, but he was a sneaky bastard – always sniffing around, sticking his nose into other people's business. I told Doctor Locke that. Peter too, come to think of it.'

A shit-stirrer. Excellent. The kind of person who enjoyed breaking rules might fetch a dead man's belongings for a stranger. If that stranger had enough time before the five o'clock ferry. He checked his phone – twenty minutes once he factored in the walk. Could always run it.

'Maybe you can help me,' he said. 'D'you think you could get me Taylor's things? Books, papers, anything like that.' He waited so the last part would land. 'Without anyone knowing, that is?'

Bare seconds to consider the request. Her craggy face lifted to his. 'Of course. Meet me at the old incinerator. Past the water tower.' She slipped inside the clinic.

The incinerator was tucked in the trees at the far edge of the front garden. The only structure on the grounds not visible from the main building. Not a freestanding firebox, but a redbrick shed with a towering chimney. Its timber doors were long gone, vines growing through cracks in the mortar, reaching for gaps in the tiled roof. A cavernous fireplace was set hip height, littered with leaves and grit, but a sheen to the walls as though the bricks were wet. He touched one: smooth, the silica fused into glass. Why would anyone need a fire hot enough to do that? Oh. Hospital crematorium.

He stepped away. Recoiled as something stroked the back of his neck – a vine tendril. Great, now even the plants were sneaking up on him.

Lara came through the doorway, plastic bag in hand. 'Great, isn't it? No mucking around in those days. Pity they let it go, though I guess it would've been grim for the other patients. That smoke would've blown all over the island.' She grinned. 'The water tower, too.'

Definitely a troublemaker – the concrete tower must have been built decades after this crematorium was abandoned. But he might avoid the water, just in case.

Lara handed over the bag. 'That's all I could find, apart from his clothes.'

A field guide to birds and a pair of expensive-looking binoculars. Caleb leafed through the book: no contact details in the front, no receipts or ticket stubs between the pages. Damn. There were a lot of Peter Taylors in the world. If he wanted to find out more about the man he'd have to ask a delicate favour from a mate in homicide.

Lara's eyes were magpie-bright. 'Tit for tat, what have you discovered so far?'

Just keen for intrigue, or did she have another reason for asking? Difficult to imagine the tiny woman slaughtering foxes and dumping them on doorsteps. Less difficult to imagine her knowing the perpetrator's identity and keeping it secret.

'A dead fox,' he told her.

'Another one? That's a surprise, I thought they were for Peter. What did the note say?'

'*I'm watching.*'

'Goodness, how dramatic.' Still bright-eyed, leaning towards him as though they were having a good gossip. 'Not very clear, though. What do you think it means? Not to talk to the police about Taylor?'

Solid theory, but interesting she'd gone straight to it. 'You mean Locke?'

'Anyone, I suppose. Do let me know if you find any more clues.' She left, her long hair streaming behind her.

An odd encounter with an odd woman. Not entirely sure what to make of her. Except that, like Ant, she didn't want to leave the clinic, despite the threats. Locke had to be doing something right. Still a deep unease at leaving Ant on the island, but he had to dig into Taylor's life, speak to friends and family if possible, do some research on Locke. And it wasn't like he could drag Ant onto the ferry – he'd need a car for that, cable ties.

———

The ferry was moored by the time he reached the bottom of the hill. Picturesque, with the nestled houses and bay, the low sun skimming the water with silver. Vehicles were coming off the ferry, a few making their way across the quayside towards it. Enough time for him to photograph that row of oversized letterboxes – get a record of the islanders' names. Many of them would be as unsearchable as 'Peter Taylor', but it'd be a good start. After a check for beanie-clad men and fence-menders, he pulled out his phone, made his way along the line of tin boxes and old fridges. Stopped in front of a metal chest labelled *Skye & Arlo Reid*.

He lowered the phone. A bullet hole in the middle of the door. New, not there when he'd noticed the letterboxes. Another bullet hole further down the line, and others. *Dr Ian Locke, Joyce Kaplan, Gideon Matthews*: everyone he and Ant had questioned.

11.

No one followed Caleb onto or off the ferry, but he walked a long and circuitous route to Kat's anyway, threw in some sudden about-turns. Not that there was any real danger. Not until he returned to the island; a clear message to back off delivered and received.

He'd sent Ant a blunt email on the ferry, complete with photos of the bullet-riddled letterboxes, outlining all the reasons he should leave. Not much hope of that – once Ant dug his heels in, he was immovable.

The phone buzzed as Caleb reached Kat's driveway: his mate on the force, Uri Tedesco, answering his plea for information on Peter Taylor. Quick work, he'd only messaged the detective twenty minutes ago.

—*Police records cannot be accessed for private use.*

Ouch, not even a contraction. Tedesco's texts always had the manner of a retired headmistress, but this one had an extra snip to it. A man with firm ethical boundaries, and Caleb couldn't risk breaching them with the truth – if Tedesco thought Ant was involved in a murder, he'd go straight to his colleagues in homicide. Which meant it was time for a very uncomfortable Plan B: emotional blackmail. Let Tedesco think he was still on the hunt for Ant. He typed quickly, pressed send before he could change his mind.

—Looks like a guy Ant knew years ago. Be good to talk to his family, see if they know anything.

A long wait for Tedesco's reply, seconds stretching towards a minute. It finally came.

—*I'll get back to you.*

Not a yes, not a no. Decent chance he'd come through; the detective had relaxed a lot under the influence of his boyfriend of a few months, Luke. A relationship that already seemed long term.

Tempting to push things and ask about possible warrants on Ant. Maybe not. It'd be good to know if Locke's hints were true, but not at the risk of drawing police attention to Ant. He put the phone away.

The kitchen light was on, the room much calmer than during this morning's pancake gathering. Surfaces wiped clean, toys packed away. Kat's mother, Maria, was working at her laptop at the table, grey-streaked black hair pulled back in a bun. The Bay's first Koori doctor, and owner of the local clinic, Maria had always been accepting of his whiteness and deafness, but they'd had some illuminating conversations about his other traits over the years, with a score card of Maria: one million, Caleb's ego: zero.

As he entered she gave him a brisk nod, then returned to work. He crossed to her. Not the most relaxing person to chat with at the end of a stressful day, but if Maria didn't know Locke, she'd at least have heard of him.

'Can I interrupt?'

She looked up, her barely lined face composed. 'It would appear so.'

Maria: one million and one.

'Do you know anything about the rehab place out on Muttonbird Island?'

'I'm aware of it but not across its details.'

'What about the guy who runs it, Locke? Heard anything about him, professionally or personally?'

Her eyebrows rose slightly. Same blue eyes as Kat's, but somehow more piercing.

'It's for Ant,' he said.

'I see. While I haven't had any dealings with Ian Locke, I have heard positive things about his work. Would you like me to make some enquiries?'

'Yes, please. Are there any other rehabs you'd recommend? Without wait times.'

'He's finished detox?'

Ant's sweat-slicked face, trembling hands. 'Possibly not.'

'Ah, that limits our options somewhat. There are generally long waitlists for detox.'

Oh shit. They were stuck if he couldn't find another place.

Maria studied him. 'I'll make enquiries about that as well, shall I?'

'That'd be great, thanks.' He paused. Should take this opportunity to say more. He'd known Maria half his life, but he suspected it sometimes felt a lot longer for her. A month of him coming and going was no doubt wearing thin by now. 'Thanks for putting up with me camping out here, too.'

'You're always welcome, Caleb. Particularly when you don't track mud and blood through the house.' She returned to the computer.

One million and two.

He made a swift retreat up the hall to Kat's room, was nearly bowled over as she swept into the hallway, already signing. 'Thank God. I was about to start gnawing on my pencils. *On my way*, he texts the hungry pregnant woman, nearly an hour ago.' Dark curls swept up in a red scarf, a touch of lipstick, slinky knee-length dress he hadn't seen before. Very slinky, its sun-warm colours hugging her new curves.

'You look amazing.'

'What, this old thing?' She grinned, gave his woollen jacket and soap-smeared jeans an examination and shake of her head. 'Lucky you're hot, Caleb Zelic. Come on, you can tell me more about how great I look while I waddle to dinner.'

Sitting with Kat in the glass-walled restaurant overlooking the bay, brightly lit targets against the night sky. 'We might need to put that on hold.'

Instantly serious, the shine gone from her eyes. 'Is it Ant? The murder?'

He'd wanted to talk to her face to face, hadn't quite factored in how long it would take to reassure himself he hadn't been followed, how excited Kat would be about their dinner date. How much to say and when?

'Precis, then fill in,' she said without him asking.

'The dead guy was a patient at Ant's clinic. They've been getting threats there – notes, dead foxes. Probably shot. Probably connected to the murder. Ant and I questioned some people about it.' He stopped. Better not sign the next part, enact the sniper pulling the trigger, the trajectory of the bullets. He said out loud, 'And someone shot bullets through all their letterboxes.'

Kat stared at him. 'The killer followed you to the island?'

Hadn't occurred to him he might have been targeted from the beginning. Kat's lateral thinking could sometimes reveal terrifying gaps in his own. He quickly revised the morning's search along the foreshore for Ant. No: he'd been on high alert, watching for Sergeant Ramsden. No one had tailed him on land, or onto the ferry.

'No, they were already on the island. It's OK,' he added, at her tight expression, 'no one followed me here either.'

'I know that – you're obsessive about that – I'm thinking about *you*. They know who you are.'

'It's just scare tactics. And I'm off the island.'

He stopped himself listing more points. The problem with being reassuring was the flipside. Kat was going to push back hard on cancelling the restaurant. She always did when he tried to manage her safety, especially since she'd been hurt.

'But we should cancel the restaurant and eat here,' he said. 'Just to be careful.'

A slower than usual response, her eyebrows pinched together as she thought. 'Let's try for a healthy balance,' she eventually said. 'Sensible precautions, not paranoia. Or I'll spend my life cowering inside. So, a restaurant with more walls? And we drive?'

Night time, and an impromptu visit; a sniper who sent warning notes instead of indiscriminately killing. And it wasn't fair to try and control Kat's life because of his own fears. But he could ask her to live some of it with airbags, ABS braking and a more anonymous car than a pornographic Beetle.

'OK.' He almost kept the smile from his face. 'Ask if we can borrow Maria's Volvo.'

———

They settled on Kell's Kitchen, a new place on the outskirts of town with a potato-based menu and an ambience to match. Plastic blue gingham tablecloths and steam-fogged bain-maries, the air thick with the scent of oil. Not exactly the glamorous date he'd originally planned, but it had a private carpark out the back and curtained windows. The spacious room was crowded with people happily tucking into plates of starch. A very pale group of diners, almost as monochrome as Muttonbird Island's population. Kat got a few stares, possibly not just because of her glamorous outfit and advanced pregnancy.

'Sorry,' Caleb said when they were seated. 'Wasn't expecting it to be so whitebread.'

An easy wave of her hand. 'I love seeing gubbas in their natural environment. Fascinating people.'

No idea how she did it. Noticeable and noticed in so much of her life, but always true to herself. Even now, he had to steel himself not to switch to speech to avoid the attention signing brought with it. His father had been right about that.

The food came quickly, and in great quantities. By unspoken agreement, they didn't discuss the murder or island while they ate, Kat managing to sign seamlessly about family and artwork, while putting away an impressive amount of food. Gnocchi, gratin, wedges, with a touch of potato salad as palate cleanser. Caleb almost kept pace, feeling slightly tranquillised as the stodge hit his stomach.

She finally lowered her fork, rubbed her stomach. 'Sorry, boorai, must be squished in there.' Murmuring, her voice too faint to catch, but she was the easiest person to read. Even easier than Ant. Words falling straight from her soft lips into his brain. She sat back, signed, 'OK, time for your honest and yet carefully-edited-not-to-worry-Kat rundown.'

How had he ended up with a woman this smart? Blundering through life and he'd found someone who could see straight through him. Terrifying. Wonderful. He went through it all minus graphic details about fox entrails. Kat had relaxed enough to snort when he told her about Skye's offer to cut his hair, but was looking sombre by the time he'd finished. Her gaze went to the curtained windows, the direction of Muttonbird Island. 'Poor Ant, he must be so scared. He will leave, won't he? If Mum finds another rehab?'

'Maybe. But you know Ant – too stubborn for his own good.'

'I know a couple of Zelics, yes.'

Sudden inspiration – Ant might leave the island if Kat told him to. 'Have you got a problem with us being there? Culturally?'

'No. I mean, I could lie to him, but you're just passing through. It's not your place.' She thought for a moment. 'Tread carefully, though. Don't go stomping all over the muttonbird burrows.'

According to the turtle-mouthed Gideon, Taylor had been out looking for the birds when he'd been run off the road. 'Is it too early for them to be back?'

'Early, but possible.' The slightest of hesitations. 'Let me know if they are? It's a good sign for the breeding season.'

The small brown birds flew halfway around the world to nest in sandy burrows, raised just one chick each year. A very vulnerable state of existence. Maybe Kat was more apprehensive about the ultrasound than he'd thought. He'd certainly been trying to keep his concerns from her. Excitement usually outweighed the fear these days, but it was always there beneath the surface.

He touched her hand, the lacework feathers of her tattoo. 'OK?'

'Yeah. Most of the time really good. But you going back to the island –' She shook her head. 'That makes me nervous. Taylor might have been killed in town, but the threats are coming from there.'

Leave

Leave

Final warning

I'm watching

Notes directed to a patient at the clinic, to the doctor, to Ant? 'I can't just leave Ant there.'

'No. No, of course not. It's Ant.' Her fingers ran through the air in a one-handed version of Ant's childhood sign name. 'But you can't arrest anyone. What's your plan? How do you see this ending?'

Fair question. Exit strategies hadn't been a big feature of his past cases, or even a feature at all. But he'd been paying a lot of attention to them over the past seven months.

'Ends with the cops,' he said. 'I just need to get enough evidence to point them towards the killer, away from Ant, and I'm out.'

She scowled. A flicker of panic before the realisation she was looking over his shoulder.

His parents' old next-door neighbour, Mrs Naylor, had come into the restaurant. Twig-limbed and ancient, casually racist in the way of white Australians raised on a White Australia policy. And irreversibly under the impression he'd lost most of his brain along with his hearing. But he should suck it up and speak to her. Mrs Naylor kept a close eye on everything; she'd know about the clinic, possibly even have a contact on the island.

Getting to his feet, he told Kat, 'Stay here. I have to talk to her.'

No, too late, Mrs Naylor had caught sight of him, was barrelling towards their table like a happiness-seeking missile. 'Goodness, you're enormous,' she told Kat.

Kat remained seated. Her polite smile didn't dip as she signed, 'Thirty seconds, then I feign labour.'

'I'm glad I ran into you,' Mrs Naylor said. 'I need to tell you about rats.'

Rats? Must have misread that. 'Sorry, what was that?' He braced himself; Mrs Naylor had never understood that volume didn't equal clarity.

'RATS. I said, RATS.' His aids sent her yell spearing through his eardrums.

Heads had turned at nearby tables, a couple of diners looking at the floor in alarm.

'I saw it in a magazine. RATS attacking BABIES. They eat their faces.'

Well, he was never going to get that image out of his mind. A quick check showed Kat faintly horrified but holding back laughter.

'Good tip, thanks. Do you know anything about the clinic on Muttonbird Island?'

Mrs Naylor took the change of subject in her stride. 'Of course. Jennifer Maldon wanted to go there for her pill problem, but it was full. Lucky for her. I SAID IT WAS LUCKY.'

'Why?'

'My hairdresser's friend used to work for the doctor there. She had nothing good to say about him. I said, SHE HAD NOTHING GOOD TO SAY.'

The exact opposite of Maria's anecdotal report. Odd to be more swayed by Mrs Naylor's hearsay than Doctor Maria Anderson's, but perfectly reasonable. Nothing at all to do with Locke's weighted pause between the words 'Ah' and 'Caleb'.

'What's the name of your hairdresser's friend?'

'Something silly. Terrible, these modern names. You should name your baby after your father. He was a saint, that man. A SAINT. So hard for him with you. I do hope your child's normal. I said, I HOPE IT'S NORMAL.'

Kat stiffened.

'Always a delight, Mrs Naylor.' He dropped a handful of cash on the table and helped Kat to her feet, her back rigid against his arm. Guided her away as Mrs Naylor went to speak. When they were in the dark safety of the Volvo he said out loud, 'Meningitis isn't hereditary.'

She switched on the overhead light to sign. 'You think I'm concerned about that? If, by some freakish coincidence, the baby's deaf, we'll be fine. All set up and ready to go. I'm angry she upset you, the old bat.' In full fight mode: rarely witnessed, always impressive. Kat was going to make a spectacular mother.

'I'm not upset.'

'Well, I am. She's a horror, and your father wasn't much better. I know he did it for the right reasons, but he never stopped hounding

75

you and Ant. Nothing ever good enough, no love unconditional. Jesus, refusing to let you be deaf. No wonder you've both got barriers up like brick walls.' She stopped, stricken. 'God, sorry, I didn't mean to rip into your father.'

The half-submerged fear rose to the surface, slicking his thoughts like an oil spill – that his own attempts at parenting would be just as well intentioned, just as destructive.

'All true. Maybe don't tell Mrs Naylor, though, it'd crush her.' He snatched his phone from his pocket as it buzzed, looked away from Kat's still-troubled face. Tedesco getting back to him, not in his usual formal style.

—*Cal. No luck yet with the next of kin but I've got some bad news about your brother. Sorry, but he's wanted for questioning in Queensland – agg burg*

Aggravated burglary. Ant had broken into an occupied building. Or worse, he'd been armed. Locke's pointed hints had been right. Ant would struggle to face a charge like that sober; stressed and strung out, he'd crumple at the first question, end up back in jail. A six-month sentence last time, Ant emerging from it hollow-eyed and shattered, reaching for the needle with new desperation. At least two years for an agg burg, potentially a lot more. Wasn't worth imagining.

12.

On Tuesday Caleb rose early, intending to do a quick run before collecting his repaired car. Ended up running the whole way to the mechanic's. Looping wide around the town in the pre-dawn light, he tried to shake the restlessness from his limbs. He'd spent the previous day working from a makeshift office in his old house; slipped over to Kat's last night. A backlog of cases cleared, invoices chased, but zero progress made on Taylor's murder. Nothing noteworthy discovered about the man, the clinic or the islanders. Caleb was stuck until Tedesco came through with Taylor's next of kin.

Even Doctor Locke was a dead end. Mrs Naylor's hairdresser's friend might have her doubts about the man, but he appeared to be a fully qualified psychiatrist with a solid reputation in treating addiction. And the doubtful friend was unfindable until the hairdresser returned from holidays.

Ant wasn't helping by ignoring his emails. Not totally unexpected after the way they'd parted; still unsettling.

Caleb arrived at the mechanic's out of breath but calmer, his top sticking to his back. Slightly less calm at the sight of the billboard out front advertising the Numbats' annual fundraising drive, generously sponsored by the local realtors where Jarrah worked part-time. Feature photo of Jarrah in action, ball just kicked, clearly a goal from the jubilant faces of his teammates. A large board, well positioned to catch traffic to the nearby hospital.

So Jarrah could kick a footy. Big whoop, Caleb could do that too. Turning his back to the sign, he went to find his mechanic, aka Peanut Butter Man in the Numbat photos. A two-for-one trip this morning, getting his car while doing some much-needed work on the footy club problem for Kat's cousin, Mick.

Greg Darmon was in the service bay, switching on lights and machinery. An excellent mechanic, member of the local council, and treasurer of the Numbats. A man with his finger in many pies, including the one he was holding. Caleb's heart sank. Greg was great at remembering to face him while speaking, less so at remembering not to do it while eating.

Greg gave Caleb's running clothes a slow up and down. Limp ginger hair, skin the colour of the pastry flakes down his overalls. 'Bit keen, aren't ya?' A brown slurry in his mouth.

'Mate.' Caleb gestured to his own mouth.

'Man's gotta eat.' Greg proved it. Spoke around the sludge. 'Car's out the back. Good as possible.'

'Words to instil confidence.'

'What can I say? It's a piece of crap, get a new one. In the meantime, give me more of your hard-earned cash.'

Those council meetings must be fun, all those lengthy parking-meter debates through half-masticated Arnott's creams.

Caleb followed Greg into the office, a cramped booth with a fingerprint-smudged desk and computer. Blue-and-black Numbat colours on display in a wall calendar and peeling posters. He cringed at the total of the bill Greg handed him. 'Speaking of fraud, I hear you're the Numbats' treasurer.'

'Yep.' Greg settled behind the desk. 'This about Numbatgate? Mick said you were helping out.' Not looking overly concerned that he'd been portrayed pleasuring himself with the aid of a jar of extra-smooth peanut butter.

'People aren't really calling it that, are they?'

'Guess it is a bit off with this whole Robbo thing. Thought it was a joke until he got smashed up. Poor bastard, hear he's in a bad way.'

The young player who'd been hurt in the car crash. That, at least, Caleb didn't have to worry about. Yesterday he'd stopped by the police station to make a statement about his 'morning run' near the scene of Taylor's murder, worn Sergeant Ramsden down with a few well-timed questions while he was at it. Young Robbo's accident was officially confirmed, complete with dash-cam evidence.

'It's not connected,' he told Greg. Interesting that there'd been no more doctored Numbat photos since Robbo's accident, though.

'Yeah? That's a relief. Been feeling bad about laughing. So what d'you wanna know?'

'Did you instigate the whole thing to hide your dodgy bookkeeping?' Just two mates bantering; not an investigator watching for signs of relief or tension in an interviewee.

Greg's mild expression didn't change. 'Definitely. Love meself some debt.'

'How bad is it?' Mick had said the club was in danger of folding, but that could just be Mick fretting about his beloved Numbats.

'Pinkish shade of red – rent's overdue on the oval – but we'll be in real trouble if you don't clear this up soon. It's killing the fundraising drive.' Greg pulled a smeared ledger from a drawer and dumped it on the desk, added another one from a filing cabinet. 'Last two years – feel free to have a look.'

Caleb would be doing that, but first he had to ask a man about his close personal relationship with a sandwich spread. 'The, ah, peanut butter? Any truth to it?'

'Well, not before I saw that photo.'

Moving right along. 'Got any theories about why you were targeted? Anyone with a grudge?'

'Nah, me customers love me.' Greg thought about it. 'Family, too.'

'What about the council, anything upsetting people there? Changing bin night? Cancelling the Chrissie decorations?'

'Good point, everyone hates the council. Cuts left, right and centre.' He pulled a Mars Bar from the desk drawer, began unwrapping it. 'But nah, nothing recent.'

There might be a lot of angry ratepayers in town, but Greg was one of six councillors, hard to see why anyone would focus on him. Caleb certainly didn't want to – the mechanic had the wrapper open, was taking a bite.

'OK, thanks,' Caleb said. 'Let me know if you think of anything.' Ledgers in hand, he beat a hasty retreat, did some juggling to grab his phone as it vibrated. At last – Tedesco about Taylor's next of kin. A short message, along with a phone number.

—*Peter Taylor's body was identified by his son, Harry. I've explained the situation, and Harry might be willing to speak to you today. He's in Melbourne.*

That 'might be' wasn't great. A seven-hour round trip to meet a man who could end up stonewalling. But his only hope of a lead. More than that, he needed to find out if the cops knew about the clinic. If Taylor had mentioned it to his son, or left a brochure or unsecured laptop lying around, it was all over. OK, Melbourne it was. Hire a satellite phone while he was there, grab his picks from his flat, too. Lock picking was a new skill, or the beginnings of one, but some of those clinic doors had looked like they'd be good to practise on.

After some hunting, he located his old Commodore on the warehouse-lined street at the back of the mechanic's. He'd found it there before – the place Greg dumped vehicles he deemed not vulnerable to theft. Thieves had had a go anyway, jemmying the lock on the boot. They'd gone away disappointed unless they liked five-year-old Melways. He did a check for dog shit and used condoms. Gave the lid a couple of hard slams to get it shut. Paused on his third attempt.

Across the road, a white van was reversing from an angled parking space. Rust-flecked duco and a green-and-white bumper sticker: the *Fuck a Greenie* van he'd seen on the island. The van slowly straightened and chugged away, belching smoke.

No reason to think it'd been following him; islanders came into town all the time. And he'd left Kat's before dawn, going out the back way and cutting through the park. But the van driver could have spotted him when he'd done the long loop of the town, running down the highway, exposed on all sides.

He got in the car, shoved his phone in the holder to video-call his computer expert. Not his favourite way to communicate with a non-signer, but Sammi Ng had recently taken to ignoring written requests for things like illegally obtained regos. Including those via encrypted apps. He wasn't sure if the change was so she'd have video evidence against him if it ever came to that, but he wasn't going to ask: at seventeen, Sammi had limited patience for the slow-wittedness of men in their thirties.

It took almost a minute for her to appear, wearing a blue school uniform, black hair tied in a neat ponytail. Poster of a labelled plant cell on the wall behind her. Huh. He'd assumed she'd quit school, always available in her computer-filled lair above an internet café.

'You're at school.'

She looked down at her uniform and did a mock double take, her spoken 'Oh my God' clearly readable.

How did he always manage to live down to her expectations? Holding back the urge to ask why she'd answered her phone in class, he made an attempt to defend himself. 'I thought you'd quit.'

She flipped to the back page of her textbook. Scribbled something, held it up to the camera: *deal w the olds*.

So she did have parents. He'd wondered about her home life over the two years he'd known her but had never asked. A care not to overstep boundaries he was only now realising may have come across as disinterest; she probably looked up to him as an older brother, a father figure. Her disdain certainly had the acid touch of a teenage daughter. 'You got brothers or sisters?'

A brief nod as she tapped an imaginary watch.

'Older or younger?'

She went to disconnect the call.

'OK, OK. I need a rego done.'

With an expression of bored disappointment, she wrote the details he dictated. Lifted the textbook to the camera again: *Urgent?*

'Not with your fees. Sometime today will be –'

She'd already gone.

He emailed Ant to let him know about the lurking van. Still no reply to the previous two days' messages – this incommunicado thing really wasn't working for him. Contact Ant's on-again girlfriend, Etty? Explicit instructions not to, and he'd been called an 'interfering prick' a few times over the years, often by people called Anton Zelic. He sent Ant a blank email instead, subject line *ANSWER ME YOU ARSEHOLE*, felt a little better.

13.

Caleb had a newsflash-worthy run of good traffic to Melbourne, arriving at Alberto's Café with twenty minutes to spare and an urge to buy a lottery ticket. An old redbrick warehouse with a vaulted ceiling, it was his favourite place in Melbourne and a hub for the Deaf community. A strategic choice of location for his interview with Peter Taylor's son. Most hearies were so disarmed at seeing a roomful of people signing they dropped their barriers, and he sensed that Harry was going to be a tricky interviewee. The man's text messages over the past couple of hours had flipped between enthusiastic and non-committal in a way that hinted at panic and, hopefully, information.

The café was busy, a constant ripple of colour and movement around the room: people signing as they ate and drank, discussing kids and pets, problems with work. And loud. So loud. Diners smacking down plates and thumping chairs, some kind of saucepan-bashing competition going on in the kitchen down the back. No group noisier than deaf people, particularly those who didn't wear hearing aids. Caleb turned his own down, made his way through the scattered sofas and tables towards a free table near the kitchen.

Tight muscles loosened as he returned a few greetings, every expression readable, every communication effortless. No voices here, only Auslan, the natural language of a community where deafness was part of an identity, not an impairment. Where 'Deaf' was signed with pride and written with a capital D. He'd brushed up against the community in his school years but had only found his way back recently, still wasn't sure where he fitted. Not Deaf, not hearing; something in between. But it was enough for now.

He was going through the real estate listings on his phone when Alberto appeared by his side. A nuggetty man who looked like a bantam-weight boxer, which was exactly what he'd been fifty years ago. Big smile, sinewy arms thrown wide. Caleb stood for a lung-bruising hug, tried not to wheeze. The café owner only came up to his chin but had a strength-to-weight ratio that deserved scientific study. The hugs had been even more effusive since Caleb had helped save the man's business and family from ruin a few months ago.

Alberto finally released him with a hard thump to the back. 'Thought you'd forgotten us. It's been ages.' He stretched an invisible line from one finger, cheeks puffing to emphasise the enormous length of time that had passed.

'Four days,' Caleb told him.

Alberto had already moved on, grabbing Caleb's phone from the table. 'More houses? You haven't found one yet?'

Hedging his bets. Kat might have agreed to inspect the shortlisted houses next week, but her lack of eagerness wasn't sitting right. Hadn't broached it with her yet, talk of Ant and snipers trumping the topic.

Swiping through the photos with his thumb, Alberto signed with his other hand. 'Too dark, too small, too ugly.' Standard Deaf directness, no mucking around. Alberto on the blunter side. Born into a multigenerational Deaf family, he was untouched by hearie conventions. 'You'd better get a move on, the baby will be here soon.' He paused in his scrolling. 'Any news there? Everything OK?'

'On schedule.'

'And you're sure the baby won't be deaf?' A hopeful expression, keen to welcome a new community member.

'Sorry, just the usual odds.'

'Don't worry.' Alberto gave his shoulder a reassuring pat. 'CODAs are precious to us too.'

Caleb had no doubt. A child of a deaf adult was a link between the two worlds, equally at home in both. The best gift he could give as a father.

Alberto's attention went to the café's entrance. 'One of your confused hearies?'

A man in his late twenties was standing just inside the door, gazing around as though he'd stumbled into an alternate reality. The same snub nose and thatch of pale hair as Harry Taylor's social media profiles, but looking a lot more dishevelled in a crumpled suit and shirt.

Caleb waved him over, flinched as the saucepan-bashing went up a notch in the kitchen behind him.

'Can we close the hatch?' he asked Alberto. 'It's getting really loud.'

Alberto shrugged. 'Turn off your ears.'

Not an option when he was about to interview a stranger, but Alberto was dismissive of his choice to work with the 'signing impaired'.

Harry reached the table after a few bumps along the way, the yeasty smell of beer wafting from him as he shook Caleb's hand. So maybe not reluctant, just totally munted. Which was either very good news, or very bad. Alcohol could make people reveal themselves; could also make them incomprehensible.

'Coffee?' Caleb asked.

'Yeah, latte, thanks. Better make it a strong one, I'm pretty pissed. Saw the funeral director this morning. Shook me up, I guess.' Mushy consonants, but not too spitty, and obviously in a confessional mood. He nodded approvingly as Caleb gave the patiently waiting Alberto their orders. 'That's cool,' he said when the cook had gone. 'Where'd you learn that?'

'School.' Thanks to his mother. Must have been a hard-won fight convincing Ivan to let him transfer to a Deaf school. Or maybe not; his failure to cope at the local one, undeniable.

Harry bobbed his head. 'Nice they let the guy work here. Is he, like, differently abled?'

'Deaf.'

'Oh. Mate. I don't think you're meant to say that.' Harry squinted blearily at him. 'What's your deal again? Cop, yeah?'

So tempting, but he could feel Tedesco's glare. 'I work with them sometimes.' He handed Harry a business card, the one that gave him the vague title of 'consultant'. 'I'm sorry about your father. Were you close?'

'Haven't heard from him since I was ten. Well, sent me a birthday card coupla months after my eleventh. Bit surprised when the cops turned up asking me to ID him, can tell you. I said they should get somebody who, you know, actually knew him, but they reckoned there wasn't anyone. What a sad bastard.'

Not someone who'd be able to give any insight into Taylor's movements, friends or enemies. Or possibly even accurately identify him – and if Taylor's identity had been stolen by the murder victim, that would mean all kinds of trouble.

'That's rough,' Caleb said. 'Hard recognising him after all that time?'

'Just b'tween you and me, was worried about that. Took a photo with me just in case, but I knew him straight off. Same nose.'

'Can I see it?'

'Yeah, s'right here.' Harry went to touch his snub nose, missed. 'The photo.'

'Oh, right. Did wonder.' After some patting of his clothes,

Harry made the apparently surprising discovery of a breast pocket in his suit, the phone inside. 'Tall bloke's him. Others are my grandparents. Died yonks ago. Photos are weird, hey?'

A few decades younger than the photos of Peter Taylor shown in news reports, but clearly the same man, same nose as Harry. Posing with an older couple in front of a shop window that had gold lettering on the glass: *Taylor & Sullivan Drapery*. Triple confirmation of Taylor's identity, didn't get more solid than that.

Returning the phone, Caleb tried to think of a way to get a handle on the dead man. No one close to him, by the sounds of it. At least, no one the cops or Harry knew about. 'Did your mum stay in touch at all?'

'Yeah, we see each other most weeks.'

Ambiguously phrased. Caleb tried again. 'Did she stay in touch with your father?'

'Nah, he dropped out of sight.'

'Any other relatives around. Of your father's,' he added as Harry went to speak. 'Living ones.'

'Oh.' Harry's mouth closed for a second. 'Don't think so.'

Massive spanner in the works. Jammed right in there, bringing the whole thing to a grinding halt. But, being the positive person he was, Caleb was going to focus on the good news that Taylor's family couldn't have told the cops about the rehab centre. Maybe the man's home would yield some information. Harry should have the keys if he was next-of-kin.

'What's your father's address? I'll need to go through his things.' Presenting it as a foregone conclusion.

Harry flapped a hand towards the ceiling. 'Darwin. Gunna go with Mum when she gets back from holiday.'

Four thousand miles away. Might not be popping there this afternoon. On the plus side, it'd be the local cops in Darwin searching the place, not Victorian homicide detectives, and some interstate bureaucracy to navigate before that happened. Should slow things down nicely. He was getting good at this positive thinking stuff.

'She's coming back early for the funeral,' Harry told him. 'Dunno why. Always said we were better off without him, all the stupid stuff he did.'

'Because of his gambling problem?'

Rheumy eyes blinked at him. 'What?' News to Harry that his father may have had a gambling addiction.

'What kind of stupid stuff did your dad do?'

'Just, stuff.'

'Illegal stuff?' Caleb asked.

Harry's pasty face instantly shuttered. Damn, gone in too hard and hit the solid band of childhood loyalty. Always seemed to be there, just below the surface, no matter how old the person, how bad the estrangement. Nothing for it now but to try and smash through.

'Bit of a bastard? Smacked you and your mum around?'

'No! Course not. Just stupid money stuff, that's all. Got her sacked.'

A moment for Caleb to be proud of – goading a drunk, recently bereaved man into telling the truth. Definitely going to be recounting this to his kids one day.

Alberto appeared with their coffees, cheerful smile dimming as he read the mood. He set the cups gently on the table and left. Harry didn't seem to notice Alberto or the coffee, his gaze on the front door. Only seconds before he decided that talking to a 'police consultant' wasn't something he needed to do.

'What happened with your mum's job?' Caleb asked. 'Your dad steal from her employers?'

Harry straightened hunched shoulders. 'Course not. Just found out stuff about her boss. That's all.'

So a whistleblower or a blackmailer. The older woman at the clinic, Lara, had talked about Taylor's snooping. A frank description of a man she'd called a sneaky bastard, *always sniffing around, sticking his nose into other people's business*.

'Blackmailed them?'

Harry's bloodshot eyes slid away. 'What? No. Toilet's over there, yeah? Beer, you know, can't buy it, only borrow it.' A slight stumble as he got up. Headed for the short corridor next to the kitchen, walked straight past the toilets towards the staff exit.

Caleb let him go. He'd come across a few blackmailers over the years, everything from straightforward extortionists to an overly ambitious employee trying to bargain his way into a promotion. Different desires and personalities, but they'd all had something in common: they'd enjoyed the power. If Taylor had got a kick out of blackmail once, odds were he'd done it again. To the wrong person.

14.

Ant finally called while Caleb was trying to survive traffic outside the Bay. In the fast lane, petrol tanker up his arse, logging truck ahead. Impeccable timing as always. A video call instead of an email meant Ant wanted to discuss something, but he had the patience of a gnat; twenty seconds max before he hung up.

Eyes on the road, Caleb stabbed at his phone in the dash holder, said out loud, 'Hang on.' He risked getting made into vehicular turducken by slowing to ninety and escaped across to the gravel shoulder, some sweat lost along the way. Letting out a breath, he turned to the phone.

Ant was shifting restlessly on a teal-coloured wooden chair. Shelves of mosquito repellent and fishing tackle behind him: calling from the shop's computer. 'Took you long enough.'

'Likewise. You want to try returning an email occasionally?'

'You emailed? Haven't checked yet.' Looking a lot healthier than he had the other day – colour in his cheeks, hands steady as he signed – but darting glances away from the screen, as though wary of people approaching.

'Not another dead fox?' Caleb asked.

'Nothing like that. Someone broke in this morning, when we were in group session. Or walked in, I guess. Not like the door's locked. Trashed the place but I don't think they stole anything.'

Might have just been an islander unhappy about the rehab.

Whether it was bad news or not depended on the level of destruction. 'Smashed things or just made a mess?'

'Just a mess.' An uncertain frown; half-upset, half-relieved. 'Well, Lucky Louie got smashed.'

The possessed cherub figurine; a vandal with good taste. 'Get all the pieces. Might respawn.'

Ant smothered the beginnings of a smile. 'The break-in's kind of weird. Doesn't feel random – they went through all the rooms, dumped out drawers. Like they were looking for something.'

The killer searching for blackmail evidence against them? His gut said yes. A high-risk move, breaking into the clinic. No guarantee a patient wouldn't leave mid-session, or a staff member wander by. Unless, of course, the killer was a staff member. Unlikely – far easier to slip a threatening note under Taylor's pillow than risk dumping a dead fox on the porch. But good to confirm.

He grabbed a pen and paper from the glove box. 'Give me a list of staff.'

'It wasn't them. They work mornings in the Bay.'

'Names?'

Ant slapped through a couple of misspelled names. Husband and wife already on Caleb's list, basic profile done. Ant was right about them working on the mainland; employed by a hotel as cook and cleaner. Easy to confirm if they'd been there today, and when the last fox had been dumped.

'What about the nurse?' he asked Ant.

'She starts later too.'

Direct answers and Ant; like opposing magnetic poles. Caleb went to ask again, stopped. Difficult to tell with the small screen, but Ant seemed to be putting a lot of effort into looking casual. 'Something else happen?'

'Kind of.' Ant glanced down the aisle. 'It's probably just for show but they, um, left a bullet. Stood it on the banister in the foyer.'

Not good. Extremely not fucking good. An escalating threat with no clear target – either the killer hadn't found what they wanted, or there were even more layers to this. 'You have to leave. I think Taylor was blackmailing the killer. They –'

Ant hung up.

Caleb stared at the blank screen. That was it? One toe nudging the line and it was over? The little shit.

———

The rubbish truck was doing its slow trundle down Waratah Street when Caleb turned the corner. A day of trucks and vans, this one hours late for collection, council budget cuts apparently affecting waste disposal now. He nabbed a bin-free parking spot just down from Mrs Naylor's, ducked into his house. Grab his overnight bag and computer, then he'd say goodbye to Kat before heading to the ferry. Hard to say goodbye after only two nights together, but at least he'd managed to grab a sat phone in the city. Just had to work out how to forward his calls to it now. And how to turn it on.

He did a quick whip around the house. Went to the hall cupboard, the resting place for old towels and third-best sheets. Pulled the ziplock bag from the top shelf. An emergency kit he'd hidden six months ago: a phial of naloxone and a syringe, instant counteraction to a heroin overdose. Just a precaution. People could OD fresh out of rehab, their old dose too strong for clean veins. They could do it after being clean for years too, having been dragged into a case by someone who should have known better.

Back out on the footpath, a warning signal from his reptilian brain: movement in Mrs Naylor's garden, the elderly woman coming down her front path. Polyester headscarf firmly in place, coat buttoned to her wattled neck. Bare second's hesitation before he stepped behind a tree. Took her a fair while to shuffle through the gate and down the street, plenty of time to ponder his life choices. A shadow fell across him as he re-emerged.

Mick. Broad brown face creased in a grin. Keys in hand, car parked in his driveway opposite. 'Shame job. You seriously hiding from Mrs Naylor?'

'Very seriously.'

'Guess I can't say I'd never considered it.' He nodded at the bag in Caleb's hand. 'Any chance of an update before you're off?'

Complete brain freeze before he worked out what Mick was talking about. A giant numbat, not snipers and blackmail. From the terrifying to the ridiculous.

'I'll go through the books tonight,' Caleb told him. 'but I'm wondering if that young player, Robbo, might be behind it all. Haven't been any photos since his car accident. He get on with the other players?'

'Well, the white ones. But you're on the wrong track there – he's back in surgery, and we just got another photo.' Offering his phone, Mick added, 'Bit different.'

Very different. No faces photoshopped onto the numbat suit this time, instead an image of an erect penis. Pinkish white and strangely shaped. Was that real? He enlarged the image, winced.

'Yeah,' Mick said. 'You gubs really that crooked?'

'That's crooked?'

A reverse-image search came up blank. So probably not a grab from the internet, but someone's private photo. A boastful dick pic from the instigator, or a direct hit at someone? Either way, it felt like they'd come to the centre of this whole charade. Find the man behind the penis, and Caleb might find the reason for Numbatgate.

He returned the phone. 'Know any white lefties?'

'You reckon that's from wanking? I mean, mate, you'd have to be tuggen at it pretty hard.'

'Guess I'll have to find out.' Going around asking footy players about the shape of their dicks; should be getting danger money. Which raised a question he should have asked earlier. 'Who's paying me if the club's skint?'

'Me.'

No. Not comfortable with that at all. 'It's free if it's for you.'

Mick shook his head. 'Nup. Puttin me money where me mouth is. Want the club to be around for the young uns. Being bottom of the ladder helps keep 'em on track.' Real pain beneath the jokes, sadness at the thought of losing the club.

This debacle meant a lot more to Mick than he'd realised.

'The club helped you?' Caleb asked, as his phone began to vibrate in his pocket, the continuous pulse of a video call. He pulled it out, eyes still on Mick.

'Saved me, I reckon. Coach back then worked with ex-cons, got me into it. Pauline's dad.' A smile at the memory. 'Married her a year later. Anyway, I'll let you answer that.' Mick turned for his house.

Not a problem at all. Just had to work the case until he solved it or died.

He checked the phone as he headed for the car: Kat. Answering, he spoke out loud. 'Hey, I'm just on my way –' He took in her tight expression, the bathroom tiles in the background. No. Please no, not again. Trying to wrestle his face into blankness. 'It's going to be OK. Have you called the ambulance?'

'I'm fine,' she signed quickly. 'The baby's fine.'

He leaned against the car, the ground unsteady, made an 'it's OK' gesture to Mick who'd pivoted sharply back towards him. 'What's wrong?' he asked Kat. Might not be a medical emergency, but she was upset about something.

'There's a cop here, waiting to take you to the station. He's a little overzealous, didn't want me to call you. It's OK,' she added as Caleb went to speak, 'he's just a young guy taking his job too seriously.'

Maybe, but cops and Kooris could be a volatile mix. Not enough centuries since the last police-led massacre, not enough weeks since the last black death in custody. And if it was that aggressive young cop he'd seen on the foreshore the other morning, Kat would have good reason to be distressed.

'Probably just about my statement,' Caleb told her. 'Stay in the bathroom. I'll be there in five.'

Mick was at his side, braced for action. 'Katy OK?'

'Yeah, but a young cop's there for me. Overeager.'

The lines on Mick's forehead deepened as he nodded at something behind Caleb – a patrol car coming down the road, Ramsden's stocky silhouette at the wheel. Only two cop cars in town, both deployed for Caleb – that felt more serious than wanting to check a statement.

'Might have a word with him,' Mick said. 'Tell him about a parking infringement I witnessed the other day.'

Caleb hesitated. Mick's brown skin was more of a target to some cops than his prison tatts. Not always clear to Caleb which cops.

Mick pulled out his phone. 'Polite man, Sergeant Ramsden. 'Specially when I livestream our convos.' Walking slowly up the middle of the road, he raised the phone in a stop sign.

———

Caleb made the six-minute drive in four, took the turn into Kat's driveway too fast, the boot flying open as he hit the kerb. He parked behind the patrol car, was out and halfway to the house when his thoughts lined up. The jemmied lock on his car. That'd happened this morning, like the break-in at the clinic. And now the cops were inexplicably keen to see him. Another bullet, this one fired from a murder weapon?

Back to the car, shining his phone torch into the dark recesses of the boot. No metallic glint, nothing stuck to the roof or hidden in the lining. Maybe underneath, the tyre well. He found the recessed handle, lifted the panel. Not a bullet, a rifle.

15.

Sleek black stock and barrel. Jammed into the space where the tyre and toolkit usually lay. Nothing like the knockabout .22 rifles he'd seen around farms. Expensive and accurate. Lethal. Owned by someone who took their weapons seriously. Smart move, planting it in his car – distract the cops and keep him off the island. Must have hurt to dump it, though. An unusually disciplined person, or someone with a large arsenal. Both.

Someone was coming out of the house – the thin-necked cop from the waterfront. Speaking into his shoulder radio as he walked. Caleb slammed the boot. It didn't catch. Another go, shoving down hard, palms slick. It stayed shut.

Slow exhale. He faced the cop: Constable Lloyd, according to his name tag. Soft pink cheeks, hard shine to his eyes. Kat had downplayed his keenness. 'Mr Zelic? I've been asked to take you to the station for an interview.'

'Sure. I'll follow you there.'

'With me, please. There's a search warrant for your car.'

Caleb froze. Even if he wasn't arrested, he'd be caught up in the mess for days. Ant alone on the island. Had to be a way out of it: distract, bribe, run.

Lloyd's thumb caressed the edge of his holster. 'Now, please, Mr Zelic.'

Across at the house, the front door was open again, Kat coming outside. Caleb tried to keep his face blank, signed quickly, 'Go back in. He's got a search warrant for the car. Someone's planted a rifle.' Turned to the cop as Kat faltered, the young man bristling beside him while staring at his hands. 'Sign language. I'm deaf.'

Kat was waddling across the driveway, one hand on her lower back, feet splayed. 'I need the car,' she said out loud. 'Got a doctor's appointment.'

No. Not going to let her get involved in a stand-off with an armed and amped-up cop. Caleb grabbed his keys, shoved them at the constable. 'Let's go.'

Kat reached their side, breathing heavily. 'I need the car. Mine's dead.'

'Don't,' Caleb signed, but Kat's gaze didn't leave the young man's rosy face.

'I'm sorry,' Lloyd said, 'but Sergeant Ramsden's on his way with the warrant.'

'With it?' she asked. 'You haven't got it here?'

The constable's expression wavered for the first time. 'The sergeant's on his way with it now.'

'So, not here. In which case, I'll use the car to get my extremely pregnant self to the doctor.' A cold smile as Lloyd hesitated. 'Unless, of course, you'd like to explain to the media, the Aboriginal Legal Service, and my mother why you illegally prevented a pregnant Aboriginal woman from obtaining medical care.'

Lloyd dropped the keys in her hand as though burnt.

'This is a bad idea,' Caleb signed. 'What if they pull you over?'

Her lips trembling slightly, she kissed his cheek. 'Don't stress,' she said out loud. 'I'll let you know how it goes.'

They kept him waiting. Fifteen minutes, twenty, twenty-five. Sitting at a gouged desk in the brightly-lit interview room, years of fear-soured breath and coffee fumes off-gassing from the plasterboard. Caleb angled his phone away from the two-way mirror, searched for local places a gun enthusiast might have trained or be known. No nearby army barracks, or training grounds, no gun club, not even a rifle range. Didn't need one when you could practise in an empty paddock.

Skye's comment about rifles. *'Half the island owns one.'*

Pointless trawling the dark web for gun-smuggling sites: too many, too secretive. He did it anyway. Nothing else to distract him from imagining all the things that could have gone wrong for Kat. Even if she didn't get caught, her body, the battlefield for two lost pregnancies, could betray her – cortisol, heart rate, and blood pressure spiking. He should have stopped her. Grabbed the keys from Constable Lloyd, admitted to everything.

His phone rattled on the desk. Sammi, not Kat, giving him the details of the *Fuck a Greenie* van. Unregistered, last known owner one Mary Howard from Muttonbird Island. Died last year, aged ninety-two.

The door swung open; two men came in. Bland suits and expressions, the smaller one striding in dick first. Damn, Caleb had been hoping for Ramsden. Vague statements about morning runs along the foreshore might appease a local cop who knew and almost trusted him; homicide detectives would be a lot harder to deflect.

The taller cop settled himself unobtrusively at the desk. Dick-first slapped down a thick manila folder as he sat beside him, the thud reverberating through Caleb's arm resting on the desk. Nice trick, but the neatly aligned edges of the copy paper padding the file were too obvious. Always better to use old print-outs. 'Thanks for coming in, Mr Zelic. I'm Detective Senior Constable ... and this is Detective Senior Sergeant ...'

An OK read, but those names were impenetrable. Leave it, or

ask? Too important not to ask. 'Can you write down your names?'

The silent cop passed him a business card without comment; a pause before the smaller one did it. Making a production out of the simple act, he slid the card slowly across the desk, kept his finger on it while he spoke. 'Sergeant Ramsden said you might have trouble understanding us. Is there a carer we can call? Someone who can help you?'

Caleb eased clenched jaw muscles. Just the usual bullshit meant to rattle him. Half-hearted too; the cop hadn't even gone to the trouble of over-enunciating. His superior officer was the one to watch. Sitting back, biding his time. Lean face impassive beneath blunt-cut hair.

'You're not that bad,' Caleb told Dick-First. 'Just work on your fricatives.' Ignoring the detective's hard stare, he looked at the cards: the silent cop was Nikolas Katsonis, the dick, Thomas Chabon. With a Ch or a Sh sound? Not going to ask.

Chabon was speaking again. '... you know why you're here?'

'No.'

'No?'

'No.'

'You're aware there's a warrant to search your car?'

'Yes.'

'Do you know why?'

'Assume you've got your reasons.' He'd love to know them. Not many magistrates would issue a warrant on the strength of an anonymous tip and a jog near a crime scene. Love to know who'd been driving that greenie van, too, because they'd almost certainly planted the rifle.

Chabon leafed through the folder again. 'Let's start with the morning of Taylor's murder, shall we? You claim you were in the vicinity due to an early morning run.'

He slid a page across the table. Not a copy of Caleb's statement, but a glossy close-up of Taylor's water-puffed face and slack mouth, a hole where his right eye should have been.

Caleb looked away, met Katsonis's flat gaze. Eyes like a freshly caught fish.

Chabon tapped the photo. 'What do you know about Peter Taylor?'

'Nothing.'

The cop glanced at his superior officer. 'I don't think he understands. Maybe we should call his wife – she must be finished with his car by now. Probably given it a good clean-out, too.'

Don't bite, just let the bait drift past.

Detective Katsonis spoke for the first time. 'You've been involved in a fair bit of violence over the past few years, haven't you, Mr Zelic? Friend and business partner killed, wife hurt.'

Seemed so bloodless when put that way. A litany of mistakes and pain; mainly his mistakes, other people's pain.

He snatched his phone from the table as it lit up. Kat at last: a thumbs-up emoji. Positive, but how positive? Still driving around with the rifle? Safely rid of it? He typed quickly.

—You OK? Where are you?

The table shuddered as Chabon smacked his palm down. 'If we could have your attention ...'

Phone buzzed.

—*All good. Jarrah's studio xx*

Jarrah's? What the fuck?

The detective banged again. 'Mr Zelic. What do you know about Peter Taylor?'

'Nothing.'

'Then why did his son inform us that you just drove all the way to Melbourne to ask about him?'

Caught in a lie. He'd broken the first rule of interrogation: shut the fuck up. A lifetime safely cocooned by silence, and he'd chosen

101

now to speak. No point trying to spin a story, just leave before he made it worse. He stood.

'Sit down, Mr Zelic,' Chabon said, 'we are nowhere near finished.'

'Am I under arrest?'

'Not yet.'

'Then I'll be happy to come back later with a lawyer.'

Katsonis looked at him, spare features expressionless. 'The words of a careful man. And you should be careful, Mr Zelic. Because the person who killed Peter Taylor will almost certainly kill again.' His glassy eyes didn't blink. 'And you're already in their sights.'

16.

Jarrah's studio was a more organised version of Kat's one in Melbourne: an expansive tin shed filled with paintings and towering bronze figures, neatly stacked pipes, timber and tools. Hot, a fire burning fiercely in a cast-iron stove fashioned like a human face, glass door for a mouth. Kat and Jarrah were standing at a nearby workbench, heads bent together as they examined a small sculpture. Burnished skin sheened with sweat, Kat's face alight as she spoke, sketching shapes in the air.

Jealousy wound its clammy arms around him, squeezed tight. They looked up as he closed the door hard behind him.

Kat tensed. 'What's wrong? Did something else happen?' Signing across the room despite Jarrah's presence; unusual enough to pull Caleb up, get his expression under control.

'No, everything's fine.' He reached her side just as Jarrah decided he had things to do at the back of the shed.

The work they'd been studying was a model of Kat's new self-portrait, a simple outline of her pregnant figure crisscrossed with red threads. Just scrap wire and cotton, but it held the power of the future work. So she'd spent the time working instead of fretting about him. Almost certain that was a good thing.

'Did you have trouble?' he asked. 'Took you a while.'

'No, I just drove around for a while to make sure I wasn't followed. It's all sorted. We poured acid into the barrel and cut it down, chucked it all in there.' Gesturing to the fiery mouth.

'The serial number was already filed off.'

We? He stared at her. 'You told Jarrah?'

'Just that I needed to get rid of it.' She touched his arm. 'Don't worry, he's safe. He's mob.'

A lot of history in that short phrase: more than eighty thousand years of culture, two and a half centuries of fighting dispossession. But she was wrong about her actions being safe. Someone like Jarrah, whole and undamaged, wouldn't understand the consequences of a misspoken word. He could tell a mate, who'd tell a mate, who'd mention it down the pub to a man with a rifle who now had Kat in his sights.

'You can't guarantee that! What were you thinking?'

'That I was driving around with a murder weapon and needed to get rid of it.'

'Which is why you shouldn't have taken it! I knew I shouldn't have let you.'

She waited a beat. 'Maybe you should go for a run, come back when you've cooled down.'

It'd have to be a long run, an ultramarathon through mountainous terrain. And now Jarrah was walking towards them with a tray of tea and snacks. What was it with this man and food? Always presenting Kat with little morsels like a cat dumping a dead mouse on the doorstep. Or, in this case, a tempting arrangement of brie and figs. Figs, for fuck's sake, could he have chosen a more erotic fruit?

'Kat can't eat that,' he said as Jarrah set the tray on the bench.

She turned glacier-blue eyes on him. 'Yes, she can.'

'Soft cheese. Listeriosis.'

'It's vegan, Jarrah knows the rules.'

Not all the rules. An important one missing there.

Kat had plucked a wedge of brie from the plate, was eating

it slowly, savouring each bite. She thanked Jarrah once she'd finished and began gathering her things.

Caleb waited for her inevitable trip to the toilet, then jerked his head for Jarrah to follow him to the door. A stack of fundraising flyers for the Numbats sat beside it, printing sponsored by the local real estate company, the same ball-kicking photo of Jarrah as on the billboard outside the mechanic's.

Up himself. Knew there was a reason he didn't like the man.

Jarrah caught his look, gave a lopsided shrug. 'Boss's joke, likes to embarrass me.'

That's right, Jarrah worked part-time as a realtor. Was there something in that? The footy field had to be worth a fair bit despite the recession: centre of town, great views. Jarrah could kill off the already shaky club and handle the sale of the oval, pocket the commission. Except the council owned the land, not the Numbats. Have to bribe all six councillors. Be no money left. But Caleb could still see Jarrah as a con artist; he was certainly shifting uneasily right now.

'Thanks for helping Kat out,' Caleb told him as she reappeared at the far side of the room. 'She tell you it was important to keep it quiet?'

'Yeah.' Jarrah's gaze went to her, lingered. 'Don't worry, I won't tell the cops.'

'Not just the cops – anyone. Could be dangerous.'

Jarrah faced him, but didn't speak immediately. No hint of his usual smile. 'I'd never do anything to hurt her,' he said slowly. 'Can guarantee that.'

———

It was raining hard on the way back to Kat's house, windscreen-wipers going full pelt. Just after sunset but already dark. Kat sat very still in the passenger seat, eyes on the white-streaked windscreen as he told her about the break-in at the clinic and his conversation with the cops. She interrupted once, asking him to speak up because of the rain, but didn't go through any of her usual questions. A faint reflection of the bad years, Kat slowly withdrawing after he'd shut her down too many times.

Both her parents' cars were in the driveway when he pulled in. Pity they hadn't been home earlier; this whole mess would have been avoided. He edged around Maria's Volvo to park near the porch's security spot, left the engine running, heater on. Half an hour before the ferry left. Last one of the day.

Kat went to get out, turned back as he touched her arm, her composed expression just visible in the rain-filtered light. Too dark to lip-read, almost too dark to sign, but he didn't want to sit in a brightly lit car. Just nerves. The sniper clearly didn't want the attention another murder would bring, had shown no sign they even knew Kat existed. Her part in the disaster only because Caleb had brought the trouble to her front door.

'I'm sorry,' he signed. 'I shouldn't have taken it out on you.'

'No, you shouldn't have.' She lowered her hands to her lap, stayed turned to him, as though waiting.

OK, more was obviously needed. Hammer away at that wall she'd accused him of still keeping up. 'I was scared for you. Last time I fucked up, you got hurt. I'm terrified of doing it again.' He gestured to her stomach. 'And now there are two of you.'

'There are three of us. I get to protect you, too. That's partly why I'm angry. No, don't go looking all relieved, I'm mostly angry because you were being an arsehole. But I couldn't just stand there and let you get arrested. We're a –' She searched the air for the right sign. Brought her fists together, thumbs upright, swept them like two people dancing: partnership. That was a good sign. A sign to ease his heart.

'You're right,' he said. Didn't add any of the caveats. 'I'm sorry.'

'OK, good.'

Argument over?

'That it?' he asked.

'What?'

'We're good? Inexcusable behaviour excused? No more discussion needed?'

One eyebrow rose in a perfect arch. 'Oh, I think we'll be discussing your hatred of soft cheeses in the near future, but yes, we're good. I'm focused on the rifle right now. The timing.'

To think, he once would have avoided a conversation about fear as though it were an acid bath. He glanced at the dash clock: still had ten minutes. 'What about the rifle?'

'If it's supposed to keep you off the island, why do it now? It's only been a couple of days since they shot up the letterboxes. You've barely spoken to anyone since then, don't know anything.'

'Harsh, but true. What's your theory?'

'The bullets weren't meant for you – no one could have known you'd look twice at those boxes. They were for the islanders, to keep them in line.'

A lot of sense in that, particularly with the escalating warnings at the clinic. Which meant at least one person on the island knew what was happening, could lead him to the killer. The anonymous text messenger, maybe? No word from them since that first morning, and no guarantee they'd be trustworthy.

'Thanks,' he said. 'You're a woman of many talents.'

'I discovered a few new ones today. Can't believe I just destroyed evidence in a murder case.'

Couldn't quite move on from that himself.

She patted his knee. 'Well done keeping that thought to yourself. Hope for you yet. Come on, I'm exhausted. You can cuddle me while I have a pre-dinner snooze. See how we go from there.'

Stay with her. Dampen the terror still rippling through him from when he'd thought they were losing the baby. 'I can't. I have to catch the ferry. Feels like things are ramping up with that break-in.' He stopped at her fallen expression. 'You OK with me going? I'll be back Friday for the ultrasound. Hopefully before.'

'How can I say no?'

That didn't feel like a rhetorical question. '*Are* you saying no?'

'No. But I'm worried about you. And me – what if I go into labour while you're over there?'

Definitely should have laid that all out for her. 'The sat phone will get me anywhere, anytime. I'd be here within the hour. Steal a tinnie if I had to. Swim.' Taking her hands, he said out loud, 'But I won't have to.'

She clasped his fingers, pulled free to give him a quick hug and a kiss. 'Don't forget the first part – be careful.' Jacket over her head, she got out, managed a slow run to the house.

An almost physical sensation as she closed the door, his body stretched tight, pulled in opposing directions.

17.

It was a close call with the ferry, the shaggy-haired pilot having to re-lower the ramp for him. Mixed feelings about his success as soon as they were underway. Welded tin can floating into heaving darkness. No idea how big the waves were, but the ferry was fighting them. Lifting high and thudding down hard, his car shuddering with each impact. Which was fine. Be laws for this kind of thing, certificate of vessel storm-worthiness or something. The chances of being trapped in the wreckage and suffocating on the long drop to the seabed were probably small. Tiny.

He'd have company on the way down. Five other vehicles as ballast, all fully laden, including a white van. Some excitement when he'd first seen it, but no *Fuck a Greenie* sticker on the back. Sammi's revelation about the greenie van being unregistered was an issue. He'd spot it quickly in a place as small as the island, but he'd rather know who the driver was before running into them on a dead-end track. Could ask the ferry operator, Max. Not an islander, so a lot less chance of word getting back to the van owner. But Max's claim he was 'a bit shit' at recognising people had turned out to be full-shit prosopagnosia. He'd given Caleb a blank-eyed stare on the return trip the other day despite their earlier conversation about seasickness and carrot chunks. Still, worth a try.

After a pause for another belly flop, he darted through the rain to the pilot's cabin. Ruined the dismount by slamming through the door and skidding inside. Small metal and glass booth plastered with photos of the ferryman's sporty-looking kids. One lifejacket.

Max turned from the console, eyes widening in alarm. 'Mate, don't you come in here spewin'. Pay at the other end.'

'Non-spewer,' Caleb told him. 'Caleb. Came over the other day.'

'Caleb. Gotcha. Guess you can pay now, then.' Standing wide-legged on the pitching deck as though on dry land, *Best Dad* coffee cup in hand. Lidless, didn't spill a drop. How was that possible? Laws of the sea trumping the laws of physics?

Caleb handed him the money, wedged himself next to the console as the ferry tilted not all alarmingly to one side. 'I'm looking for one of your passengers. You know who drives a white Toyota van? Sticker on the back says, *Fuck a Greenie.*'

'Half the island, I reckon. Comes over all the time. Probably the only roadworthy one they've got.'

'You know who's been driving it the past couple of days? Went across this morning?'

'Jeez, mate, that'd be challenging the brain cells. I'm not real great with faces.'

A series of popping vibrations beneath his feet, like a seam of rivets giving way. 'That meant to happen?' he asked Max.

'What?'

Very reassuring. Like seeing the flight attendants chat easily during turbulence – of course, you had to assume they weren't fans of freefall skydiving.

'Never mind.' Caleb examined the photos lining the cabin. Two boys with the same scruffy brown hair as Max, running races and holding trophies aloft. No Numbat uniforms, but it seemed nearly every other sport was represented.

'Your boys, any chance they play footy?'

'The youngest. Star of the under-twelves. Eldest is more into fencing and pentathlon these days.' Pride in the flash of Max's teeth. 'Following in his dad's footsteps, can't do anything practical.'

The open-hearted acceptance some parents seemed to have with their kids. Could probably learn it.

'You heard about the Numbat photos?' Caleb asked.

'Numbatgate? Who hasn't?'

'Any rumours about who's behind it?' Trawling for inspiration; the sure sign of a clueless investigator. But he was willing to grasp anything after this afternoon's conversation with Mick.

'Plenty, but my money's on the mayor.'

Eighty-six year old Edith Partridge, five times mayor. 'Why?'

'Wants to sell the oval, doesn't she? Pocket the money.'

Caleb's own theory, with a few more flaws thrown in. Couldn't make it work, despite his best efforts. Nothing in it for Mayor Edith and the other councillors except a very modest bribe and the undying hatred of the town. It'd be generations before locals stopped hoping for the club's resurrection, lukewarm pride turning white hot. The end of anyone who voted to sell its home ground. But he'd be going through the Numbat ledgers tonight to see if Greg the mechanic-come-councillor had found a different way of making a dodgy buck.

The nose of the ferry suddenly tilted to the sky. Grabbing the edge of the console, he stopped himself sliding onto his arse. Steep angle, airborne – had to be airborne – smacking back down. Absolutely fine: Max calmly drinking his coffee, not reaching for the lifejacket or emergency radio. The ferryman drained the cup, gestured to the door with it. 'Might want to buckle up. Gunna get a bit rough soon, and I already lost a load today.'

'*Get* a bit rough?'

'Yeah, storm's on its way.' Max frowned. 'Probably should've cancelled the run. She's not really up to the big seas.'

They reached land intact. Not dry land, though – the clearing by the pier was flooded, water covering the running boards of the vehicles ahead of his car. He edged slowly forward, the rain hard slashes in the Commodore's headlights, got just past the shop before the tyres started slipping. A murky waterfall coursed down the hill, turning the dirt road to mud. He eyed the trees whipping overhead, gave up any idea of making it to the clinic that night. High chance of a very cold reception even if he got up there in this weather. Non-visiting hours on a non-visiting day, to a brother who hadn't asked him to come. Who'd all but told him not to.

He did a hundred-point turn, headed back for the shop. Hopefully he'd be able to get a feed and rent one of the holiday lets he'd seen advertised the other day, otherwise it'd be a long night in the car fine-tuning the heater between hypothermia and carbon monoxide poisoning. The shop's veranda was dark, but lights were on inside, flickering as though the generator wasn't quite up to the job. A few people visible, including Skye and her husband sitting by the window. Caleb made a quick dash for the steps, jacket collar up in the vain hope it would stop water gushing down his neck.

He slowed as he reached the darkened veranda. Skye and Arlo were mid-argument, Skye over-enunciating the way hearies did when they whispered, Arlo hunched over his beer. No black beanie today, the back of his bald head gleaming. More than an argument? Skye looking anxious, fair skin blanched in the harsh light. Caleb edged closer to the window, stopped short of the light pooling on the boards. Tricky to lip-read with the distance and lack of helpful intonation, but he eventually clicked into Skye's steady speech rhythms.

'Then. What. About. Bovis?'

OK, maybe not quite clicked. Although, a strong chance 'bovis' was a name – Bevin, Marvin, Boris? Too many similar shapes, he wouldn't get it without more context.

Skye shook her head, leaning towards Arlo, her palms flat on the table. 'Because. I'm. Scared.'

Headlights swept across the veranda, pinning Caleb in their beam as the car parked directly behind him. Timing. Skye's eyes widened when she caught sight of him, but she smiled and gave him a wave, her husband turning to stare. OK, spying was obviously over for the night. Caleb headed to the door, was two steps inside when Arlo barrelled into him, speaking quickly, chest thrust forward. Hard focus to his deep-set eyes – not drunk, just hair-trigger angry. Too overheated to reason with, too many mates here to fight. Try to distract.

Caleb backed up so he could see the man's face and fists. 'I'm after a room. Got one free?'

'You're … fucken … are ya? … staring at my wife … fucken perv.'

Skye still at the table, face alight. Four men looking on in interest. Keen to see the city-boy get smacked around, maybe help out if Arlo went down.

With a last, wild-card, attempt to diffuse Arlo, Caleb got ready to run. 'Shit no. I'm looking for that arsehole Locke. He here?'

Unexpected success: Arlo loosening his stance, backing off. 'Not if he knows what's good for him.'

General aggression, or a real grudge there? Arlo seemed more the type to bash in the clinic door than take the time to kill and dump a fox, but maybe he had a calmer side.

'Got a problem with Locke too?' Caleb asked.

'None of your fucken business what I've got. Caravan's by the beach. Fifty a night. Nah, make that sixty.' He strode to the door, held it open.

Time for a tactical retreat. Wasn't that hungry anyway.

He found the caravan in a clearing by the beach's retaining wall. Another 1970s original, with the aerodynamic lines of a block of wood. What was it with this place and the 70s? No other vans or huts visible by the light of his phone despite the shop's sign advertising 'holiday lets'. Possibly blown away, this one tethered to its concrete slab by ominously thick steel cables.

It was musty inside, but the fluoro lights worked. Fake wood panelling and a bare mattress with what were hopefully rust stains. Tiny wall-mounted TV and VCR player, tapes stacked on top: *Highlander II*, *A Very Brady Sequel*, *Super Mario Brothers*. Not the most depressing place he'd stayed, but making the top five. Excellent choice, giving up a night with Kat for it.

Eight-thirty. Nothing for it but to work. After a quick strip and change into dry clothes, he took his bag to the table, sat under the two-bar heater. Almost certain it was working, a distinct smell of burnt dust. He texted Kat from the chunky black sat phone to let her know he hadn't drowned. Actual buttons to push. Would've been nice to have a long video chat, but the thing didn't get internet. Because it was 'a tool, not a toy', according to the salesman; definitely not a toy himself.

Goodnight message received from Kat, he tucked the phone away, grabbed the Numbat ledgers from the bag. Underneath them, the binoculars and birdwatching guide Lara had fetched from Taylor's room. Forgotten about them. A decent chance Taylor had used birdwatching as an excuse to spy, but it could have been a genuine hobby. Might be possible to retrace his movements if he'd recorded when and where he'd been twerking. That wasn't the right word. Jerking? Tweeting? Twinging? Birdwatching.

A leaf through the book firmed up the idea Taylor had only used it as cover. No writing, drawings or even dirt marks. But a fine stubble at the back where a page had been torn out. The blank notes section, a faint indentation of handwriting on the preceding page. Too indistinct to try the pencil trick. He stood, carried it to the overhead light. No convenient list of locations or copy of a blackmail note, just a few downward strokes of letters. Maybe the word 'son', maybe his subconscious revved up and raring to go.

Rain-scented air swept in as the door flew open. Skye bustled inside wearing a hooded raincoat and gumboots, carrying something covered in a plastic sheet. She shook the hood from her pale hair, smiling easily as though she hadn't just seen her husband about to wipe the floor with him. 'Oof, that rain! Thought you might like . . .' She unwrapped bed linen and a foil container from the plastic, chatting as she moved about the caravan, putting things in place. '. . . kitchen's closed . . . lasagne . . . towels.' Brushing too close with each pass, even given the tight space.

So he hadn't misjudged her reaction back in the shop: bored and reckless, looking for entertainment. Possibly information. Which would work both ways if he was careful and assumed everything he said would get back to the islanders. And that Arlo would kick his head in if he encouraged her too much.

Giving a pillow a last plump, she turned to him. '. . . tell him I asked around about a rifle. No luck, I'm afraid.'

A wild moment thinking she meant the one planted in his car, before he remembered Ant's concocted story about wanting to borrow a gun for the 'fox problem' at the clinic. 'Because it'd be for drug addicts?' Caleb asked. 'Or –' What had that woman in the cardigan called outsiders? 'Or incomers?'

'Both, but mainly the incomer part. Three generations in the ground to call yourself a local around here.'

'That why your husband doesn't like Locke?'

'You still worried about your brother? I wouldn't be. Arlo's just bitter because he wanted to turn the old hospital back into a hotel.

Like that was ever going to happen. Can't even make money with the shop. I hope –' The rest of her words were lost as she gazed around the caravan.

He hesitated. Probably couldn't hide his deafness from her for much longer but revealing it would put a stop to his spying sessions. Worse: from what he'd seen of Skye, she'd respond with cringe-inducing pity. 'Sorry, what was that?'

Smiling, she came closer. Her slanted cheekbones caught the light, revealing a faint dusting of freckles. Interesting face; Kat would enjoy drawing it. 'I hope you won't be bored out here by yourself.'

He lifted the book. 'Got homework. Thought I'd learn the local birds like Taylor.'

'Oh no, not another twitcher. Muttonbird fanatics everywhere.'

Twitcher, that was it.

'Taylor was interested in muttonbirds?'

'Always seemed to be off watching them.' Fingertips brushed his arm. 'You're a very attentive listener, aren't you? Or do you just like the look of my mouth?'

OK, shut it down. 'Sorry,' he said. 'Didn't mean to embarrass you. I'm lip-reading. I'm deaf.'

A full three seconds as she took it in, worked out how to respond. 'That's amazing, how clever. I never would have known. Well, I'd better be getting back. See you in –' Pulling the raincoat over her hair, she left.

The unlatched door whipped back and forth, smacking against the side of the caravan. He pulled it closed, slid the flimsy lock into place. He'd been wrong about her response. No pity in her expression, just fear.

18.

He drove to the clinic after breakfast. Slow going, having to veer around water-filled potholes and fallen branches. Getting out a couple of times to drag larger limbs to the side of the road, his Commodore too wide to pass where smaller cars had. A miracle the ancient caravan had survived intact. It had rocked and shuddered all night, but there'd been no actual airborne moments, the guy ropes doing their job.

The clinic's ironwork gates were open, a familiar Hyundai hatchback parked alongside the usual few vehicles. Ant's girlfriend, Etty, was here. Nice for Ant, but a concern with the escalating threats. Interesting too, given Doctor Locke's claimed ban on weekday visits and the fact it was Wednesday. Bendable rules for friends and relatives who weren't investigators?

Leaving the Commodore parked discreetly behind the brick fence, he walked to the gate. Spotted Ant immediately. Hard not to: in a bright pink shirt and tight leggings, he was executing a passable headstand in the gazebo he'd been repairing the other day. Ant doing yoga? Etty's influence, no doubt, a physiotherapist with lots of excess energy to burn. No sign of her, but a second yoga mat next to Ant's. A brief reprieve. The woman had to have some residual anger towards the man who'd pushed Ant back into using.

Caleb skirted around the soggy lawn to the rotunda. Ant lowered his legs and stood, tugging at the too-tight crotch seam of the leggings. Had to be borrowed, their form-clinging material leaving nothing to the imagination, nicely offset by Ant's oversized Hawaiian shirt.

'Your dick'll fall off.' Some mime necessary to sign it – showing Ant's member tumbling through the air, plopping onto the timber boards – could've been more generous with the sizing.

Ant grinned. 'Nah, I keep it in hand.' Relaxed stance and movements, no obvious objection to Caleb being here. Even the sharpness of his face seemed softened. Big difference in only a couple of days.

'I see Etty's here.'

'Yeah, she comes Wednesdays. I didn't think to cancel. Hanging out for it, I guess. Don't worry, she's catching the next ferry.'

'So there's no problem with me being here, then?' Caleb asked. 'The whole Saturday visiting hours thing?'

'Nah, that's just the official line. Meant to keep problem family away.'

Problem family. Right. He was liking Locke less and less.

Ant's face lit up as he looked past Caleb. 'Sprung bad. I'm meant to be finishing my poses.'

Etty was coming up the path, gym bag slung across one shoulder. Wiry, with no-nonsense brown hair and a long stride that didn't match her height.

'How much does she know?' Caleb asked.

'Everything. No secrets, no lies. I stuff up again, she's gone for good.'

Including the aggravated burglary in Queensland? Maybe hold off on mentioning that and everything else until later: if Caleb fucked things up between Ant and Etty again, it'd be very bad news all round.

She'd reached the gazebo. Bright smile instead of the glare he'd expected, scattering words like confetti. '... see ... here ... great ...'

'Sorry, what?'

'Ahshit, sorry. Alwaystoofast. I'm so glad you'rehere. I didn't realise Ant had finallyasked you to come.' Beaming at Ant. 'Well done, sweetie.'

'I didn't.'

'He didn't.'

She looked at them. 'The two of you are completely shit at communicating.'

'Hey,' Ant said, 'I'll have you know that my talking has been called both incessant and annoying.'

'Yeah, but you're just talking to cover your fears. And you,' she fixed on Caleb, 'only talk when interrogated.'

No idea how to respond. Play it for laughs? Honesty?

'There you go, proving my point. I don't know how Kat stands it. Right – Caleb, Ant wants your help. Ant, Caleb wants to help. The rest you'll have to work out by yourselves, I've got a ferry to catch.'

Ant glanced at his watch. 'Shit. Yes. Got to tell Locke I'm going. Back in a sec.' He set off towards the clinic.

When he was a few metres away, Etty turned to Caleb. 'I'm so relieved you're here. He really needs you.' She went to add something but stopped. Unusual for Etty to hold herself back – then again, he didn't really know her as well as he'd like to or should.

After giving her a few seconds, he asked, 'How do you know Doctor Locke? Ant said you recommended him.'

'Yeah, isn't he great? Ant's doing so well with him. One of my clients was a patient here, told me about him. He seemed exactly what Ant needed. Kind but firm.' Her gaze went to the clinic where Ant had stopped to chat to someone by the door. One of the wobblier patients, accompanied by a strapping woman in a uniform-style blue top who looked like a country vet but was probably the nurse. Good timing. If Etty knew her name, he'd have the last staff member ID'd. The cook and cleaner seemed to be in the clear, their employer in the Bay confirming by text this morning that they'd been at work during the break-in, and the day the last fox had been dumped.

'You know the nurse's name?' he asked Etty.

'Melissa.'

'Surname?'

'Um, Wadleigh.'

One of the easier names to search: four kids, no criminal record, an islander by birth.

Etty's attention had returned to Ant. An unnatural stiffness as she watched him disappear inside.

'You OK?' Caleb asked.

'Yeah, I just – I can'tstopthinkingaboutthatday, you know? When he OD'd. And I can't –' A fist to her chest. 'I can't breathe.'

The beginning of Ant's fall. Slumped on the bathroom tiles, needle in his arm, a terrifying stillness to his chest.

'God, sorry,' Etty said. 'I didn't mean to upset you. Don't worry, it'll be all right. Locke's the best. He'll sort him out.'

———

Caleb followed Etty's hatchback down the hill. The water on the quayside had drained, leaving a scummy layer of mud. A small queue of vehicles was waiting to board the ferry, more parked along the sides of the clearing, including the *Fuck a Greenie* van. He pulled up near enough to give it a once-over but not show overt interest. No one in it or near it, doors closed. Too many people around to look inside, the islanders taking advantage of the calm sea to do their errands in town, some in their own boats. An older tinnie was pulling alongside the smaller of the two almost-derelict piers, piloted by Not-a-Total-Prick Gideon, the man who claimed to have helped Taylor after he'd been run off the road near Muttonbird Cove. A potentially honest broker of information given Skye's confirmation of Taylor's interest in the birds.

Caleb made a 'stay there' motion to the oblivious Ant and Etty, entwined in her car, and headed for the tinnie. An obstacle course of mud-holes and tree litter on the way, his canvas Volleys waterlogged within four steps. Should pack gumboots next time. Should buy gumboots.

Debris was strewn along the usually pristine beach. A high-water mark of leaves and water bottles, tangled plastic, the not-at-all disturbing sight of a yellow biohazard bag. He reached Gideon as the man climbed from the tinnie. Box of shopping already on the pier, the distinctive orange logo of Best Buy Cellars on the side, a few soup tins tucked between the vodka bottles.

Gideon hoisted the box easily, gave Caleb the country handshake: slight lift of the chin. Very slight.

Caleb replied in kind. 'The white van over there. Know who's been driving it lately?'

'Nup.' Gideon moved around him, kept walking.

Question answered, nothing volunteered. Some uncomfortable self-recognition there. Etty was right, that was obnoxious.

He squelched his way back to the car, pulling the sat phone from his jacket when it buzzed. Kat's mother, with an unexpected amount of information.

—*Caleb*

Re: Doctor Locke. He is well regarded in the field of addiction management.

Re: Clinics. The below places come highly recommended but do have significant wait times. Please forgive me if this is an overstep, but as I know the director of Turning Point, I asked for special consideration.

If Anton wished, he could start there next week, on the twentieth.

A seven-day wait wasn't perfect, but a great back-up plan if things got worse here. Maria was a wonderful person.

—Please book Ant in. Thank you. Really owe you

—*My pleasure. You can repay me by placing the cutlery handles downwards in the dishwasher as we discussed last week.*

Ant and Etty had made it to the outside of the car. Side by side, arms around each other, Ant like a bereft flamingo in his leggings and pink Hawaiian shirt, a jacket hanging limply from one hand.

Might be a good time to mention Turning Point, get him prepared to leave, get Etty on board with it too. Caleb opened his mouth, closed it as Ant gave him the stink eye. What was with the mind-reading? Was he that predictable?

Etty unwound herself. 'Well, I'd love to stay and watch you two say fuck-all to each other, but I have to go.' She planted a kiss on Ant's mouth and hopped in the car, took off towards the ferry.

Ant gazed after her. 'Is it weird I get turned on when she's snippy?' Automatically signing now Etty was gone.

Caleb went to stop him. Left it. By now, everyone on the island knew who they were and what they were doing. Might as well get respite from all the lip-reading he was going to have to do today.

He brought Ant up to date as they walked to the Commodore, giving him the basics about the planted rifle, and more detail on his blackmail theory, that the killer had been hunting for evidence at the clinic.

A sceptical look. 'Why leave the bullet if they were just after evidence?'

That was the question. Warning they'd be back, or to keep quiet, or something far more tangled?

Caleb opened the car, did a hip-block to stop Ant getting behind the wheel.

After a brief tussle Ant headed for the passenger side. A bounce to his step, even after his lack of success and farewell to Etty. The old Ant shining through again.

'So where to?' he asked as he got in.

'Quarry. See if their CCTV caught who was chasing Taylor that night.' Caleb paused as Ant made himself comfortable. Some manspreading going on, the garish shirt falling open to reveal more anatomical detail than could be comfortable. Or, perhaps, legal. 'You want to change first?'

Ant tugged at his crotch. 'Why?'

19.

The quarry was a scooped-out hill of pale limestone. White dust drifted across its barren surface despite last night's rain, coating the roadside eucalypts with fine powder. Not much to it, a couple of sheds and a silo, lone excavator working in the distance. Ant's attempts at the intercom didn't get any response. He kept jabbing the button, a little welcome-to-my-world frustration Caleb wasn't above enjoying, even with his uneasiness about that ridgeline and silo. Might as well go home now if he was going to get twitchy about potential sniper lairs. Highpoints all over the island: the hills and the clinic's water tower, houses, even the pines with their broad, climbable limbs.

He glanced over his shoulder. Only paddocks and the farmhouse down the road where the goat cardigan woman lived.

Ant gave the intercom a final jab. 'Fuck this for a joke.' He gripped the fence's wire strands, scrambled up to the small solar panel mounted by the CCTV camera. Brief inspection, then he disconnected something. The gate sagged open. He jumped down, looking pleased with himself. 'Magnetic lock. Easy.'

So easy, it didn't bode well for the quality of the CCTV or the number of break-ins Ant had done recently. Not a topic of conversation Caleb was looking forward to, but he had to know what they were facing. He looked at Ant as they headed for the sheds. 'So, agg burg in Queensland.'

A hitch to Ant's footsteps. 'Of course you know about that.

First thing you would have done was look for all my fuck-ups.'
He took a slow breath. 'OK, give it to me – is there a warrant?'

Caleb stopped himself from signing 'not yet'. 'Wanted for questioning.'

'OK. OK, thanks.'

'How's it "aggravated"?'

'Family was home. Didn't even know they were there, I was pretty off my – One of the little ones woke up, started crying.' An unfocused look. 'I came here a few days later.'

'You weren't armed?'

'The fuck? No. Course not.'

That was something, at least. Ant would have to face up to the cops eventually, but it was hard to see that happening under the threat of a massive jail sentence. 'Anything else I should know about?'

'How to get that stick out of your arse would be a good start.' Ant lengthened his stride, heading for a hulking machinery shed. Two men inside, cutting stone.

Caleb followed, winced as a squeal dragged across his ears. A tense moment before realising Ant had his hands over his own ears – not tinnitus, just the aids amplifying real sound. Easily fixed. He pulled them out: silence. Like slipping into a warm bath. How did hearies bear not being able to do that?

As he and Ant approached the open mouth of the shed, the two stonecutters glanced up for a second. Returned their attention to the slab of limestone they were guiding through an enormous circular saw. Industrious men. Very large, industrious men. Possibly not the type who'd appreciate being forcefully interrupted. He kept walking, reinserting his aids, Ant already two steps ahead and moving towards a nearby portable.

A regular-sized man was working inside the cluttered cabin: *B rt Lanning, M na g r*, according to the peeling sign on the door.

Burt raised a finger telling them to wait, his eyes not leaving the chunky desktop computer as he pecked one-handed at the keyboard. Not comfortable with technology, the quarry obviously more of a paper-based business. Dusty folders were piled on every filing cabinet and shelf, a stack teetering near Burt's elbow.

Ant positioned himself in front of the desk so Caleb could lip-read them both. Oh shit, he was intending to lead the conversation. Nope, not after his train-wreck attempt with Skye.

'Sorry to barge in,' Caleb said. 'Couldn't get anyone on the intercom.'

Burt looked up, mouth open. Ruddy face and a high, hard gut, a few days on from his last shave. 'It's busted.' He gaped at Ant's clothes, an aviator jacket with a sheepskin collar now completing the ensemble. 'You an actor or something?'

'Aren't we all in some way?'

Caleb stepped forward to give the manager a business card, made sure he landed hard on Ant's foot in the process. 'We're after info for an insurance claim. Car accident near here. Could we see your CCTV footage from last Saturday?'

'Nah, mate, not worth me job. Boss is a stickler for that kind of thing.'

Caleb pulled out his wallet, held it by his side. 'How much would it be worth?'

'Sixty-four a year, plus super.'

Right. Seventy-four grand was slightly out of his price range. He tucked the wallet away. 'Any chance you saw something? Yellow jeep speeding past, around eight-thirty?'

'We knock off at four. Well, three-thirty.'

'No night shift?'

Burt gazed around the cramped space. 'Night shift?'

'Your boss on site?' If he was one of the surly stonecutters, they might be out of luck.

'Dave? Nah, he's sick. Heart stuff, you know.'

'Where's he live?'

'You know, the limestone place.'

Might need more detail than that. 'Got an address?'

But the manager was studying Ant, his flushed face wrinkling. 'Hang on, aren't youse from the clinic?'

'Is it the clinic you don't like?' Caleb asked. 'Or someone in it?'

Burt's reply was lost as he turned back to the computer.

Ant flinched. He rallied quickly, gave a genial smile. 'Got to correct you there, Burt – only some of us are junkies, the rest are pill poppers and alcos.' He walked out, left the door open.

Caleb caught up with him just outside, kept pace as he cut across the yard towards the gate.

'Let's find the owner,' Ant said. 'Can't be too many limestone places around.'

An untroubled expression, but Caleb was almost certain he should say something. A supportive comment to soften the manager's insult but not draw attention to it. Something encouraging but not patronising; light-hearted but not dismissive. Impossible.

'Woman down the road first,' Caleb told him. 'Goat cardigan.'

———

They drove the short distance to Joyce's farmhouse. From the few minutes he'd spent in the woman's company at the shop, it seemed unlikely she'd witnessed a car chase and not mentioned it. But sometimes people didn't know what they were seeing.

Joyce's property looked like an ad for a cleaning service. Not a glamorous place – a stump-sunk weatherboard with peeling paint – but everything meticulous. House windows shining, lawn raked, driveway cleared of twigs and leaves. As though last night's storm hadn't happened. No sign of a car, but they knocked anyway, went around the back. A long, grass lot with a milking shed at the far end, goats in the adjoining paddock. The shed was empty, a hand-painted sign on the door advertising raw goat's cheese for sale. So there was a reason for Joyce's watchful-eyed goat cardigan, if not an excuse.

A spark of an idea – maybe the missing word in Skye and Arlo's whispered argument had been 'bovine'. Though it was hard to see how anything to do with cows could be worthy of blackmail. Cattle rustling? A cover-up of mad cow disease? He tested the shapes in his mouth. Bovine, bovis, bovine, bovis – identical.

'You having a stroke?' Ant asked. 'Can you smell burnt toast?'

'Trying out some words.' He explained about the argument at the shop and Skye's fearful reaction to him having witnessed it.

'Sorry to burst your bovine bubble, but I haven't seen any cows since I've been here.' Ant contemplated the house's faded boards. 'You know, I feel Joyce may have misjudged her market somewhat. I mean, who'd want to eat homemade unpasteurised goat's cheese?'

Jarrah, probably, when he wasn't procuring vegan brie and ripe figs to feed Kat.

'That's quite a scowl,' Ant said. 'Raw goat cheese a step too far for you?'

Ignoring him, Caleb headed up the long driveway towards the car.

Ant followed. 'OK, now I *need* to know.' He smacked Caleb's arm, kept smacking. 'Come on, what's got your goat?'

God, Ant wouldn't stop when he was in this kind of mood, would just keep on and on until Caleb either caved or smothered him. 'Jarrah.'

'Jarrah? What'd he do, smile at you?'

'At Kat.'

'Wouldn't be alone there. Although I can see the appeal from her point of view – trade up emotionally damaged goods for a spunky black artist with good taste in clothes and an appealing nature.'

Well, that certainly dragged Caleb's fears into the cold, hard light of day.

Ant's grin faded. 'You're not really worried, are you? Kat's not like that.'

No, she wasn't; far too honest to hide things. So why was he letting Jarrah get to him? He grabbed the first idea that came to him. 'She's stalling on buying a place together.'

A pause as Ant took that in. 'Asked her where she wants to live?'

'What d'you reckon? Yes, detailed list of streets and suburbs.' This conversation was over. Why did people say you should talk about things? Shit advice. He pulled out his keys as they reached the car.

Ant slid between him and the door. 'Still doing that looking-away thing, huh? I meant, here or Melbourne. You considered she might want to make the move here permanent but she's concerned about you? I mean, it'd be pretty shit for you – your business, the Deaf community. Weird she hasn't mentioned it, though.' He stopped at something in Caleb's expression. 'You dickhead. She has, hasn't she?'

A few weeks ago. Not Kat's usually forthright style, but an oblique approach he now realised was a gentle sounding out. He'd smacked down the idea without thinking, not one that had been raised before. But it made sense. Family, friends, culture, Country – of course Kat would want to raise their family here. OK, that was a problem, a fairly large problem, but a manageable one.

'You're welcome,' Ant said. 'And hey, if you go with it, you can buy me out of the house. Reckon it's time for me to move on.' He snatched the keys from Caleb's hand.

20.

They spent the morning trying to find the quarry owner's house. Getting lost on nameless muddy tracks that wound through the scrubland in baffling directions, coming across sudden dead ends, houses built from asbestos and salvaged timber. Bare dirt yards with salt-bitten veggie gardens, graveyards of rusty cars. People not home, not answering doors or incapable of giving clear directions.

Back at the shop, Skye finally came to the rescue with an overpriced map and detailed instructions. Her usual smiling self, no hint of last night's fear in her face.

The house was visible a long way off, a neat limestone cottage set close to the road. On the far side, a thick hedge acting as windbreak. Flat grazing land around here, Merino sheep and knock-kneed lambs in the paddocks.

Caleb stomped on an imaginary brake as the car slewed towards a fence post. 'Fence.'

Ant looked at him. 'Nervous much?' He tugged the wheel, getting them back on the waterlogged road. A lot less perky as the day wore on but he'd still won the last two tussles for the keys. Not doing so well on the whole hands-on-the-wheel thing though, keeping up a flow of Auslan without bothering to adjust for the driving conditions. 'So anyway, we decided she'd visit once a week, take things slowly. But it hasn't been slow in bed. Right back into it. We even –' He sighed. 'That damn phone's going again.'

'Yeah.' Already reaching for it, and not just to avoid the conversation; the tone might be too high-pitched for him to hear, but the satellite phone's super-charged vibration made him jump every time. Should have just given the number to Kat and her family instead of forwarding his usual number to it. Constant interruptions from clients, real estate agents and the so-called Tax Office Department urgently advising him to CLICK THIS LINK.

Slightly different spam this time, Mick with another dick pic, the image fortunately unviewable on the phone. No idea what to do next with the investigation. A thorough hunt through the club's ledgers last night hadn't unearthed anything except debt and well-kept records. Which left the unlikely theory the whole thing was just a vendetta against the coach, Ross Greene.

Caleb sent a 'working on it' message to Mick, kept it short to stop Ant from crashing as he tried to read it. 'Need me to read it out?'

Ant looked unabashed. 'No, I got it. What's up with the Numbats?'

Probably worth telling him; Ant had trained under Greene as a junior player, had mates in the Numbats. He explained about the photos, waited for Ant to stop laughing before continuing. 'Ross Greene must have a few enemies. Who'd be your pick?'

'Nah, Greene's OK. I mean, he's got the sensitivity of a block of wood, but he loves the team. Just pushes too hard because he flaked out when he tried to go pro.'

'We talking about the same Ross Greene? Walking, talking arsehole?'

Ant gave him a look of mock sympathy. 'He mean to you? Make you cry?'

'Thinking of yourself, maybe? The time you dragged Mum up there to tell him off.'

'No dragging necessary, given I was her favourite. Her delinquent eldest son out stealing cars.'

'One car. And I was twelve.'

'Five,' Ant countered. 'And you were fourteen.'

Damn, nothing to throw back at him. 'What'd you mean about Greene flaking out? I thought he was injured? Had to stop playing.'

'Yeah, he's got a few scars he likes to flash around, but they're nothing much. Pretty sure it was all just an excuse for him to pull out, not risk failure in the big league.'

Complete speculation, but Ant's instincts for people were good. And someone who'd concoct a face-saving myth like the coach's might just be the kind of man who'd go to the trouble of photoshopping a giant numbat suit.

The car slowed, Ant peering at something through the windscreen.

Caleb followed his gaze. The cottage was up ahead, something slung over the barbed-wire fence opposite. Soft shape, like a coat. Hairs plucked the skin on his arms. Another fox.

Ant crept forward until they were alongside. It was hanging by its hindquarters, front paws dangling to the ground, the grass below its muzzle dark with blood. Not dead long. Killed since the storm, possibly while they'd been driving around the island asking for directions.

A cold spot on the back of Caleb's neck, the vulnerable divot where the top of his spine met his head. He scanned the area. Treeless paddocks, and the house, its front windows just metres from the road. Nowhere for a sniper to hide.

'Could be a coincidence,' Ant said. 'Lambing season, farmers'll be on the lookout for them. Remember the fox fence? Still freaks me out.'

On the back road to the beach. Foxes strung along it in varying stages of mummification, bags of bones stiffening in the sun.

Culled to protect the flock, displayed to ward off others. Ivan had pointed them out whenever they'd passed the farm, made some comment about necessity or facing reality. No idea how Ant knew what they'd looked like – he'd screwed his eyes shut every time.

'Could be,' Caleb said. 'But park in the driveway.' Only a few metres ahead, tucked behind that nice thick hedge.

A woman around their age answered the door, toys strewn along the hallway behind her. Heavy eyes, a milky stain down her mis-buttoned shirt. She was stirring the steaming contents of a dinosaur-shaped bowl as though her life depended on it. Momentary confusion, as though she'd been expecting someone else. Her gaze didn't go to the fox hanging on the other side of her garden. Might have seen it earlier, seen a hundred dead foxes strung from fences; he'd still anticipated some reaction, an 'oh yeah, there's a new dead fox outside my house'.

'Yes?' Mild irritation in tone and face.

Ant glanced at the fox, went to speak. Caleb made a subtle 'shut up' sign, snapping his hand shut like a beak; Ant's mouth closed. Magic. Should try that more often.

'Dave in?' Caleb asked her.

'No.' Adding a few cooling blows to her whisking. 'He's on the mainland. Heart surgery.' The same slow speech as most islanders, thank God. The tinnitus had been sliding in and out of his ears all day.

'You're his –?'

'Daughter.'

'You running the quarry while he's away?'

'No fear, I'll be getting out of here as soon as he can get someone to mind the damn dogs. Quarry's running itself. For what it's worth, which is about two cents.'

Living on the mainland by the sounds of it, which hopefully

meant she wouldn't be as invested in keeping secrets as a current resident. He started going through the story about the insurance claim and CCTV footage, but she interrupted him. 'Sorry, you'll have to wait until Dad's back.'

'We could log on here if you're not comfortable giving us access codes.'

'Power's out.'

No mains power on the island. He called her bluff. 'Generator broken?'

'Out of diesel. Delivery's late.'

Two large, very hairy, dogs raced past the end of the hallway, a toddler running in their wake. The spoon whisked faster. 'I have to go.' She went to elbow the door shut.

Caleb rested his hand on the frame. No guarantee she wouldn't slam it on his fingers, but most people wouldn't.

The thought flashed across her tired face, but she sighed. 'The camera's probably not digital anyway. Dad hates computers. Only uses them when he has to.'

That exhausted impatience could be a cover for nervousness, but analogue tapes fitted with the quarry's paper-filled office and old computer. Which meant this was over. Ancient, re-used tapes would barely capture anything in daylight; at night, there'd be nothing but static.

He looked at Ant, pale again, but obviously still desperate to ask about the fox. Passed him the conversational ball with a flick of his hand.

'What's the deal with the fox?' Ant said quickly.

Impressive. They were getting good at this.

'What?' Blank gaze, as though she hadn't understood the question.

'Dead fox? Hanging from the fence?' Gesturing to it as he gave her his most charming smile. The one that had skipped every other

134

Zelic male in living memory and had most recipients offering him their hearts.

'They're pests.'

'But why hang it there?'

'Not my fox, not my fence.'

Caleb whipped his hand from the door as she slammed it.

'Not my fox, not my fence,' Ant repeated out loud as they turned from the door. 'Not my fox. Not my fence. Neither one of them mine.' He changed to sign. 'Let's just steal the tapes. Clinic's got boltcutters – nice pair, good edge on them.'

'Not worth the risk, tapes'll be shit.' Caleb made for the driver's seat, got ready for the usual scuffle.

But Ant turned meekly for the other door, began rolling a cigarette as soon as he was seated. He paused as the sat phone jolted Caleb's arse cheek. 'Give it to me, I'll turn off the sound.'

'No.'

'It's annoying. Really whiny.'

'Yeah, you should work on that.' Caleb grabbed the phone. Private number.

—*half moon bay now*

Had to be the same anonymous messenger. Someone who'd almost certainly saved Ant's life last time, but there was no way of knowing their motivations. Or if this message was a trap.

He angled the phone away from Ant as he typed.

—Why do you want to meet?

After a short wait, he tried again.

—Why should I trust you?

Still no answer. Their only possible lead; had to go. But by himself – Ant was slumped in his seat, hands trembling as he tried to light the rollie. Hanging out for his dose of methadone. If the shakes got as bad as the other day, he'd be a serious liability.

'Got some work stuff on,' Caleb told him. 'I'll drop you at the clinic while I sort it out.'

Lit cigarette between his lips, Ant signed casually, 'Cut me out of things, and I'll spread it around the island you're a kiddie fiddler. See how far you get then.'

Jesus, nuclear first strike. Had to admire it. 'Bit over the top, don't you think?'

Ant picked a speck of tobacco from his bottom lip. 'Mutually assured destruction is the only thing you understand.'

Caleb grabbed the map from the back seat. Chucked it at Ant. 'Find Half Moon Bay.'

The track to Half Moon Bay petered out on a clifftop. Old grazing land, the remains of a post-and-wire fence blocking their way. Caleb parked beside it and grabbed Taylor's binoculars, got out. A featureless plain marked only by a few arthritic grey tea-trees. No nearby hills or bushland for a sniper to hide in, no cars following them from the low scrub.

Slinging the binoculars around his neck, he turned to the car. Ant was leaning against the door, ashen, his sweat-darkened hair plastered to his forehead. That had to be more than the lingering effects of detox.

The old terror gripped Caleb. All those years Ant had injected poison into his body, all the damage he might have inflicted. 'Are you –' He stopped, hands midair. How to form the shape of his fears? 'Are you OK?'

Ant shoved himself upright. 'I'm not going to stuff up this meeting, if that's what you're asking.'

'No, I mean, health wise. In general.'

'Oh. Yeah, this is just me weaning off the 'done. Been on a high dose. Locke did a full exam when I got here. Some dodgy veins and stuff but otherwise all clear – no HIV, no hep.'

A shaky breath. 'Great. That's great.'

'What are the odds? Got another chance. More than a chance. Feels different this time, you know. Like I'm really going to kick it.' Ant's eyes filmed with tears. 'Then again, thought that before.'

OK, definitely time to say something supportive. 'You'll be right,' he said. Winced at the inanity.

Ant gave him a long, deadpan look. 'You could charge for that kind of pep talk, you know. People'd pay thousands.'

They climbed a toppled section of the fence and crossed to the land's edge, sharp saline wind in their faces. A sheer drop to the slamming waves below. The ocean side of the island, water surging in from a deep basin. Half Moon Bay was a little way along, where the cliff face sloped at a gentler angle. A cradle of white sand and tumbled rocks, seagulls fighting over something at the high-water mark. The path to the beach was gone, swept away by an old landslip. Have to scramble down. Or not. Someone had been there, clear footprints coming from the next bay along. An odd waver in their passage; the person had suddenly veered to the tideline as though to examine something, before running back the way they'd come, feet leaving deep depressions. Unease stirred.

Ant was peering over the edge. 'Shit, they've already gone.'

Caleb raised the binoculars. Adjusted the dial until the sand sprang into sharp relief, crisp grains flecked with shell bits and mica. He traced the footsteps along the beach to the tide mark, the squabbling seagulls. Red eyed and open beaked, pecking at something in the tangled kelp. Flesh. White bone protruding from one end. An animal. Had to be.

Dark discolouration on the pale skin. He slowly brought it into focus – a tattoo.

21.

Part of a body, a forearm. Blue-white and bloodless. Chunks torn from it by sharks and birds. Not bloated yet, but the skin was beginning to slip from the flesh, elongating the tattoo: two black lightning bolts. Coarse brown hairs and defined muscles. Young bloke, probably. Killed then dumped at sea in the past couple of days, borne back by last night's storm.

Caleb lowered the binoculars. The shriek was growing louder, higher. He ripped out his aids. Fuck, only partial relief.

Ant was shifting restlessly. 'Come on, let's go. They've pissed off on us.'

'It's not a meeting, it's a tip-off. There's a, um, a body part down there. Man's forearm.'

'What?' Ant pulled back. 'No. You sure? Not from a mannequin or something? Stuff gets washed off those container ships all the time.'

'I'm sure.' So, their anonymous helper had found the arm. Or some other beachcomber had, the story of their find passed from islander to islander until it reached the messenger. Caleb held out the binoculars. 'There's a tatt – see if you recognise it.'

Still looking dubious, Ant raised them to his eyes, lowered them abruptly. 'Oh shit, it really is.'

'Recognise the tatt?'

'No. Well, I know what it is. SS bolts, yeah? Reckon I'd remember seeing that around.'

They both would. That double lightning design was the type of thing white supremacists inked on their skin.

Who the hell was the dead man? Taylor's blackmail victim? A weak link who'd been silenced? Not questions for Caleb to answer – time to accept reality.

He faced Ant. 'We have to call the cops.'

'No.' Instant reflex response.

'I'll deal with them, keep you out of everything.' When Ant didn't reply, he kept going. 'Another man's been murdered, and I've got no idea why or how to stop it happening again. We can't just ignore it and hope it'll all go away.'

Ant sucked in air as though drawing hard on a cigarette, released it slowly. Gave a small nod.

'I'll find a way down to the beach, keep the arm safe.' Caleb went to give him the sat phone, stopped. No, the cops would ask who'd made the call. 'Go to the shop, make an anonymous call from the payphone.'

'I can't call! Those things are recorded.'

'Well, I can't do it. Just call via Legal Aid or something.'

But Ant was looking back towards the car, braced like that morning on the foreshore, about to run. Calculating the quickest way to disappear, end his rehab, his future.

A surge of panic-tinged anger. 'For fuck's sake, Ant, take some responsibility for once.'

Ant's face wiped of expression. 'Yeah,' he said. 'Fair point.' He turned for the car, head high.

An image of him at seventeen, walking away from the house without a backwards glance. Their father watching from the doorway, the word 'ashamed' hanging from his lips. A man of firm convictions, Ivan Zelic. The kind of man who'd watch someone he loved walk away, instead of offering help. The kind of man it was easy to walk away from.

Hands to his mouth, Caleb yelled, 'Ant!'

He turned, outlined against the lowering sky, the wind snatching his hair.

'You're right,' Caleb signed. 'It's not worth the risk. Stay here, I'll handle the phone.'

———

The quayside was bustling, ferry just docked, shop crowded with returned islanders, a couple in Res Bay High uniforms. Caleb parked opposite, tentatively put in his aids – still wailing, but faint. Faint enough, anyway. He crossed to the shop's forecourt, not entirely sure of his next move. His usual emergency services technique of repeating the word 'ambulance' or 'police' wouldn't cut it: he needed a messenger. Too many people in the shop to risk asking Skye, not to mention the possibility of her involvement. Not Arlo, either. A schoolkid? Might have to be. Couldn't leave Ant alone and strung out much longer, almost half an hour already.

A woman was suddenly in front of him. The older patient, Lara. Magpie eyes fixed on his, long white hair blowing about her face. How the hell had she snuck up on him again? Appeared from nowhere both times they'd met. Well, not quite nowhere – the bright yellow jeep was parked in front of his car.

'Sorry,' she said. 'Didn't mean to startle you. I just wanted to see if Anton's all right. He's usually at the clinic by now.' Concern in her bright eyes.

So Lara and Ant were mates. Could see them getting along well with their shared sense of humour. And she was a rule breaker who didn't seem to mind keeping important information from the cops. Perfect.

'He could use your help,' Caleb said. 'With a phone call. Did he tell you I'm deaf?'

'Oh, so I'm allowed to know? Wasn't sure. You put a lot of effort into hiding it. Self-defence, I assume? People can be such arseholes.'

'The call?'

'I'm banned from the shop, but Locke's got a landline in his office if it's urgent.'

How did a seventy-year-old woman get banned from the only shop on the island? Arlo's temper at work?

'Banned? Why?'

'Misunderstanding.' A dismissive wave, the sleeves of her flannelette shirt swallowing her hand. 'Who do you want me to call?'

'The cops. But it has to be a public phone. There's a body part washed up at Half Moon Bay. Ant's there, guarding it.'

She studied him. 'You're really serious?'

'Yes.'

'No one'll thank you for bringing the police here.'

'Which is why you need to make it anonymous, keep Ant and the clinic out of it.'

An unreadable expression as she thought it through, came to a decision. 'Well, they can hardly chase me out, I guess.' She traipsed up the veranda steps, shirttails swinging like a cocktail dress as she went.

Wait or go? Should wait, debrief with her afterwards, make sure there weren't any nasty surprises. He turned for his car, leapt back as a white sedan zipped past, Ugly Cardigan Joyce at the wheel. A faint note joined the tinnitus: car horn blaring. Coughing, heart and dust in his mouth. People were staring at him from the shop and jetty. A curtain twitched in a house opposite. Like he was five again, learning the dangers of silent traffic. So much for being discreet.

On the second attempt he reached the Commodore safely. Sat

inside trying to work out what to tell the two homicide cops when they arrived. Somehow point them towards the clinic, but not Ant. Had to be possible, because if he fucked things up for Ant now … God, he hoped he hadn't just made a terrible decision.

Lara was crossing the street towards him, giving a thumbs-up. He opened his door, but she went straight to the yellow jeep and got in. Took off in a smart U-turn, accelerated up the hill. He stared after her, one foot still on the road.

People always asked questions in times of danger and intrigue – Who? How? Why? – and Lara, with her keen mind and opinions, would absolutely want answers about a body part on the beach. Yet she'd raced back to the clinic. To warn Locke about the cops? Agreeing to phone them just a ruse to buy time.

Follow or get back to Ant? If Locke was involved in the tattooed man's murder, that changed everything. Had to follow. He started the car.

22.

The jeep was parked at the far end of the clinic when he arrived. No sign of Lara. Try the garden or inside? No one around to point him in the right direction – apart from Ant and Lara, the patients seemed to stay huddled in their rooms. He jogged to the jeep and peered around the corner: an old orchard, fruit trees pruned hard to their trunks. Faint smell of smouldering leaves, maybe a bonfire. Or something else. Lara's words the first time he'd met her: *That smoke would've blown all over the island.*

He sprinted back across the lawn, kept going past the water tower to the redbrick shed hidden at the far corner of the grounds. A wisp of smoke was coming from the incinerator's towering chimney. Lara was inside. Standing in front of the yawning hearth, her back to the open entrance, blowing on a scrappy fire to get it to flame. Piled twigs and smoking leaves, what looked like balled-up pieces of paper. Burning evidence of some misdeed, or the evidence the blackmail victim was searching for? One last piece of paper in her hand.

He crept across the leaf-littered floor, lifting his feet and placing them carefully. Brushed a vine from his face. She whipped around, crumpling the last page in her fist. Did she have bat genes? Appearing from nowhere, aware of everything.

'Sorry,' he said. 'Didn't mean to startle you.' Using her words to him.

'Startle? You scared the crap out of me.'

'Guilty conscience?'

'You could say that. I'm burning my regrets. Doctor Locke's suggestion. Embarrassing, really, but it does help to watch the words go up in smoke.'

Keep her talking, keep that piece of paper out of the fire. 'What kind of regrets?'

'Today it's my grandsons. You and your brother remind me of them. Or so I imagine, I'm not allowed to meet them.' Actual tears in her eyes – could she really turn it on that easily? 'Anton said you've got a baby on the way. You should be with your wife, not all the way over here.'

'It's not far.' He edged closer.

'Believe me, it's not that distance that counts.' A tap to her forehead with a bony finger. 'It's this one. Then again, what would I know?' She tossed the scrunched paper into the fire, watched while it smouldered then flamed. A satisfied smile as she left.

He ran to the hearth, swept the paper onto the floor with his hand. The ashen layers disintegrated as he tried to ease them apart. Fragments of print. Not a list of Lara's regrets unless she'd typed them up and printed them earlier, written in code. Seemingly random letters and numbers. He photographed each segment and zoomed in: *RBV, 508320, 850N*. Meaningless.

The clifftop was empty when he arrived. He parked by the old fence, got out. Ant had probably gone down to the beach to keep their gruesome find safe. No reason to think he'd panicked, was halfway back to the mainland.

Caleb set off along the fence, running too fast for the terrain. Slowed to climb a fallen section by a gnarled tea-tree.

Heat splintered his face. Trunk and branch shredded.

Down on the ground, arms over his head. No thought, body moving before his brain caught up. Pressed low in the grass, heart pounding, legs tangled in the fence wire. Where the hell was the sniper? No hills, no high points.

Ant.

Bleeding, dying, dead.

Caleb lifted his head. 'Ant! You there?' Only the bone-coloured grass rippling across the ground. Hadn't heard him, that's all. Voice probably didn't carry very far outside. He raised himself higher. 'Ant!'

Shrapnel sprayed above him, slivers of wood peppering his neck and head. Down again, cheek pressed to the spikey grass. Couldn't just lie here. Had to move, help, do something.

Faint beats beneath him. Stomach-lurching fear, but the vibration wasn't footsteps, just the fence wire moving against his thigh. Steady pattern, as though someone was tugging it. One-two-three, stop. One-two-three, stop. Wilting relief. Smart, very smart. Always said his brother was the smart one.

He scrambled around, gripped the wire with both hands. 'One for yes, two for no,' he yelled.

A single beat.

'You OK?'

Slight delay, then a yes. That hesitation was a concern. Hurt but not badly? Obviously clear-headed enough to think of the fence, make his way to it from wherever he'd been sheltering.

'You close?'

Another yes.

'To the east?' No response. For fuck's sake – Ant and his lack of directional knowledge. Caleb tried again. 'Use a clock face. If the cliff is six o'clock, are you at three?'

Yes.

A quick look, still no sign of him.

'Where's the sniper?' He went through the same routine, got a solid yes for a south-west position.

Good news, a rise in the land between them. Be safe if he stayed low, let the swaying grass disguise his movements. Hopefully.

'OK, I'm coming.' Caleb stopped. Unlikely someone with a rifle would need to lure him closer, but it didn't hurt to be sure. 'Safety check. Is Mrs Naylor a cat?'

No.

Maybe a double verification. 'A cow?'

Instant yes.

He dragged himself across the ground on his stomach, braced for the slam of the bullet. Sting of sweat in his eyes, rocks and burrs biting. Nearly fell on top of Ant as the land gave way in a sudden fold.

'Took you long enough,' Ant said while Caleb untangled himself.

Sitting half-propped against the embankment, shaking, skin like parchment. One arm wrapped around his ribs, pink shirt stained red beneath it. Shot. How much blood had he lost?

Caleb scrambled upright, shrugged off his jacket to get to his T-shirt for a makeshift bandage.

'It's OK,' Ant signed. 'Almost stopped bleeding.' Sweat rolled down his forehead, splashed onto his Hawaiian shirt.

Going into shock. Caleb gripped his T-shirt hem, went to lift it.

Ant kicked his ankle. Hard. 'Seriously. Calm the fuck down, it's exhausting. Just withdrawal and fucked nerves, overreact to pain.'

Definitely not dying with that pissy attitude. But the injury could be a lot worse than Ant was letting on. That knee-jerk denial of weakness was a family trait – and one Caleb was beginning to suspect might not be the character strength he'd thought it was.

'Show me,' he said.

Giving an exaggerated sigh, Ant gingerly lifted the shirt to show his blood-smeared side. A short, deep gouge across his ribs, the surrounding flesh swollen. No bright arterial spray or shards of bone, but it'd be a miracle if a rib or two weren't fractured. He wouldn't be able to run if the sniper came to finish them off.

'Happy?' Ant lowered the shirt.

'Yeah, you'll live. So, contingency plan. If the sniper comes closer, stay here. I'll draw them away.'

'Won't happen. He's just keeping us away from the beach. Motorboat turned up a few minutes ago – still there now.'

Someone getting rid of the arm. 'You see who?'

'No, sniper drove me up here.'

Caleb went to run, fell back as Ant grabbed his wrist.

'Don't!' Ant said. Eyes wide, he signed one-handed. 'That's how I got hurt. Bullets weren't even close until I did a you and ran back to see the boat. He gave me a few warning shots, hit me when I kept going.'

Could run a lot faster than Ant. The clifftop wasn't far; only be exposed for five, six seconds.

No. Men with families didn't do that. They stopped and remembered they had a very great need to stay alive.

He lowered himself to the ground. 'Do a me?'

Ant released him, sagged against the rocky embankment. 'Don't worry, the fuckwittery's all yours from now on. Too painful.'

Some pain involved in being smart, too. Sitting here, letting whoever was in that boat get away with the remains. The accomplice he'd suspected they were up against, the one who'd rammed Taylor's car. Right outside the turtle-mouthed Gideon's house; a man who owned a tinnie. As did most islanders.

'Two people in on it,' he told Ant. 'Maybe more.'

'Yeah, did the maths. How'd they find out so fast? You broadcast the news?'

Quite possibly. A chance Lara had tipped off the killers, but an opinionated islander like Cardigan Joyce was more likely. Zooming past just after he'd spoken to Lara. If she'd overheard them, she'd have spread the information far and wide.

'I asked Lara to call the cops,' he told Ant. 'Think Joyce heard me.'

'Two strikes for you, then. No way Lara called them. Hates cops.' Exhaustion as well as relief in his expression. 'So anyway, bit of a wake-up call. Reckon I might leave, go to another rehab. Don't know why you didn't suggest it, really.'

Fuck. Fuck.

Ant was looking at him. 'Long wait?'

'Seven days.'

Panic flashed across Ant's face. 'I can't –'

'No. I'm hooked now, anyway. Have to see it through.' He kept going as Ant started a half-hearted objection. 'Boat still here?'

'Yeah. Leaving, I think.'

Get Ant back to the clinic and hunt for the sniper's lair. South-west position, according to Ant's earlier answers, but no high points there. Shooting from the top of a vehicle? Not much height, they'd have to be close.

'How –' He broke off as he realised Ant's eyes were shut, started again in English. 'How close is the sniper?'

Eyes still closed, Ant signed wearily, 'Maybe a kay.'

A kilometre? No. Didn't want that to be true. Not an improbable distance, but it put the sniper's abilities at a whole new level. Particularly with the strong wind. A highly skilled marksman. Or woman.

'Sure it's that far?' he asked Ant.

'Yeah.'

'How?'

Ant opened bloodshot eyes. 'Did you miss Year Seven physics? Because I can barely hear the shots. Because there's a big gap between the sound and the bullets hitting things. Like, you know, me.' He flapped a hand towards the ocean. 'Boat's gone. Stick your head up, see if he shoots.'

Caleb used his jacket instead, waving it from side to side in the air. Nothing.

He grabbed the binoculars from beside Ant. Raced to the cliff's edge. Restless grey sea stretching to a wide horizon, no boats. On the beach, one set of crisp footprints led from the waves to the high-water mark and back. The arm was gone.

23.

By the time they reached the clinic gates, Ant was doubled over in his seat, breathing shallowly. They'd had to stop twice for him to vomit by the side of the road. Locke was in the driveway, climbing stiffly from the unpolished Jag Caleb had seen the other day. He straightened as Caleb pulled in sharply beside him and got out.

'Ant's hurt,' Caleb told him, kept moving to open Ant's door. 'Gunshot. Shallow, but maybe some cracked ribs.'

Locke's composure didn't waver as his gaze moved rapidly across Ant's face and bloodstained shirt. 'Come with me.'

A slow shuffle into the garish foyer, Ant's arm heavy across Caleb's shoulders. The doctor led them past the staircase to a closed door. Steel-plated with excellent locks, a white-tiled surgery inside. Reassuring security in a rehab. The wide-shouldered nurse, Melissa, was there, doing a stock check of the drugs cabinet. Flyaway brown hair escaping its ponytail. Light reflected off her glasses as she turned, obscuring her eyes, but a sense of decisions being quickly made. A pause to secure the cabinet, and she strode to help Caleb get Ant onto the examination table. Gave Ant's arm a comforting pat once he was lying down. Cautious and caring; Ant was in good hands. If those broad hands hadn't recently been holding a rifle. Exactly how bad was her eyesight?

After a few unintelligible words to the nurse, Locke faced Caleb. 'Perhaps you could give us some privacy.' No edge to his soothing voice but clearly an order.

Caleb stayed where he was.

Ant waved to get his attention, face damp with sweat or tears. 'Go. Meet you at the shop tomorrow morning. At eight.'

Went against every instinct to leave, but Caleb wouldn't want anyone watching while he puked and cried either. And he had a doctor's office to search.

He followed the nurse to the door, slightly too close, got a look through her lenses as she opened it: large magnification and distortion. Doubtful she could shoot well with astigmatism that bad. Could pilot a boat, though. Did the timing work? Get from the beach to the quay, dump the dismembered arm, zip back to the clinic and be calmly sitting in the surgery before he and Ant arrived? Possible, but highly unlikely.

Out in the foyer, he stopped her from closing the door. Spoke quickly as he hunted through his wallet for a business card. 'Could you let me know if there are any problems? Text, don't ring.' He found a card, was met with a confused expression when he held it out. 'Don't voice call,' he explained as she took it from him. 'Text.'

A briskly sympathetic smile to match the pat she'd given Ant. 'Sorry, love, but I'm not too good with accents. Can't understand you. I'll give the doctor this, but I'm sure he'll talk to you afterwards if you're concerned about Anton. Just wait in the foyer.' She closed the door.

Fuck. Just, fuck. Cottonwool voice. Years of speech therapy meant it rarely happened, but tiredness and stress could still thicken his words. Particularly when he rushed. Couldn't hear it himself, but he could feel it. Made sure he felt it. Except, apparently, today.

He strode away from the door, took the orange stairs at a run.

The office lock wasn't as sturdy as the ones on the surgery door, but it put up a fight. Exposed position at the top of the landing didn't help. Had to concentrate on the bumps and vibrations of

151

approaching footsteps, as well as the slight clicks of the tumblers; lost all his work twice when he had to duck away from the door. Finally got it open, checked the time: eleven minutes down, make it fast.

A light-filled room renovated into comforting blandness. Floorboards polished, walls painted in colours that would have names like Whisper Hush and Tranquil Dove. Someone had been heavy-handed with the lavender essential oil. An age-softened timber desk with a laptop and landline phone, silver picture frame. The photo of a dark-haired woman, early forties, serious eyes beneath the smile. Girlfriend? No mention of a wife or sister in any research. He gave the laptop's password a go, but none of the usual guesses worked: Locke's name forwards, backwards, 12345, PassWord, PA$$W0RD. No papers or files in the desk drawers, everything either stored electronically or in another room. Not a man who left notes lying around; unlikely Locke was the owner of those printed pages Lara had burnt.

Nothing else in the room. Through the deep-silled windows, a spectacular view over the island's hills and winding tracks, slightly ruined by the hulking concrete water tower next to the front fence.

A disturbing idea crept into his mind. You'd need good elevation to shoot a target a kilometre away. High enough to allow for the falling arc of the bullet. He went to the window. At the far edge of the building, a direct line of sight to Half Moon Bay in the distance. Only a smudge to the naked eye, but it'd be a lot clearer through a telescopic sight on top of that water tower. Perfect sniper's lair. Could easily sneak up the ladder on the far side of the base, lie hidden on top.

Locke as the sniper? Calm and considered, quick to respond in an emergency. But it made no sense for him to leave threatening notes and damage his clinic, harm his patients.

A change to the building's rhythms, the steady beat of footsteps under the wind's shifting vibrations. Caleb moved into the middle of the room as Locke entered.

The doctor started. 'How did you get in here?'

'Door was open. How's Ant?'

Locke didn't respond to the barefaced lie. He crossed to the desk, winced slightly as he eased himself onto the chair. 'I ... he ...'

Damn it. Not a big fan of feeling like a schoolboy being called up to the headmaster, but lip-reading wasn't a distance sport. He went to stand in front of the desk. 'Say that again.'

'My apologies, I said he's resting comfortably.'

Solicitous fuck. 'He told me his nerves overreact. What are you using for painkillers?'

'I'm sure he'll tell you if he wants to.' Locke opened his laptop to check the screen, another slight grimace as he shifted it to one side. Maybe that slow walk to the surgery hadn't just been for Ant's sake. The doctor caught his look. 'An old back injury playing up.'

A man who'd so far offered no personal information, suddenly hurt, suddenly willing to divulge his medical details to a patient's brother who'd just broken into his office. And not looking like someone who'd be able to lug a rifle to the top of a water tower. An alternative scenario presented itself: Locke not as sniper but hero, trying to stop the shooting. Anyone could access the tower – straight up the hill and in through the open gates. Even better, over the fence.

'You would have heard the shots,' Caleb said. 'They came from near here.'

'Yes.'

Unexpectedly easy. 'So who was it?'

'I have no idea. I'm afraid I didn't pay much attention. There's often rifle fire – farmers and hunters, I suppose. It echoes in the hills.'

Words Locke could repeat to a solicitor. Not that he'd have to. No legal obligation for him to volunteer information to the police, or even to answer if asked outright. Keeping silent was a risk-free position. As long as you didn't mind ignoring the murder and attempted murder of your own patients.

Locke was studying him, a slight frown marring his usually smooth brow. 'Anton was talking about a body part – an arm washed up on the beach, then removed by someone in a boat. Is that correct?'

'Yes. There was an alt-right tattoo on it, black double lightning bolts. You know anyone like that?'

'I don't believe so. This is all deeply concerning. Have you called the police? Oh, my apologies, of course you can't –'

Give him nothing: no change of expression, stance or tone. 'I asked Lara to call, but I don't think she did.' Almost certainly hadn't – no sign of them when he'd stopped to check the quayside from the top of the hill.

'I see.'

'You could ring them now,' Caleb said.

'That's a decision for you and Anton to make.'

Teflon man, every emotion sliding right off his face. When prepared for questioning, anyway – he'd looked shaken that first day, when Caleb had told him about the dead fox, the note. *I'm watching.*

So rattle him, go for the one personal thing in the room. Caleb picked up the framed photo of the dark-haired woman, examined it. Locke stilled.

'Who bashed you today?' Caleb asked as he met the doctor's gaze.

'No one.' The doctor's gentle smile had settled back into place. 'As I was saying, today's events are quite troubling. You're obviously concerned for your brother, and I'm sure you have the best of intentions, but I've noticed a worrying change in Anton since you've been here. He's reckless, trying to prove himself, his actions today the most obvious example. Given your history with him, I hope you'll put some thought into that.'

Acid bit Caleb's stomach. Couldn't be angry with someone for telling the truth.

Locke opened his laptop. 'Now if you'll excuse me, I have work to do.' Already focused on the screen.

Caleb set the frame on the desk. Walked out, closing the door gently behind him.

Dusk was falling when he reached the quayside. Houses all shut tight, no one in the shop or on the street. Every person here would have heard those shots or know about them, would have seen the bullet-riddled letterboxes outside the shop. They'd all have theories and suspicions about the sniper; some would know the truth. An urge to bang on all their doors, but he wouldn't get answers. Not now. A conspiracy born of fear. Going about your farming, fishing, cleaning, knowing that any second a bullet could rip through you. Or through your child, partner, parents. No reason for anyone here to risk that for outsiders. He wouldn't.

He parked facing the bay, bruised sky and sea dissolving into darkness. So far out of his depth with this. Any hope the sniper wouldn't kill on the island, gone. Not just the tattooed man, but Ant as well. The intention might not have been to kill, but no marksman in the world could have guaranteed that wouldn't be a fatal shot. A slight shift in the wind, a miscalculation, and Ant would have been dead. Lost to Caleb like so many others.

'Given your history . . .'

Two opposing thoughts flipped like a neon sign in his head: Call the cops/Don't call the cops/Call the cops/Don't call the cops.

Homicide detectives who distrusted him, no evidence, no leads. Ant would be arrested at worst, scared away from rehab at best. A long way down if he spiralled out of control again, not much chance he'd ever claw his way back out.

Decision made.

The tight-clenched feeling in his chest didn't ease, the fear he was going to regret whatever he did.

24.

Arlo was unloading the ute when Caleb got to the shop the next morning, beanie on. He paused to give Caleb a long stare, then returned to work. A system to his packing, rustier barrels of diesel separated from the veggie crates by a folded cardboard box. Good thinking, wouldn't want the food to contaminate that fuel. Caleb stopped by the veranda steps, snapped Arlo's photo while pretending to check reception on his usual phone. Never knew when a photo ID would come in handy. One islander down, around seventy to go.

Ant wasn't inside yet, just Skye and a couple of customers. Ten past eight. Only ten minutes later than Ant had said he'd be here. Not late for Ant. Far too soon to start worrying about sepsis and blood clots. Give it a few hours first. Just twitchy after yesterday and unable to go for a calming run. He'd made do with a few sniper-safe jump squats and push-ups in the rocky caravan; they hadn't really cut it.

He bought a vegetable-free breakfast roll from Skye, retreated to the computer. Not all that comfortable working in public, but at least no one could sneak up on him, his back hard up against a shelf of fishing tackle and mosquito repellent. The murder victim first – a chance someone with an alt-right tatt would be known to the police. Less chance a police mate with strong ethics would be forthcoming with their details. Caleb emailed Tedesco anyway: a request for info on a possible missing person, along with a stock photo of an SS bolt.

While he searched local tattoo parlours' websites, he started on the roll. Surprisingly good: bacon, egg, goat's cheese. If the cheese was from Ugly Cardigan's farm, she knew her stuff. Possibly knew a few other things, too. Next on his list of people to visit, followed by the boat-owning Gideon.

The sat phone buzzed as he ate the last bite. A forwarded text from his usual number, someone called Annabelle. Who was Annabelle and why did he have her number saved with the sidenote, *Mrs N hair*? That's right, Mrs Naylor's hairdresser. Back from holidays and replying to the messages he'd left at the salon enquiring about her friend with a dislike for Doctor Locke.

—*that was Willow i think she's a nurse. she used to work with him in melbourne but i don't know why she doesnt like him. i don't really know her much. please stop leaving messages*

Good old Annabelle and Mrs Naylor, coming through with the goods.

City of five and a half million, but it took him two minutes to discover Willow's surname, phone number and date of birth. All available due to a complete lack of privacy settings on one of her social media accounts. Barely twenty-one. Hadn't her parents told her how dangerous the world could be? Going to wrap his own child up so tightly they wouldn't be able to breathe. So he was obviously going to be seeing his therapist as soon as this was all over; the man who'd worked miracles on some pretty shit PTSD symptoms had to be able to steer him right on a few parenting skills.

He texted Willow Lane an ambiguously worded query, as though vetting Locke for a job. Hopefully she'd get back to him quickly, with some decent info, because he wasn't sure how else to get a handle on the man. Trusted by colleagues, Ant, patients, medical boards. Caleb seemingly the only dissenter.

Someone entered the aisle: Skye. Coffee cup in hand, fair hair artfully disarrayed, fresh lipstick pink against pale skin. He switched tabs away from the tattoo as she stopped, a few strides short. 'Would you like a top-up?' Nothing like her usual speech patterns: inaudible, mouth movements exaggerated. It clicked – a little re-enactment of the argument he'd witnessed. Testing to see if he'd understood her whispered conversation with Arlo, maybe that word 'bovis'. Which he hadn't. Unless the tattooed victim had liked cows, or his name was something like Boris, Maurice or Marven, there was no apparent link to anything.

Caleb peered at her. 'Sorry, didn't get that. Could you come closer?'

She set an insipid-looking coffee next to him, rested a hand on his shoulder. 'I said, I thought you might like a top-up.' Still standing too close.

Over at the counter, Arlo had turned to watch, open vulnerability on his face. Caleb averted his eyes. Unexpected sympathy for the man.

Skye was studying the computer screen, the news report on racial violence Caleb had changed to. 'Some light reading?'

Could tell her, test her. 'Research. Another man's been murdered.'

Colour drained from her face like a retreating tide. 'Where? Who?'

Impossible to fake a reaction like that. Not involved in the murder, or scared that he knew about it?

'Young guy,' he said. 'Know anyone with a tatt like this on his arm?' Keeping his gaze on Skye, he switched to the SS bolts.

No involuntary widening of her eyes or hitch to her breathing. So the man probably wasn't an islander, and Skye probably wasn't involved in his murder. Probably, probably.

'No,' she said. 'That's a skinhead thing, isn't it? What happened? How was he killed?'

'I don't know. There's no body.'

'Oh. So it's just a lead or something?' Relief softened her mouth. 'That'll be a mainland thing. You should look over there. We don't have people like that here.' She collected his used coffee cup and left, her gait loose.

Nearly nine o'clock. Pity he'd been so muffle-mouthed with the nurse; could have sat back, relaxed in the knowledge she'd let him know if anything was wrong. Five more minutes, then he'd go and hammer on Locke's door. But Kat first. He'd managed to get enough service on the pier to video-call last night, told her about yesterday's events. Not sure he should have dumped that much bad news on her, but she'd taken it reasonably well, as though she'd been bracing herself for something much worse.

She appeared onscreen, ear protectors slung around her neck, standard messy-work outfit of paint-stained overalls, the front straining across her stomach. Black singlet under the overalls, long-sleeved shirt yet to come.

'You look unbelievably hot,' he said.

'Wait till you see me in my welding visor.'

He took in the corrugated-iron background: Jarrah's. Of course, where else could she be working with power tools? Which was fine. Cheese-boy didn't stand a chance. 'You've started on the new piece?'

'Yeah.' Only a half smile at the prospect, something undercutting her usual new-project excitement.

'Having problems with it?'

'Just not really feeling it this morning.' She glanced off screen. 'Hang on, Jarrah wants to talk to you. Something about the Numbats.'

Numbatgate, the gift that kept on giving.

Jarrah came into view, standing beside Kat, bare arm almost touching hers, easy smile. 'Hi, Cal ... I ... tell you ...'

No chance of piecing together the missing words, not via the flat pixels of a video. Could ask Kat to translate. No, he couldn't.

'Text me,' he told Jarrah, then signed to Kat, 'Have to go. Talk to you later.'

Surprise in her face as he logged off.

Great. Handled that well. Very mature. And Ant was now an hour late. Caleb cleared his search history, headed for the car.

He got halfway up the hill before he stopped. Ant would resurface when he could; he'd be feeling like shit, trying too hard to cope, and doubting his ability to do it. Storming in there and taking over wouldn't help. Much as Caleb really, really wanted to.

Turning back down the hill, he went to see a woman in an ugly cardigan about a dead body.

Joyce's white sedan was parked in the driveway, freshly washed. Driveway, too, by the looks of it, the fine dust from the quarry stopping at the gate. Excessive but reassuring standards in a woman whose unpasteurised cheese he'd likely just eaten. He gave his grimy Commodore a pat and a promise as he got out. Definitely going to clean it one of these days.

It took a few knocks before Joyce cracked open the door, mousy hair pulled back from her faded face. Same scent of bleach he'd picked up on their first meeting in the shop, but stronger. Half a knitted goat stared at him through the narrow gap, its tufted chin hair blowing slightly in the breeze.

Joyce was talking before he'd quite tuned in. '... the middle of the cleaning. You'll have to excuse ...' Chatting like they were old friends but holding the door like a shield.

The back of his neck prickled. A glance behind him – no water tower, the clinic safely behind the ridgeline of the quarry.

She was still going when he turned back. '... like to buy some cheese?'

'No, I'd like to know who you told about the body part at Half Moon Bay.'

Her dry lips clamped tight. Most of the island, judging by her expression. Best to move on to something more specific: her story about the blackmailer nearly crashing into her on the way from Muttonbird Cove. 'The night Peter Taylor sped past here, did you see who was following him?'

'He was being followed?' Genuine-seeming surprise, though she pulled the door closer. Maybe not scared, but trying to keep him out? That bleach smell was very strong. Cleaning up after some fox shooting? Or worse. Sharks weren't the only thing that could sever a human arm. Hard to envisage the talkative woman as a killer, but he'd been fooled before.

'Can I come in?' One step forward and she instinctively shifted, releasing the door.

Cramped living room with mismatched furniture. He kept moving down a dogleg corridor, glancing through each doorway: small bedroom, bathroom, laundry. Everything neat and painfully clean.

He opened the last door – an empty kitchen. Ancient oven and cupboards, linoleum stapled in one corner. He'd disturbed her halfway through scrubbing out the fridge. Small wheels of paper-wrapped cheese were stacked on the table, each with a sticker of a creepy cartoon goat, laughing with oversized teeth. An eye-stinging stench of bleach, but no troubling ghost-stains on the walls or floor, just more evidence of long-term cleanliness.

Far beyond food-handling care, the kind of clean that came from a deep-seated compulsion.

In the doorway, Joyce was wiping red-raw hands on her cardigan, scanning the room as though ready to defend it.

Easy to weaponise her discomfort. He leaned against the wall, arms crossed, as though settling in for a long chat. The cardigan goats glared judgementally at him. 'Who wanted Taylor dead?'

'I don't know. How would I know? Lots of people were against the clinic. Disgusting place. Shouldn't be there.' Eyes widening, she quickly said, 'But it was probably an incomer.'

Interesting response. 'Who was most against the clinic?' When she didn't answer, he pushed himself away from the wall and went to the table, pulled out a chair.

'Gideon Matthews,' she said quickly, looking uncomfortably close to tears.

Even more interesting. 'Why?' he asked.

'I don't know. You won't tell him I told you, will you?'

'You scared of him?'

'Wouldn't hurt a fly. But he likes his privacy. He's on a pension or something, doesn't like us knowing his business.'

Us. 'He's not an islander?'

'No. Only been here a few years.' She grabbed a wheeled packet from the table, shoved it at him. 'Here, have a sample.'

He bought a kilo of guilt-cheese. Escaped to the car. A strong chance Joyce had thrown Gideon at him as a sacrificial outsider – or incomer – but there were enough possible links to take the accusation seriously. No info on the man, the common surname stymying research; time to throw money at the problem. As in, ask a price-gouging schoolgirl to do it.

Caleb texted Sammi from the sat phone, hoping she wouldn't ignore a message from an unknown number. Or be in the middle of PE.

—using sat phone. No internet, can't vid call. Need tax office info. First name: Gideon Sur: Matthews Address: Muttonbird Island, Vic Age: approx 40 yrs. Will pay outrageous $ for immediate turn around C Zelic

An almost immediate reply

—*K*

Hopefully a busy young hacker's version of 'OK', not an accidental mistype as she'd LOLed

He waited in the car, wound down the windows to get the stink of bleach from his nose. Chalky limestone dust settled almost immediately on the dashboard. It'd be a constant job for poor Joyce to keep that driveway of hers clean. Trying to control the uncontrollable.

The sat phone's small screen lit up.

—*doesn't exist. emailed you fat bill*

Gideon Matthews was living under a false name.

25.

Caleb went to stake out Gideon's house from Muttonbird Cove. Slowly picked his way across the windy dunes to a grassy hiding place, mindful of Kat's warnings not to stomp on the birds' burrows. Lots of them here, deep holes suddenly opening up in the sand-slipping mounds. Completely defenceless against introduced predators. Like foxes.

Be good to be able to tell Kat the birds had returned, but there were no obvious signs. A sniff at one of the burrows only got him a lungful of briny sand. He was only just now realising why she'd seemed off this morning – working on the first self-portrait she'd done of this pregnancy, and the final ultrasound was tomorrow. He'd been trying so hard to put it out of his mind, he'd pushed her needs out of the way too. And possibly been a bit of a dickhead about Jarrah. Again. At least there was no need to talk to the man; Jarrah had already texted what he'd tried to say on the video call – an update on the Numbats' fundraising drive. A dismal failure, not enough money raised to cover this quarter's rent for the oval, or the one they already owed. The question of why Jarrah was delivering the news, not Mick, was made clear in a follow-up text.

—*uncle mick didn't want to hassle you but I thought you should know*

No, Mick wouldn't hassle him, would probably never speak of the case again if Caleb didn't mention it.

Finally finding a sheltered spot in the dunes, he hunkered down for the rest of the day, slapping at mosquitos, regretting the lack of insect repellent, and the half a kilo of goat's cheese he'd eaten for lunch.

Gideon didn't go out much. A few minutes in the garden but no trips off the property, so Caleb couldn't go in and snoop. Couldn't even get close, the timber hut like an eagle's eyrie with clear views all around. A visibility that worked two ways. Taylor could easily have witnessed something he shouldn't have with his high-powered binoculars.

When dusk fell Gideon appeared, backlit in the window, and drew the curtains. Caleb waited for the last of the daylight to ebb. Stood, shaking out stiff limbs. The wind had died away. Clouded sky, the dunes just visible under a half-hidden moon. Back to the shop for an early dinner, then go and very politely enquire after Ant.

He walked along the hard sand of the beach to avoid the burrows, rock-hopped towards the road. The night sky came alive. Shadows flying at him, swooping, flapping. He ducked. Birds. Hundreds of them, thousands. A teaming, heaving mass. Coming in low and fast, without warning, their wings stirring the air by his face.

Be embarrassing for a grown man to run from a few birds. He did it anyway. Stumbling over the rocks, arms over his head. Beside the road he stood flat against the embankment, out of the muttonbirds' flight path. Jesus. The sniper shouldn't have bothered shooting Taylor, just left him to go birdwatching.

———

No sign of the yellow jeep when he reached the shop, but he got out to check the caravan anyway. At the buzz of the sat phone, he backtracked to read the newly arrived text inside the car. Unlikely a sniper would try to pick him off in the dark, but the words 'safety, efficiency, fun' were running through his head – the hierarchy of priorities from his childhood, one of his father's favourite sayings. Right up there with: 'If your best isn't good enough, try harder.' Have to come up with some better ones for his own kids. Something about being cautious but brave. No, terrible idea. Buy a book of quotes instead, add it to his growing number of bewilderingly conflicting ones on parenting.

Safely in the car, he read the text. From Tedesco. Not an answer to his request for information on the tattoo, just a sentence.

—*We should talk next time you're in town.*

How could such a deliberate communicator be so cryptic? Sensitive information that wasn't urgent, or just 'let's catch up sometime'? Put it in the think-about-later pile.

When he got to the clearing, the lights were on in the caravan, curtains drawn. Ant, finally. Caleb jogged across, opened the door: Etty. Sitting at the table, her greyhound frame wound tight, leg jiggling.

He shot up the steps. 'What's happened? Is Ant OK?'

She started in surprise, then got to her feet. 'I ... Ant ... you ...'

'Slower.'

'Sorry. Sorryhe'sfine. MiserablebutOK ... fractured ribs.... tellyou he won't be around fortwoorthreedays.'

Caleb worked it out: fractured ribs but all right, lying low for two or three days. OK, breathe again. 'But nothing major?'

'No, it's just hard withthewhole pain thing. Nothing he's allowedto have works that well. GodCal, hecould'vedied. Ifeelsick. I wasatwork when Doctor Locke rang, justranstraight out and ontotheferry. What haveyou found out? How can I help?'

'By staying safe. Ferry goes soon, I'll drive you to it.'

And be on it himself. Be with Kat before, during and after the ultrasound. Amazing. The pulled-apart tensions of the day gone in an instant.

They waited with one other car on the pier. The ferry only ten minutes late, but Etty shifting restlessly the entire time, her fast-running motor seeming to do extra revs. The same feeling he'd had the other day that she was summoning the courage to tell him something.

When the ferry finally docked, she turned her pointed face to him. 'I ... you ... something.'

He switched on the overhead light. 'Little slower.'

'SorryI'mnervous.' She exhaled slowly, made an obvious effort to settle. 'I have to ask you something, but I don't want you to tell Ant.'

So much for the pair of them not having any secrets. 'I don't know, Etty.'

'Yeah, it makes me uncomfortable too. It's up to you, I just don't want to give him any reason to quit rehab.'

Oh no, what was she about to confess? Ant's progress was a Jenga puzzle of hopes and dreams; yank out one piece and the whole thing could come crashing down.

The ferry ramp was lowered, a short queue of vehicles disembarking. Get this conversation over with in case he needed to stay here and put out some fires.

'Can't promise,' he said. 'But tell me.'

'Ineedhelp withtheclinicfees ... gone through all my savings and the bank won't ... Locke's ... good about it but ... asking ... today.'

He tried to make sense of it all. Etty had been paying clinic fees but had run out of money? 'I thought it was free. Big discount from Locke, and Ant's working off the rest.'

'Yeah, I lied.' A teary laugh. 'No discount. It was the only way I could get him to go. He was so down on himself, he didn't think he was worth the money. Wouldn't ask you for it, wouldn't let me pay for it. God, Cal, youshouldhave seen him. Ididn'tthinkhe'dla stanotherweek.'

Hadn't wanted to ask his own brother for help. Understandable. There'd been too many years of having his hand slapped away, of judgement. Thank God for Etty. 'I'll take over the payments. You've done enough.'

'Really? That'dbeamazing.' Her bright smile dimmed. 'You sure Kat'll be OK with it?'

She'd be concerned about the money, but she would always find a way to help family. 'Yeah. How much are we talking?'

'Probably another twenty by the time he's finished.'

'Thousand?' Jesus, no wonder Locke seemed so smug. Time to push for a meeting with the man's unhappy ex-receptionist, Willow. With that kind of money at stake, Locke's motivations were a lot murkier than those of the altruistic saviour Ant had described.

An uncomfortable thought surfaced. Someone else's motivations could be at play here, too. Easy enough for Etty to send him fake invoices and keep the money.

'Don't worry,' he said, as she looked stricken, 'I'll work something out. Email Locke, tell him to send the invoices directly to me.'

'God, thank you. I can't tell you what a relief it is.'

He relaxed.

'Can I ask one more favour?'

Knew he'd let his guard down too soon. 'Sure.'

'I'm going on a retreat tomorrow. A work thing, can't have my phone for three days. If I give you the emergency number, will you let me know if Ant gets worse? I don't think he'll call it. You know what he's like.'

There were times Caleb had a real fear there was something fundamentally broken in him. 'Sure. He's lucky to have you.'

'We're both lucky. Sure he's a fixer-upper, but I've got a few cracks too. We bring out the best in each other.'

The last of the cars had disembarked, Max waving for the Commodore to board. Caleb drove to the far end of the ferry and parked facing the water, the faint lights of Resurrection Bay strung out along the waiting shore.

26.

The next morning he stayed too long in bed with Kat, had to fang it up the freeway to Melbourne. Fifteen minutes late for his meeting with Locke's receptionist and still hunting for a park – not too slick. But Kat's happiness at the news of the muttonbirds' abundant return had spilled over into nervous excitement for them both last night, leaving them still hyped up this morning. Impossible to drag himself away. Probably still be there if Kat's sisters hadn't arrived en masse to whisk her off for a day of distractions. What kind of medical system scheduled ultrasound appointments at four on a Friday? Inhumane.

He finally squeezed the car into a fifteen-minute park. Ran the four blocks to Sweet Shine, arriving twenty minutes late and slightly out of breath. Not a café like he'd assumed, but a cut-price nail salon with ice-white tiles, forensic-level lighting; an attempt at a clinical aesthetic gone badly wrong. But popular, with women in most of the massage chairs and a nearly equal number of staff.

Relief that Willow Lane was still there. Sitting near the back of the room, her feet soaking in a mini-whirlpool. Looking younger than twenty-one with her mousy hair and large eyes, and very uncomfortable despite the massage chair pummelling her shoulders. She stared as he approached; a possum caught mid-scramble.

The nail technician glanced at him as he reached the chair but didn't pause in her task, which seemed to involve removing

Willow's fingernails with a miniature circular sander.

'Willow?' Caleb gave her a reassuring smile. 'Sorry I'm late. Traffic. Thanks for seeing me.'

'I'm not really sure how I can help.' Tight little words, but more than enough light for him to read her, do a spot of neurosurgery at the same time.

Salon clients to either side, more opposite: Willow couldn't have chosen a worse place for an interview. Intentionally? She'd initially seemed keen to talk in the messages she'd sent last night, asking a lot of questions about who he was and why he was interested in Locke. Backed away at Caleb's suggestion they meet at her workplace.

'Like I said, my clients are after a personality fit.' Continuing the story he'd spun about vetting Locke for a job. He angled his head towards the women in the neighbouring chairs, clearly eavesdropping as they scrolled on their phones. 'We can keep it anonymous if you like, not mention names.'

'OK.'

'I want to get a feel for what he's like as a person.' Caleb waited a moment, then prompted her. 'So what's he like?'

'Polite.'

'To you?'

'To everyone.'

'Tell me one positive and one negative thing about him.'

'He listens to people.'

'And the negative thing?'

Wide brown eyes blinked at him. Not shutting him down, not offering information.

He took a gamble. 'Why was he asked to leave the clinic?'

'He wasn't a partner, just rented rooms there.'

One of the worst sidesteps Caleb had ever witnessed. How to ease a story from someone who wanted to tell it but wasn't sure how? Maybe with the truth. 'I have to be honest, I'm not really doing a background check. He's treating someone close to me. I've got some doubts about him.'

'Oh, no.' Her lips pressed together. 'Sorry, but I can't talk about it. There was a letter and everything. From a lawyer.'

A cease and desist? Non-discloser agreement? Threat to sue her for slander? 'Was it regarding his personal or professional life?'

The nail technician looked up, tiny sander poised. Willow glanced at her, then the neighbouring customers, all staring now, phones forgotten in their hands. She whipped out her own phone, swiped quickly at the screen. This was going to be good. Evidence of some kind: photos, documents, a video. She popped in a pair of earbuds, leaned back in the massage chair, eyes closed. Slight tap to her right foot as she settled into the music.

That was some top-level ghosting. Had to resign; couldn't beat a move like that. Giving their disappointed audience a shrug, he crossed to the door, checked his phone as he walked outside. One minute, thirty-two seconds filled, hours to go.

He texted Tedesco: homicide cop, good mate and sender of cryptic *We should talk next time you're in town* messages. It'd be a quick reply if Tedesco was off duty or on call, might take days if he was on a job.

—The chicken barks three times at noon. Alberto's in 30?

Chickens on the brain after the ferry trip with Etty last night. Her relief at having unburdened herself turning into happy chatter about her plans to surprise Ant with a pet chicken when he'd finished rehab. Etty herself apparently the owner of two bantams called Elton and John. For very different people, Etty and Ant had a significant Venn diagram overlap.

The phone vibrated.

—*You should take your chicken to the vet. I'll be there in ninety minutes.*

Alberto's was much quieter today. No bashing saucepans or plates, just a lone couple arguing silently at a table by the door – he wasn't happy about her new job, she wasn't happy about his attitude. Caleb politely averted his eyes from their signing and crossed to the far side of the room. Hopefully Tedesco would be full of useful information about dead men with tattoos, or this entire trip would be a waste of time. A visit to Locke's old clinic after seeing Willow had netted nothing from the staff except stone-faced looks to his questions about the doctor. Professional closing of ranks, not fear. Whatever Willow was upset about hadn't involved threats or murder.

He put his phone face-up on the table: five hours for the three and a half hour drive to the hospital, plenty of time. Relaxed about it really. Quick look at the wall clock in case his phone was broken – still five hours.

Alberto appeared, tanned scalp shining. 'Again! Two visits in a week. We're honoured.' He gestured Caleb up for a cough-inducing hug. Settled in the chair opposite. 'I've found a house for you. A Deaf family selling. Everything already done – flashing doorbell, smoke detectors, the lot. And right around the corner. You can bring the little one by every day.'

A moment to imagine it, another to imagine telling Kat. He still hadn't raised the subject of moving back home, the idea too new, too difficult.

'Why the frown? It's good news.' Alberto wrote a number on his order pad, thrust it at him. 'Text today, they want to sell quickly.'

'The house hunt's on hold. Thinking about moving permanently to the Bay.'

'What? No, that's a terrible idea. There are no Deafies down there – how would you communicate?'

'Like I do now.'

'Lip-reading.' Alberto plucked the idea from curled lips, threw it on the floor. 'Scurrying around, picking up hearies' scraps.'

'Kat and Ant sign. The baby will too.'

'Three people? One who isn't even born yet? No, you'll stay here.' Wiping his hands on his apron as though the matter was settled. His satisfied expression dropped into a scowl as he looked past Caleb. 'Him again.'

Uri Tedesco was coming through the door, taking up a lot of space; tall and wedge-shaped, face like a slab of granite. Hearies were usually warmly welcomed in the café, signing or non-signing, but Alberto had taken an instant dislike to the detective the one time they'd met, unable to comprehend that Tedesco's lack of expression wasn't rudeness.

The detective headed towards Caleb and Alberto, sucking all warmth from the room as he studied the other diners, obviously trying to follow their signing. Not much chance of that: Tedesco might have picked up a few signs over the past couple of years, but he was spectacularly lacking in talent. He nodded to them both as he sat, a boulder shifting position. Hair slightly longer these days, at least five millimetres, off-the-rack blue suit bought in the right size. The influence of his boyfriend, Luke, no doubt – a man with a very dry sense of humour who ribbed Tedesco mercilessly for his cop ways and looks. Caleb had taken to him instantly.

'I think Alberto's in a hurry,' Caleb told Tedesco as Alberto bristled. 'What do you want to order?'

'I'll do it.' The detective stared down Alberto and signed, 'Coffee white weak sugar two.' Good hand position, correct signs, but the expression of a commander signalling the firing squad.

Alberto glared back, seemed to grow a few inches taller.

'It's his face,' Caleb quickly signed.

'I know it's his face, can see it's his face. Staring at me like a big gargoyle.'

'He can't help it.'

'Well, I can't help wanting to chisel a smile into it.' Alberto demonstrated – big chisel, hard blows. Stomped away to the coffee machine.

'Problem?' Tedesco asked.

'Maybe try raising your eyebrows next time, make it a request instead of a demand.'

The detective practised, a fierce focus to his eyes. Worse; much worse.

'Good start.' Caleb glanced at his phone: four hours, fifty-four minutes.

'This bloke with the tatt,' Tedesco said, straight down to business, 'that connected to the Taylor murder?'

A careful reply needed. Tedesco was a mate, a close mate, bonded through surviving the horrific case that had almost killed Kat, but the detective had a strong moral compass. All decisions would be aligned to it – whether that involved helping a friend, or sicking homicide colleagues onto him.

'There's no evidence to support that,' Caleb said. 'But if I find any, I'll take it to homicide.'

Tedesco waited for the compass needle to align, then said, 'No one matching that description has been reported missing or is wanted.'

'Thanks. I owe you a couple of your embarrassing coffees.'

'You owe me a few. My colleagues on the Peter Taylor murder popped by to ask about you.'

'Shit, sorry. They found out you gave me the son's number?'

'No, just looking into you.'

Not good. His friendship with Tedesco would only have come up if the homicide cops were really digging into his background.

And there was more news to come – Tedesco wouldn't have asked to meet in person to tell him what a text could have covered.

Alberto appeared with their coffees. Set Caleb's long black carefully before him, delicate biscotti balanced on the saucer, slopped Tedesco's treat-less cup in the middle of the table. Turned for the kitchen.

Tedesco gazed after him. 'My superior detection skills tell me he doesn't like me much.' He poured the milky liquid from the saucer into his cup, drank it.

Four hours, fifty minutes.

'In a hurry?' Tedesco asked.

'No. Just, last ultrasound this afternoon.' Caleb kept going in case Tedesco decided it was time for one of his supportive moments. 'What'd you tell your colleagues?'

'That you're stubborn, loyal to a fault, and lack impulse control. But that given your hot-headedness you'd be unlikely to choose a high-powered rifle as a murder weapon.'

'Jesus. You didn't have a go at my clothes too?'

'Buy some leather shoes, Volleys are for teenagers. Or so Luke tells me.' Tedesco drank his coffee, taking his time, clearly still wrestling with some dilemma. Finally set the cup on the saucer, got to his feet. 'Walk you to your car.'

Nervous about being overheard in a Deaf café. This was now officially concerning.

Tedesco was silent when they reached the Commodore in the busy shopping strip. Broad jaw moving slightly as though rehearsing his words. Caleb braced himself: another murder, a warrant, a meteor.

The big man eventually met his gaze, a pink tinge to his face; granite warming in the sun. 'Luke and I are getting married.'

A second to recalibrate. 'Mate, that's great news. Congrats.' The pair of them had only been dating a few months, though – rushed, even for someone as decisive as Tedesco. 'Three months. You two don't muck around.'

'Thanks, Mum, but we've known each other years.'

Had they? Caleb had to get better at interrogating people about their personal lives.

'We're thinking mid-Jan,' Tedesco said. 'Was wondering if you'd be best man.'

'Be honoured.' More than honoured, a bit choked up. Should they hug? Not a hugging relationship.

'Casual thing, not dressy.' Tedesco's gaze went to Caleb's feet, canvas Volleys somewhat the worse for wear from the island's mud. 'Maybe a little dressy. Good luck this afternoon.' He left. Broad shoulders cut an easy swathe through the oncoming pedestrians.

27.

Caleb drove straight to the Bay, got to the hospital with an hour and fourteen minutes to spare. New record: usually only half an hour early for prenatal appointments. OK, forty-five. At least Kat was spared the wait this time, getting a lift with Georgie, her eldest and most protective sister. Highly likely Amelia and Helen would come too. Kat's family had gathered around her like worker bees during the pregnancy, and there'd been a larger than usual turnout for the last couple of appointments.

He tried his luck in the onsite carpark – a pipedream, but he was feeling lucky. Halfway through his first loop, he spotted a familiar white van in a loading zone by the exit. Stomped on the brakes. The *Fuck a Greenie* van following him. Following him here to Kat and their baby.

Freefalling panic before he thought it through. No one could have followed him. Even when relaxed he kept a close eye on the rear-view mirror, watching for emergency vehicles and trucks with inaudible horns. And he was nowhere near relaxed.

Still queasy, he squeezed the Commodore into an illegal spot, jogged back to the van. Locked doors, nothing much visible through the smeared windows, few takeaway coffee cups on the passenger seat, a crumpled tarp in the rear compartment. No rifle or obvious hiding places for one. A distinct possibility the van driver wasn't connected to the case at all. If they hadn't followed him here, they might not have followed him to the mechanic's and planted the rifle. One of those assumptions that could seriously derail a case.

A shadow loomed over him. He turned, came face to face with Arlo. Eyes thin slits beneath the black beanie. 'The fuck you looken at?'

What was the man's problem? The world in general, or just Caleb?

'Wondering about the sticker – that pro or anti greenie?'

Arlo grabbed his T-shirt, slammed him against the rear doors. 'Leave. Me. And. My. Wife. The. Fuck. Alone.' Wanting the fight, stocky body braced.

Shit. Be pretty bad if he fronted up to Kat and her family with a black eye after his last mud-spattered appearance. But a bad defensive position, no room to throw or block a punch. Have to go the knee. He went to raise it, stopped as someone turned the corner: a young hospital orderly in a bile-green uniform. Writing on a clipboard, head lowered.

'Get security,' Caleb called to him. 'This man's assaulting me.'

The orderly's head jerked up, eyes widening as he took in the situation. Arlo glanced at the man, released his grip.

Good result, mental pat on the back for defusing the situation. Sharp blow. Stomach.

Crumpling. Jagged pain in his guts. Down on his hands and knees, puking up the falafel he'd eaten on the drive. Hadn't been prepared. He got ready to block the next blow, but Arlo had gone, the van at the exit, belching exhaust. Orderly had gone, too. Only a family of four skirting wide around Caleb on their way inside.

When he was sure he'd stopped vomiting, he eased himself upright, one hand on the hospital wall. Let his guard down, mind on other things. Not smart. A little terrifying. Should have known Arlo was angry enough to strike out. Hard to pinpoint why though, even given the man's simmering jealousy over Skye. The usual alpha male bullshit, or was he hiding something? Something beneath that crumpled tarp, maybe. Have to be small.

Think about that later. An hour to make himself presentable, brace himself for the future.

28.

The waiting room was crowded when he and Kat finally emerged. All three of her sisters and their kids, both parents, a trio of aunties. No need to make an announcement, couldn't keep the news from his grinning face if he'd wanted to. Instantly surrounded. Kat gave him a wild-eyed smile before being swallowed by a wall of nieces and nephews. Years since he'd seen her this happy. Kisses and hugs, people talking. Scary sister, Georgie, embraced him, said, 'Jesus, didn't realise you could smile. Suits you.' Then elbowed him out of the way to get to Kat. He answered the few questions he caught – healthy, could deliver today if necessary, not expected to be necessary – and received another round of hugs. A lot of relief for what was supposed to have been a standard appointment. Apparently he hadn't been the only one holding his breath.

When the initial wave of excitement subsided, he checked Kat was still happily talking. Went to steady himself against a scuffed wall. New understanding of the double-clap sign for 'happiness'. An urge to do it now; clap, laugh, cry.

Across the room, Maria had extricated herself from the throng and was striding towards the exit. Dressed in her usual immaculate black pants and silk shirt, hair in a sleek bun. Off to her clinic to scare more patients into good health. Looking particularly determined about it today. Did he really want to talk to her right now? Yes – she was his go-to for medical information,

182

and he had a photo of a crooked dick to identify.

He mentally girded his loins, went to head her off. 'Have you got a sec?'

She stopped abruptly. 'Of course. Is this about Anton? Or should I get the obstetrician?' Asking if Caleb felt he'd missed something. No real danger of that – he secretly recorded each appointment and got them transcribed – but it was a constant concern. One he'd hopefully kept better hidden from Kat than her mother.

'No,' he said, 'but thanks again for your help with Ant. It's about a case. I need some medical information about –' He stopped. A lot of non-Kat-related people in the room, sitting all around him on rows of plastic chairs, more walking past on their way to the door. Discussing his theory about a left-handed wanker was feeling like a bad idea. 'It involves a man's privates. Is it –'

'Let's use the correct terminology shall we, Caleb? It's "penis".'

Yes, let's. And let's use the same confident speaking voice as Maria, make sure those two octogenarians in the back corner heard it and turned to stare.

He tried to lower his voice in the non-existent hope she'd follow suit. 'Is it possible that excessive wank . . . ah, masturbation could cause a penis to bend significantly? Permanently?'

'It's highly unlikely, but if you've noticed any changes in your penis you should see your doctor immediately.'

Oh God. The black-garbed nonna sitting opposite looked him in the eye, then further down.

'It's not me,' he told Maria. 'It's for a case. Do you know what could cause something like that?'

'There could be a number of causes. Are you finding intercourse painful?'

Just let the sniper shoot him in the face. Get it over with.

'It's seriously not me.' Fast scrabble for his phone and the doctored photo. 'I've got a photo of a – of an erect penis. I'm trying to ID the man. D'you think you could have a look at it?'

'Goodness, Caleb, how many erect penises do you think I see in my work?' She paused. 'Or my private life.'

Growing suspicion she was just playing with him now, but seeing the phrase 'erect penis' on his mother-in-law's lips was going to play on repeat in the long dark night of his soul.

Maria studied the image thoroughly, zooming right in. Eventually returned the phone. 'This is by no means a diagnosis, but it could be that he's suffering from ...' Her mouth formed a series of unintelligible shapes. He shook his head; she already had her phone out, typing. Turned the screen towards him: *Peyronie's Disease*. Often associated with *Dupuytren's Contracture*, which causes a thickening of the facia.

Simultaneously informative and uninformative. 'If someone had it, would it show if he was –' Caleb searched desperately for a phrase that didn't contain the word 'unaroused', ended up gesturing. Maria followed the movement, along with a fair portion of the waiting room. Why had he thought that would be better?

'Are you asking if the penis would be crooked while flaccid?'

'Yes.'

'It's unlikely. You'd be better off examining it while it was erect.' A glint to her eyes. 'However if that's not possible, look at his hands. Dupuytren's can make the fingers pull inwards. Surgery is often required.'

'Thanks. Let's never speak of this again.'

'And you were doing so well with the terminology.' She swept away.

Very lucky with his family-in-law, a bonus to being with Kat. Who was coming towards him, wide smile, curls disarrayed from all the hugging. 'That looked intense,' she said. 'What were you talking about?'

'Crooked dicks.'

'Again? You two really need a new hobby.'

He took Kat the long way around to the carpark. Through featureless beige corridors that smelt of disinfectant and floor polish, his steps and heart light. She signed quickly as they walked, a flood of thoughts that had obviously been dammed until now. Baby clothes and birth plans, ideas for managing sleep schedules, the baby sling Georgie swore by. She finally slowed, nudged him with her hip. 'Enough about me. We should talk names.'

They'd made a long list the first time, stuck it on the fridge. Veto powers given, bribery attempted with sex and cups of Earl Grey tea. A much shorter discussion the second pregnancy, never again mentioned.

'Now?' he asked.

'No, I'll give you a few days to muster your failed arguments.'

Just as well, because this happiness thing seemed to have starved his brain of oxygen. He'd agree to anything right now, their child named Hospital Gurney or Clean Hands Count. Their child. A clear droplet of thought: where they should live wasn't about him or even Kat, it was about their child. Here, on Country, surrounded by family. Contentment at the decision. It was doable; done.

They were at the gift shop near the exit, a small glass kiosk whose odd array of wares overflowed into the corridor. He took Kat's hand to draw her away from the trickle of people heading to the carpark. Stopped beside a table of chunky plastic jewellery. Silver and gold balloons bobbing above them.

'Are you about to propose?' Eyes and smile bright.

He could just kiss her; he did. 'In a way. I think we should live here, in the Bay.'

'What?'

'I know I shut you down when you brought it up, but it's a good idea. It'll take me a while to transition the business, but I can make it work. We can buy Ant out of the house. It'd save us a tonne. We could –' He stopped at her troubled expression. Going too fast, taking over. 'Or we could get somewhere new?'

'The house is a great idea, but you don't want to live in the Bay. You hate it here.'

'No, I don't. Not anymore. I want us to live here. So, what do you think? D'you want to raise little Garamond on Country?'

Her lips curved. 'I'd love nothing more than to raise Helvetica here, but you need to think about it for a while. You can't make major life decisions while you're all giddy. Give it a few days until normal services have resumed.'

No extra time needed, services changed forever. His first major decision as a father, and a good one. A decision his father wouldn't have made. But she was right about the dangers of giddiness. Once he was through those doors and into the carpark he had to focus, make sure it was safe to bring the car around for Kat. Just because Arlo hadn't been following him didn't mean the man was innocent. Could easily have come back, or even alerted the sniper.

A hard slap of reality.

He shouldn't be driving Kat home. Shouldn't even be with her now.

'We need to change plans,' he told her. 'I shouldn't drive you. Ring one of your sisters, ask them to come back. Arlo was hanging around earlier, the aggro guy I told you about. In the white van.'

The light fled her face. 'He was here?'

'He wasn't following me, but I don't want to take any risks.

There's no guarantee he's not working with the sniper.'

'I'm not arguing. There's no way I can go with you.' She flinched as the balloons swayed in a gust of air. Pressed a palm to her chest. 'God, what are we doing? What am *I* doing? I can't run, I can't fight. We shouldn't be together until this is over. It'd be bad enough if you got hurt, but –'

But she could have been there with him in the carpark, cornered by Arlo, punched by Arlo. Not the worst scenario; nowhere near the worst.

Sweat broke out across his forehead, the back of his neck. This was over. Should have been over a long time ago.

'I'm done,' he told her. 'I'm going to the cops.'

'When?'

'Now. Right away.'

She didn't move, expression caught between hope and fear. 'What about Ant?'

Get him somewhere safe and isolated, organise medical support. Only five days to cover before Caleb could get him into Turning Point. Not that long. Must be possible. 'He'll be OK. I'll work something out.'

The tightness rinsed from her face as she closed her eyes. He put his arms around her; she leaned in. Standing still, nothing but the weight of Kat's head on his shoulder, her stomach pressed against his hip.

His second major decision as a parent. Much easier; harder.

29.

Once he'd seen Kat safely off in Georgie's car, he drove straight to the police station, a half plan hatched in his head, hoping more details would filter through. Had to control the timing. Avoid the homicide cops, already convinced he was involved. They'd hold him for questioning as soon as he admitted to any knowledge. Use Sergeant Ramsden as go-between, buy himself enough time to sort things out with Ant. No guarantee Ramsden would do it, but the cop knew how deep his roots were in town, knew he wouldn't be running off.

He parked around the corner, did a slow walk past the station's rear carpark. No sign of the kind of late-model sedan two homicide detectives from Melbourne would be driving, just the two patrol cars and a jacked-up SUV, along with Ramsden's black Holden. An older model with the same lumpen style as his shoes. Same colour, too. Consistency: a reassuring trait in a man you were about to ask for vital help.

The amped-up constable who'd been at Kat's was staffing the front desk, dealing with a young woman who was waving what looked like a fistful of parking fines. Constable Lloyd seemed more flustered than aggressive right now, a red rash climbing his thin neck as he tried to get a word in. 'We don't – It's not a police – We don't issue parking fines.'

A bad week for Lloyd, with the arse-kicking he would have received after letting the planted rifle slip away. Could almost feel sorry for him. But not quite.

The woman gave what were obviously a few choice last words, spun around to leave. Zeroed in on Caleb. 'Outside my own house!' Speaking in short hard clips. She held up the parking tickets. 'Friggen hospital zone, can't get a park. Not my fault the street's filled with perverts and patients, is it?' Glaring at him. 'Well, is it?'

'No. Town planning issue.'

'Damn right it is.' She strode away, her exit slightly ruined by her need to wait for the gentle glide of the automatic doors.

Perverts and patients – a woman who knew how to express herself. Reference in part to the clientele from Secret Angel, probably. The legal brothel was a few blocks from the hospital, well placed to catch the passing trade. A married man making regular visits to a place like that might choose to park elsewhere, like a nearby hospital carpark, or a mechanic's. Might get very defensive if he thought someone had discovered his clandestine activities. Secret Angel was swankier than Caleb would have expected for Arlo's budget and tastes, but people could surprise you.

Constable Lloyd had regained his belligerent expression, narrow shoulders squared as he faced Caleb. 'Can I help you?'

'I need to speak to Ramsden.'

'Sergeant Ramsden isn't available at present. Can I be of assistance?'

'I'll wait.'

'He's not here.'

'His car is.'

'He's not available.'

Caleb leaned his palms on the desk. 'Bit of friendly advice – John's a mate, good mate. He'd want to know I'm here. Particularly after that stuff-up with homicide.' Overstating his relationship with Ramsden by a factor of a hundred, but a good chance the too-eager young cop wouldn't know that, or want to risk it.

'He's at Matt's,' Lloyd said quickly.

'Matt who?'

The constable's eyes narrowed. 'Guess you'd know, if John's a good mate.'

Town full of Matts; yell out the window and every second man would turn his head, a few of the dogs. Hadn't crossed Caleb's mind he'd have to wait, the starter's pistol fired, up and out of the blocks.

'OK, I'd better not disturb him,' he told Lloyd. 'But tell him I need to see him. Tonight. He's got my number.'

Lloyd pulled a message book across the counter towards him, wrote Caleb's name in neat, small letters. 'What's it pertaining to?'

'Just tell him it's urgent.'

———

Caleb went to wait at his old house, possible future home. Did a drive-by first, checking the sightlines. Fences, trees, peaked roofs – no unobstructed views, nowhere for a sniper to hide, even one who could hit a target from a kilometre's distance. Not that there was any real danger in an impromptu visit, but today's good news shone an even brighter light on the importance of staying alive. At least Kat seemed a little reassured now things were underway, her strained expression easing when he'd called from outside the police station.

The sun had almost set, Mrs Naylor enjoying the last of its meagre warmth by bailing up a newly-wed couple outside her house. Caleb left them to her mercies. Made a quick getaway from the car to dash across the road to Mick's. Hadn't come close to solving the Numbats' woes, but he could report on the conversation he'd had with Maria, see if Mick knew anyone with the telltale curled fingers she'd mentioned. A long shot. The glaringly obvious might escape Caleb at times, but he was attuned to hands; hard to imagine not noticing someone's misshapen fingers. Far more likely the victim had already had surgery to fix the problem.

Mick answered the door barefoot and bare-chested, wearing baggy blue shorts. Fresh out of the shower, water beading his brown scalp. Door directly opposite Mrs Naylor.

A nod for Caleb, a wave for someone across the street, presumably Mrs Naylor, having a good look down her nose.

'You'll give her a heart attack,' Caleb told him.

Mick scratched the greying hair on his chest. 'Never occurred to me, Your Honour.' He nudged the screen door wider. 'Good timen. Pauline's out with the kids, so I invited a few Numbats over for a feed. Should be here soon, you can ask 'em about their wanken habits.'

'Hard to pass that up, but I just came to say that I've got a tip on the crooked dick.' He paused, rephrased. 'Info.'

'Relieved to hear it. Been checking out a few tips meself at the urinal. Not winnen me any friends.'

'The bend won't be obvious on the flop, but he might have curled fingers.'

'Now there's a phrase you don't hear every day. How'd you work that out?'

'Maria.'

Mick laughed. 'You and Maria talking about doonghis. Wish I'd been there.'

'Probably online by now, a snuff film. So, no Numbats with hand problems? Or previous problems. Apart from an allergy to the ball, that is.'

A hurt expression. 'They've been worken on the catching. But nah, nothing obvious. None of the board members, either. Here's Ross now, you can double-check with him.'

Caleb followed Mick's gaze to the road, where a dented blue Monaro was pulling in to park. Ross Greene, the bullish coach of the Numbats whose playing career had supposedly ended due to injury. A thought that had been nudging Caleb's brain broke through. Hand surgery left scars, something he was painfully reminded of every time Kat signed, and according to Ant, the coach had scarring somewhere on his body. Better be discreet, not ask Mick. Or the coach.

Mick's eyebrows were raised, as though he was waiting for an answer.

'Sorry,' Caleb said, 'didn't get that.'

'Heard things went well with the scan. Be a relief, yeah? Find out what you're havin'? Got a bet with Pauline it's a boy.'

'No. You wanted a boy?' Never occurred to him, Mick's adoration of his daughters so obvious.

'Nah, relieved if anything, given my dad – the whole father-son thing.' Mick frowned. 'Then again, a dad can really stuff things up for girls. Self-esteem and all that. Probably worse now I think of it.' He caught something in Caleb's expression, stopped. 'Got the heebie-jeebies?'

'A bit.'

'Usual stuff? Or wonderin' how a gub can raise a Koori kid?'

Jesus Christ. A lucky dip of his anxieties, this conversation. 'Mate, you're killing me.'

Mick slapped his shoulder. 'You'll be right, budj. Wouldn't stress it.'

'Not everyone is.'

'Not talken about everyone, talken about you. You might be a fudgehead, but you're a solid fudgehead. Take Katy out to celebrate, get outta ya brain.' His gaze drifted across the road. 'Lost me audience. Might finish dressen, then. Let you and the coach have a word before the boys get here.' He ambled back inside.

Ross Greene was halfway up the driveway when Caleb reached him. One hand holding a six-pack of beer, the other by his side, palm hidden. Mouth set in the same irritated line it had been the other day at training. Possible it was just an unfortunate trick of nature, the man actually in a good mood.

'The deaf not dumb Zelic brother,' Greene said by way of greeting. 'You worked out who's behind the photos yet? Fundraiser was a washout thanks to them.'

'You got any ideas?'

'Wouldn't bloody be asking you if I did, would I? What –' The coach stopped as another car pulled up, a couple of Numbat players inside. 'Get a move on, will ya?' he told Caleb. 'Club'll fold if you fart around much longer.' Hoisting the beer, he went to move past Caleb towards the house, clearly keen to end the conversation now the players had arrived.

Caleb blocked him. 'Before you go – how long's Greg Harmon been club treasurer?'

'Five years,' the coach said clearly.

'Sorry, what was that?'

'Five. Years.'

Caleb shook his head. 'Sorry, still –'

'Five! Years!' Thrusting an outstretched hand in Caleb's face to show five digits, faint white scars lining his palm and ring finger. 'Get it that time?'

'Perfectly, thanks.'

The coach stalked away, six-pack swinging. Not the kind of man who'd post a less than flattering picture of himself: the target, not the culprit. Couldn't have happened to a nicer person.

Caleb headed across the road to his house, checking messages as he walked up the front path: nothing from Ramsden. The usual battle with the front door, the key refusing to turn in the lock. Add that to the list of things to fix. Warm inside, considering the cold day, his father's well-sealed workmanship standing up after all these years. Strange that he'd once thought this place bleak; just an empty house waiting to breathe. Very different, imagining it filled with people. Sunday barbecues and swings in the backyard, kids running in and out. Kat used to talk about having a large family like her own. Three kids, four. Safety in numbers, a wide soft buffer from the sharp edges of the world.

He paced each room, phone in hand, calculating for paint and repairs. Nothing major to do – they'd be in well before the due date.

It didn't hit him until he was in the sunroom out the back. Dark outside now, the row of windows reflecting the snug room's honeyed boards, his own stationary figure. Seven weeks. Sitting on their old claw-foot couch by those windows, Kat and their child curled beside him. Everything he'd thought he couldn't have, in his arms. Unbelievable. Believable.

Just had to safely navigate this last treacherous stretch, and everything would be complete. He could do it. Had to.

30.

Caleb gave Ramsden until nine the next morning, then drove past the shops to the bunker-like police station. No chunky black Holden in the rear lot. Slack bastard – didn't reply to urgent messages, rocked up late to work. Caleb kept driving, heading for the real estate office where Jarrah worked on Saturdays. Partly to follow up on the coach's dick pic, partly so he didn't crack and go for a run.

The office was brightly lit, Jarrah visible through the large plate-glass window. Organising a display wall, somehow making the standard real estate uniform of charcoal suit and blue tie look fresh. Still, jeans and a long-sleeve T-shirt were a timeless choice, particularly when paired with a five-year-old grey woollen jacket.

Jarrah turned as he entered, looked startled. 'Cal, hey.'

Caleb gave him the country handshake. 'I'm following up some Numbat stuff. After some info on Ross Greene's exes – you know anything?'

'His exes? I'd have to think.' Back to his usual relaxed posture, leaning against the display table. 'Barb. Yeah, Barb Howard. Be a year and a half since they split, maybe two.'

A cold lead for that level of revenge.

'Bad break-up?'

'Nah, but she seemed pretty gutted. Who'd have thought, hey?'

Inside knowledge about the coach's health issues? Easy for

Jarrah to have scrolled through the coach's phone in the footy clubhouse and found some personal photos, either by chance or with prior knowledge. 'Why?'

'Just, no accounting for taste, you know.' His smile faltered under Caleb's scrutiny.

Jarrah was unlikely to be behind anything that damaged the Numbats – community leader, team captain, long-time member – but he was acting squirrely again, not quite meeting Caleb's eye. Time to re-examine the evergreen theory that this was all about land and money, Jarrah after the sales commission. If the coach quit, it'd certainly hasten the Numbats' death and sale of the oval.

'Thanks anyway.' Caleb nodded towards the perspex wall display beside them, neat aerial images of vacant rural land. 'Got anything decent in town? Thinking about building.'

'In the Bay? I didn't know you and Kat were staying.'

'Really? Thought everyone knew. You got any land in town with a water view?'

'Nothing that central, but some great new land's just been released out west. River Views. Some beautiful old red gums on it. Reckon Kat'd love it.'

She would, would she?

Jarrah coughed, glanced away. Definitely nervous.

'Anything coming up central to town? I'd spring for a deposit straight away for the right place.'

'Not that I've heard. Reckon you'd be in for a wait – land doesn't come up in the town centre very often.'

Scratch dodgy commissions off the list – no real estate agent in the world would leave a titbit like that dangling, even one who worked part-time to support his art. Particularly one like that.

'Thanks,' Caleb said. 'I'll let you get back to it.'

Jarrah walked him to the door, clearly relieved to see him off.

'Let me know if you change your mind about River Views. It's going fast – Greg Darmon's bought acres. Loves it.'

Greg the mechanic, club treasurer. Was there something in Jarrah and Greg doing business together? Be weirder if they didn't – both locals, both Numbat supporters. The interconnected circles of the town.

Another drive-by of the cop shop – two patrol cars and a motorbike. The thought had dawned on him that it could be Ramsden's day off. And that young Constable Lloyd may not have gone out of his way to alert his superior officer to Caleb's message.

Caleb did a U-turn, headed for the highway. Reasonably sure he could find Ramsden's place: the family farm, out past the old bluestone wool mill. If that didn't work, he'd throw himself on the mercy of the homicide detectives.

Ramsden's white weatherboard had a quaintly old-fashioned garden of geraniums and violets. A splash of colour in a landscape of featureless overgrazed paddocks. The cop's black Holden was parked facing the road – a cautious man, wanting to avoid reversing into traffic. Not much of it out here; a couple of tractors and the school bus would make it peak hour.

Caleb gave the horn a warning tap as he pulled into the driveway; always best not to spring a surprise visit on a cop, even one as relatively laid-back as Ramsden. The sergeant's sturdy figure didn't appear at the front window. One last beep, and Caleb got out, headed for the door, a side entrance off the driveway. Slowed as he skirted Ramsden's car.

A terracotta pot was lying broken on the recessed porch. Flowers and soil spilling across the concrete. Someone sitting nearby, an odd angle to their legs. A glimpse of ugly black shoes as he drew nearer. Navy slacks. Ramsden slumped against the doorway, staring at him with opaque eyes. Blue shirt stained black. Shredded hole in his chest.

31.

Dead. Didn't need to check. Very dead. Long dead. Meaty smell, flies moving lazily in the cold air, settling on the pulped flesh of his chest, the blood-splashed flowerpots. Killed last night: porch light on, keys in the lock. Perfectly framed as he'd paused to open the door. Clear shot across the paddocks from the old wool mill.

The thin-necked Constable Lloyd's finger on the trigger? No, too aggro, too eager. Not an islander. Couldn't have been popping over to shoot letterboxes and people without anyone noticing. Or even piloting a boat to remove washed-up body parts. But in on it. An informant – told the sniper about Caleb's message, lined Ramsden up for the shot. Good shot. Punched right through the cop's body. Sprayed pieces of him all over the door and pots of cheerful flowers. Little white petals turned brown.

Go now. Sniper might come back.

Turning. One step then the other, down the driveway, into the car. Few tries to get the keys in, engine started. Slow reverse, driving away.

The shakes hit him a few kays down the road. Clammy-skinned nausea. He pulled over, onto the long grass, window down, head back. Gulping in air to clear the flesh-iron stench from his nostrils. Ramsden dead. Dead because of him. Waved a big red warning flag with that urgent request at the police station. Made it look as though he knew more than he did, that Ramsden might be able to connect important dots if the two of them spoke. Knew fuck-all.

How big was this thing? Three people murdered; three co-conspirators, maybe more. People who were willing to kill a cop. Senior cop. No one was safe if they were killing cops. So why wasn't he dead? They must have known he'd go looking for Ramsden, could easily have lain in wait. Luck? His trips to the island? Homicide would swarm all over the place if he was murdered. Be over there as soon as they accessed his phone and credit cards. No – as soon as they spoke to Kat.

Kat.

Breathe. Breathe and think. No need to race off and terrify her, right? The sniper was analytical, not bloodthirsty. Patient enough to send warning notes to a blackmailer, plant evidence in cars and shoot up letterboxes. No reason to think a person like that would go after Kat to get to him. None at all.

But there were at least two other people in on this. One of them a trigger-happy young cop with an inflated sense of importance.

And Lloyd knew Kat was living with her parents.

Fear cored his chest.

Car into drive, stabbing at the phone as he pulled onto the road, foot hard on the accelerator.

———

Kat's bright Beetle was outside the house. Oh thank God. Hadn't known whether to come here first or the studio, Kat not answering texts. He pulled in sharply, was out and running. In through the front door and along the hallway. 'Kat!'

Not in her room, living room. No one here, no sense of movement. Into the kitchen, the open back door. There. Chatting with Georgie by the budding magnolia tree, rugged up in a red coat and bright pink beanie, obviously about to go for a walk. Safe. His world safe. Everything safe.

Trying to draw a wider focus. More people in the garden, all in coats and boots: Maria, four kids, Kat's eldest two sisters.

Kat caught sight of him in the doorway, her bright smile instantly snuffed. She stood still, waiting for the bad news he'd brought.

'Come inside,' he signed. 'Get everyone inside.'

Kat took him to talk privately in the small sitting room off the kitchen. Kids and other adults inside the house, all obviously confused, but the women quick to have responded to Kat's urging. The usually neat space was cluttered by the morning's activities; had to step over Lego and colouring books to close the blinds. Kat sat on the couch, still in her coat and pink beanie, her eyes fixed on him.

He stayed standing. No softening it, had to be direct. 'It's Ramsden. They killed him.'

'I don't understand. How's he involved?'

'I wanted to talk to him, not homicide. Left a message for him at the station to call me. And now he's dead.' No, don't fall apart. Focus. 'That young cop Lloyd's involved. Taking kickbacks or something.'

Mates with the sniper, or the offsider with the boat. The turtle-mouthed Gideon? Going back and forth to do his shopping, could easily be friends with a crooked cop.

Kat was staring at him. 'He was here. In this house.'

'Never again. I'm calling homicide right now.' Like he should have done in the first place. Meet somewhere neutral, a long way from the police station.

It was possible someone other than Constable Lloyd was the informant. That message book had been lying on the front desk, available for all to see. He found the card Detective Katsonis had given him, the senior, watchful detective.

Kat stood as he went to text. 'Better if I call. Hearies. They'll assume a text isn't urgent.'

Caught between actions. She was right; people usually answered voice calls immediately, texts eventually. But her name couldn't be listed in a phone log, her voice recognised. Not with the slightest chance Lloyd would find out.

She took the phone from him. 'Fake name. I'll say I'm your secretary.'

The best of two bad choices. 'Don't answer any questions. Just say it's urgent. Foreshore toilets in ten.' He read out the cop's number for her to dial. Kept looking at the card: Katsonis. He'd been too distracted in the interview room to notice the neat spelling of that name. But it jumped out at him now: Kat-Son-Is. Like the writing in Taylor's birdwatching book, the faint indentation of the word his subconscious had told him was *SON*. No reason to think the murdered man had written 'Katsonis'. The cop wasn't a local, only in town to do a job. But Caleb had no idea how big this conspiracy was, what it was, how deep it went. And both homicide detectives could have seen his message for Ramsden.

'Hang up,' he told Kat.

'What?'

'Hang up.' Said it out loud that time. Too much force behind the words, could hear it himself, see it in her shocked expression.

Kat ended the call. Eagle feathers showing in stark relief as she gripped the phone.

Trying to keep the panic from his face, he signed quickly, 'I don't know if we can trust them. You need to leave. Go to Melbourne. No, interstate – stay with your friend in Sydney. Mandy.'

She didn't move. 'I'm due in seven weeks.'

'Just until I sort this out. A few days. Maybe a week.'

'Cal, babies come early all the time. It could come today.'

Away from her family and carefully selected team of healthcare professionals, away from him. He'd read Maria's research, knew all the grim statistics about Koori mothers and infants.

'Your sisters, then. Just move around, mix it up.'

'Come with me.'

Yes. Be with her, never go into the world again. But he couldn't. This wouldn't end until he'd found the killers. His trips to the island might give him some immunity now, but there were too many people involved in the conspiracy. One of them would eventually decide to tie up loose ends and come gunning for him. And, quite possibly, for Kat.

She was already shaking her head. 'You can't. Of course you can't.' Face bleak. 'God, I can't believe this is happening again.'

Neither could he. Both of them caught in a recurring nightmare of his making.

He crossed to the sliding doors, opened them. All three women were standing poised in the middle of the kitchen, kids milling. No need to explain his fear; it was reflected in their expressions.

'Kat needs to stay with one of you,' he told them. 'She might not be safe here. Something to do with my work. Can you take her now?'

Kat was beside him, shoulders squared. 'No,' she said out loud. 'Not with the boorias. I'll go to the Mish, Aunty June's.'

The old mission settlement on the outskirts of town, now owned by the Koori community. Open land, one road in and out. Home to thirty or so families, all of whom bore the scars of the Stolen Generations. They'd spot an enemy within seconds.

Kat's sisters and Maria helped her pack a bag, quickly bundled everyone into the cars. A wrench when he saw the seating arrangements: Helen and the kids in one car, Georgie and Kat in the other. Doing as Kat said, keeping the children as far from his life as possible.

Maria caught him as he was putting Kat's bag in the boot. He slammed the lid. Steeled himself as he turned to her.

'Is this connected to your questions about Doctor Locke?' she asked.

No, no, no. Couldn't have Maria making connections like that.

'Disregard that question,' she said. 'I heard some unsubstantiated stories when I made my enquiries for you. Rumours he was involved in a troubling incident at his last workplace, something to do with a patient.' She inclined her head. 'Rumours I obviously won't mention to anyone else.'

'Thank you.' He tried to find the right words, but couldn't. 'I'm sorry.'

No hint of her usual resolute gaze, exhaustion dragging at her mouth and eyes. 'I really don't know what to say to you.' She turned away.

One last goodbye to Kat by the car, Georgie at the wheel, engine already running, other car gone. A short, tight embrace, Kat's fingers digging into his back.

'I love you,' she said when he'd released her. 'Please be safe.'

'I will. Love you, too. Text me when you're there.'

She gave a small nod. Got in the car. Georgie took off as he was signing 'I love you' again, leaving him standing alone, his crossed arms holding empty air.

32.

Somehow it was still morning. People going about their days, stopping to chat outside the supermarket; kids running around the playground, cheeks red with exertion and cold.

Caleb parked outside the foreshore shops, angled the rear-view mirror towards the police station. Ramsden's body would be found soon, if it hadn't been already. Everything would change then. Couldn't avoid the homicide detectives forever, but he could manage it for a while. Three, four days, maybe a week, like he'd told Kat. He had to work out a plan, move fast.

Ask Tedesco for help? A known mate, already questioned by Katsonis and Chabon; be a target as soon as he asked the first question. Wouldn't get to ask a second one. Or have his not-too-dressy wedding and happy life with Luke. Had to work it alone. Alone – and with Ant.

Jesus, Ant. This kind of stress would make even a long-term sober addict spiral. Face that problem later. Ant was relatively safe for now, tucked up inside the clinic. Enough time to follow up Maria's tip, dig deeper into Doctor Locke's past.

A flurry of movement at the police station. People running, two patrol cars pulling out of the back lot, red and blue lights flashing.

Caleb started the Commodore, drove in the opposite direction, towards the highway.

Locke's old rooms were in a small block of consulting suites, the entire place no bigger than the Muttonbird Clinic. No one was waiting in the cosy anteroom, but a couple of smartly dressed women were talking at the end of a short corridor to the left, coffee cups in hand.

Willow was perched behind the reception desk, looking even more possum-like today, in a fluffy grey cardigan, big eyes ringed with liner. Nails had come out well, neat ovals of quicksilver pink. She stilled when she saw him, darted a glance at the women. 'What are you doing here? I told you, I can't say anything.'

'That's OK. I can ask those doctors to confirm what you told me about Locke. That he assaulted two patients. I'll ask him too, of course. And his lawyer.'

'I didn't. You can't –'

As Caleb turned for the corridor, Willow shot from behind the reception desk. Blocked his way. A tight-lipped whisper, then she hurried across the waiting room, out the emergency exit. He followed, hoping she hadn't just threatened to call the cops or pepper-spray him.

She'd stopped on the stairwell landing, her back to the wall. Already speaking before he closed the door. Voice bouncing off concrete walls, steps, ceiling. Aural mud.

'Hang on,' he said. 'Can you say that again? Slower.'

'Why? So you can tape me?' Annoyed, not scared. But looking at the stairs as though about to run down them.

'I'm deaf. Sound echoes in here, makes it hard to lip-read.'

'Yeah?' Her chin lifted. 'How d'you know that if you're deaf?'

Easy to recognise those words and angry disbelief, seen them a thousand times. No idea why people got so shitty when he was the one having to lip-read. Next would probably be the

206

conviction hearing aids were like reading glasses: a simple, perfect fix. 'Hearing aids.'

'So you can hear me.'

'Like wearing bad glasses. I can't read a book, but I can see the bookshelf.' Talking bookshelf – might need to work on that metaphor.

Willow didn't look impressed by it either, still eyeing the stairs.

Suck it up. Didn't have the luxury of being squeamish. Pulling back his hair, he showed her the aid tucked behind his left ear, quickly covered it.

An abrupt switch in Willow, her face and stance opening. 'Sorry, sucks I made you do that. I used to wear a back brace, scoliosis. Hated it when people asked me to show them. One aunt, my God.' She paused. 'But I still can't tell you anything. I'll lose my job.'

'No one will know it came from me, I promise.' When she didn't speak, he said, 'Some bad things have happened. I need to know if Locke's got anything to do with them.'

She bit the edge of a pearlescent thumbnail, caught herself, dropped her hand. 'Is this about your friend? The one Doctor Locke's treating?'

'Yes. What did Locke do?'

'Dated one of his clients. Holly Evans. I mean, she was his client first. He stopped treating her before they went out.'

Maybe unethical, but not illegal. 'He threatened to sue if you talked about it?'

'Not about that. She killed herself and left him all her money. She was really rich.'

Not what he'd been expecting; potentially a lot worse. Or complete fantasy.

'Did the police treat her death as suspicious?'

'No. I mean, she did it. There were witnesses and everything.

But he talked her into it, I just know he did. He got inside her head and made her do it.'

The photo of the serious-faced woman in Locke's study. The doctor's tense reaction when Caleb had picked it up. 'Holly – was she dark haired? Around forty?'

'Yes. She was really lovely. Came in three times a week and always stopped to talk to me. We used to talk about our dogs – she had a border collie, Bruno. Brought him in sometimes.'

'How d'you know about her will?'

'I opened the letter – her, you know, last letter. She sent it here. Wrote about how badly everyone here had treated Doctor Locke. That she'd been happy with him, and it wasn't his fault.' Willow's face scrunched. 'I keep worrying about what happened to Bruno. Do you think he's all right?'

'Holly's family probably took him in.'

'She didn't have any family. Lost everyone in an accident when she was sixteen. I think that's why she was seeing Doctor Locke, but he made it worse. She looked more and more see-through every week.' Her chin trembled. 'I hope you get him.' She pushed past him, scurried out the door.

He let the door swing shut. Willow was young and clearly attached to the dead woman; couldn't take her words as truth. But she'd just described the kind of man who'd destroy people to get what he wanted. Smile calmly while he did it.

———

Caleb stopped for the night outside town, paid cash at a motel off the main road. Almost-fresh cheese sandwiches bought on the way, along with spare batteries for his aids, everything else already stowed in his overnight bag. A neat room, floral bedspread to match the chemical scent. Small white flowers on it like the gore-spattered ones by Ramsden's front door. Averting his eyes, Caleb flipped it over so the unpatterned back was showing. Opened the windows.

He sat on the bed to work, made himself eat the sandwiches while he researched on his phone. The media hadn't covered Holly Evans' death, but he tracked down a few mentions of it on a dog-lovers' forum she'd belonged to, the shocked comments confirming that she'd taken her own life. Just over a year ago. Her profile picture was still there; a smiling version of the woman in Locke's photo, arms around a keen-eared border collie.

Uncertain what to do with the information yet. If he confronted Locke directly, both Locke and Ant would shut him out.

He got to his feet, lobbed the sandwich wrappers into the bin. Stood in the middle of the room. Too late to call Kat. She'd sent a goodnight text an hour ago, would long be asleep; had looked exhausted on their video call earlier. He tried anyway, staring at the green call sign as it pulsed. It rang out.

33.

The yellow jeep was parked at a rakish angle on the grass near the caravan. A slight lulling of jangled nerves: Ant was up and about. Caleb parked next to it, jogged across the clearing to the door. Ant was inside with Lara, heater on, the pair of them chatting easily as they tucked into hot chips at the table. A whirlwind mess around them – drawers and cupboards emptied, mattress off the bed, the few things he'd left behind dumped in a pile. The killers still searching for the blackmail evidence? Have to be desperate if they'd resorted to going through his things. Deeply troubling; panicked people were unpredictable.

Ant waved a chip at the room, said out loud, 'You should tidy sometimes.' Looking relaxed in an orange-and-red Hawaiian shirt. Not aware of Ramsden's death yet. How to break it to him? Not doing too well with it himself, hard to see Ant coping.

'Well, that's me off.' Lara slid from behind the table and stood, leaving half a bowl of chips on the table. Facing Caleb she said, 'Sorry I didn't call the cops for you the other day, hon. I should've been more upfront. Like I told your brother, I get jumpy around them. Long story.'

He bet it was. Be good to know whose papers she'd been burning the other day. Had run back to burn, obviously nervous that he'd eventually get onto the cops. Hers or Taylor's? Easy to believe she'd pick through a dead man's belongings then squirrel away the evidence, just as easy to believe she had her own secrets to hide. No idea how to get through her defences to find out. He had a go. 'Any regrets to burn today?'

Sunken cheeks lifted in a genuine-seeming smile. 'Clear conscience and thoughts, I'm happy to report.'

'Not concerned that another man's been killed?'

'To be honest, by the time you get to my age, you're just glad it's not you.' She blew Ant a kiss. 'Bye, gorgeous, thanks for your help.'

Ant raised a chip. 'Likewise.'

She traipsed outside, silver hair swinging.

Like chipping at concrete with a cotton bud. Have to get Ant's help with her, hope he didn't get all overly protective about the clinic again. Which he would.

Caleb closed the door. 'What's her deal? Why's she at the clinic?'

'Keeps telling me it's for sex addiction, but I'm pretty sure it's just pills.' Stuffing in chips as he signed. 'Poor chook. Must be struggling, she's been here since the clinic opened.'

'Why's she banned from the shop?'

'Got caught shoplifting – dunny rolls, would you believe. Nicked one from a thirty-six pack every time she went. Eighteen before they caught on. Have to give her full marks for commitment.'

Or a bad cover story. 'Lara told you that?'

'No, Skye. Lara told me she'd swiped a bag of cat food. Doesn't even have a cat. Said she wanted to be prepared.' He shoved in a few more chips. Big appetite for someone with a couple of cracked ribs.

A sour thought wormed its way into Caleb's brain. Ant seemed desperate to get clean, but he'd stumbled before, stumbled often. And he and Lara had been up to something together. Better approach that subject obliquely.

He sat, casually helped himself to one of Ant's few remaining chips. 'So you were helping her shop today?'

'Convinced Skye to let her back in. And before you burst a blood vessel trying not to ask, no, she wasn't supplying me with smack in return.' He nudged a plastic bag from under the table with his foot. 'Helped me get this.' A nod towards the ancient wall-mounted TV. 'Hoping it'll work in there.'

Caleb opened the bag: a VHS tape. Dates scrawled on a peeling sticker, including the day before Taylor's murder. Cold realisation. Ant had broken into the quarry and stolen the CCTV tapes, involved Lara. The complete and utter fuckwit.

'It's fine,' Ant signed airily. 'Lara doesn't know what they are, just distracted the manager for me. I was in and out in seconds.'

'What the hell were you thinking?'

'You should really get that vein checked, you know. Looks like it's about to blow.' Ant dipped a chip in tomato sauce. 'I don't know why you're so freaked out.'

'Because they're worthless, and the quarry guy might call the cops! Jesus, you're like a child. I'm trying to save your arse and you're running around stealing useless crap. In a fucking neon shirt. Absolutely clueless.'

'Then piss off, no one asked you to come.' Ant shoved his plate away. Slammed out the door.

Caleb dug his fingers into his temples; more than one vein feeling ready to burst. Had to be deliberate. No one could be that annoying by accident. He grabbed the tape and rammed it into the machine, pressed play. Exactly like he'd suspected: static-etched darkness.

On his way out the door, he snatched a jacket from his up-ended belongings. Ant was leaning against a large ghost gum, sucking on a tightly rolled cigarette. Facing away from the quay, at least. Protected from snipers, if not himself.

Caleb threw him the jacket. Muted brown, no gaudy palm trees. 'Put that on. You stick out like a boil.' He kept moving to the car.

A solid thirty seconds for Ant to come to the car. Not wearing the jacket. 'Where are we going?'

Locke or Gideon? Both high on his list of untrustworthy people. But only one of them had the loyalty of an already pissed off Ant.

'Stake out Gideon's. He's using a fake name, owns a tinnie. I want to search his house.'

'Why? It's not like he'll have a murder weapon lying around.'

'Maybe we'll get lucky, find another dismembered body.'

Ant muttered something that looked suspiciously like 'hopefully yours', thrust his arms into the jacket.

———————

They waited in a hayshed just down the road from Gideon's hilltop house. Nearer than Caleb would have liked, but it meant they could do a discreet up and back on foot when Gideon left. If he left. Once again the man had shown no signs of it over the course of the afternoon, his silhouette occasionally visible through the windows, the front door never opening.

'Han Solo or Indiana Jones?' Ant asked. Lounging on a bale, signing in between attempts to set fire to the hay with the binoculars.

'Han.'

'Dolly Parton or the Dalai Lama?'

'Dolly.'

'Margaret Thatcher or the Queen?'

'Queen.'

Ant paused in his arson attempt. 'Incorrect but state your case.'

'Handbag as a weapon and she'd be a scrappy fighter. Lot of pent-up anger.'

'Thatcher had a handbag. And helmet hair.'

'Corgies.'

'Hairspray.'

'Still calling it for the Queen. Can I have the binoculars?'

'No.' Ant returned to the job at hand. Restless, but not hanging out for a hit – no jitters or sweating, not even reaching for his tobacco despite his obvious boredom. A deep swell of hope. There was a solid chance he'd get through rehab and out the other side if he didn't freak out about Ramsden. Or set them on fire.

Time to distract him with work. Caleb grabbed his normal phone, found the photos of the papers Lara had burned. Still no sense to be made of the fragments, a print-out of random digits and letters: *RBV, 508320, 850N*. Tossing it onto a bale next to Ant, he said, 'Look at those instead of torching us, will you? Lara burnt some papers after I asked her to call the cops the other day. Photos are what I could save.'

Ant made a why-would-you-do-that? face without bothering to sign. Not a bad effort-to-arseholery ratio.

'Might be the evidence the killers are looking for. What's left of it.'

'You can't seriously think Lara's involved? She's seventy-two and has arthritis.'

It was the unlikeliest people you had to be most wary of.

'I'm more thinking she nicked it from Taylor's room. But we can't trust anyone.'

'Must be terrifying inside your head.' Ant gave the photos a few seconds' examination. 'Looks like a shipment order.'

Caleb had seen plenty of those while poking through the guts of shonky businesses, but nothing about the fragments had jumped out at him. 'Why?'

Ant tapped the *RBV*. 'We used the same code at the bottling factory. Lot of local places do. RBV, Resurrection Bay, Victoria.'

Trafficking. Stolen goods? Drugs? The island as halfway point. Cargo dumped from container ships then picked up by locals, run to the mainland. Or going the other way. The nurse, Melissa, with that handy cabinet of drugs. Doing the stocktake, adding a few extras each time. No – not lucrative enough for this many people, you'd need a larger supply for that. Arlo? Maybe not making illicit visits to the brothel after all.

'Arlo's been hanging around the hospital in that van.'

'Nicking drugs?' Ant's eyebrows rose briefly. 'Nah, he wouldn't have shipping orders. Hospitals use more than one supplier, stuff comes in dribs and drabs. Have to swipe it from the pharmacy if you want a decent amount.' A pause. 'Or so I'd imagine.'

Might just let that slide past. OK, keep Arlo in the frame, change the crime.

'Could be sex trafficking,' he told Ant. 'He's been parking near Secret Angel, too. Might've mocked up the shipping orders for customs.'

'Now you're just getting desperate. Reckon it's just one of Lara's little secrets.' Ant sat up. 'Gideon's leaving.'

'OK, I'll be back in twenty. Stay here and keep a lookout.'

Ant stood, strolled towards the road.

Had to tell him. Couldn't let him barge into a potential cop-killer's home not knowing what he might be up against.

'Something's happened,' Caleb said out loud. 'I thought things were getting out of hand. Went to Ramsden.'

Shoulders slumping, Ant turned. 'Yeah. Figured that'd happen eventually. He at the clinic?'

'No. He's dead. Shot. Another cop tipped off the sniper. Maybe a local, maybe homicide.'

Ant's face slackened with shock. 'That's – Jesus. What do we do now?'

'I don't think we'll be safe until it's finished. Not if they're killing cops.'

'So what do we do?'

'Keep going.'

34.

Gideon's timber hut was unlocked – not unusual outside the city, but a surprise given the man's secretive nature.

Caleb had one more go at keeping Ant away. 'We need a lookout.'

'I'll hear the car,' Ant said and pushed inside.

The door opened onto a tiny kitchen. Raw timber walls and open shelves, basic crockery and food staples in neat rows. One bowl drying on the sink. The box from Best Buy Cellars was on the counter, nearly empty. Four bottles in four days.

Caleb pointed to a short corridor on the left. 'Bedroom and bathroom.' He stopped; worth going over the instructions again. 'What are you looking for?'

'Sense of self-worth, I guess, what about you?'

Caleb held back a sigh. Fears that Ant would crumble over news of Ramsden's death had well and truly passed. He'd interrogated Caleb about the shooting the entire ten-minute walk. And was now, apparently, on the upswing of an adrenaline rush.

'Shipping lists,' Ant said. 'Anything that could have Gideon's real name on it. Links to other people, particularly cops. Particularly cops called Katsonis. Alt-right stuff. Weapons.'

'Ten minutes. Don't move anything.'

Ant saluted and left.

The living room was cold despite the coals glowing in the fireplace. A large bookshelf, but otherwise like a prison cell. Bare timber walls and floor, the only furniture a couple of armchairs.

One positioned by the fire, the other by the window. No rugs, personal belongings or decorations.

Not normal. Not in any of the myriad degrees of normal he'd witnessed in his years poking through people's lives. The house of someone who'd fled their old life.

But Gideon was still human; highly likely he'd kept some link with his past. Too many books to hunt through in the time available. Structure first. He stomped along the floor to check for loose boards, moved on to the walls. Knocking each timber slat, feeling for the duller vibration that signalled a filled hollow. Nothing. Nothing slipped into the armchairs' covers or cushions, either. Nothing underneath them. He sat in the one by the fire, followed the sightlines to the bookshelf.

Biographies and novels, no obvious copies of *Mein Kampf* or *The Art of the Deal*. One leather-bound book in a wall of paperbacks. Middle row, pride of place. He went to it. *My Side of the Mountain*, a bookplate inside, dated and inscribed in a flowing hand: *To my darling Gideon. Happy 10th birthday. All my love, Grandma*. Date of birth and confirmation of a first name. Excellent. If Gideon really was on a pension like Cardigan Joyce had said, Caleb would be able to unearth his real surname.

In the kitchen, Ant was peering into a low cupboard. He straightened, holding a carton of long-life milk. 'Maybe that word Skye said really was "bovine". There's like, ten litres in there. What d'you reckon – smuggling diamonds?' His expression caught, gaze on something behind Caleb.

Gideon. In the doorway, hands loose by his sides, weight on the balls of his feet.

Caleb backed against the counter, box of vodka bottles by his left hand.

'Want to tell me what you're doing here?' Hard mouth forming each word clearly and calmly.

Must have parked his car away from the house if Ant hadn't heard it. He'd known they were watching, had let them search the house. Why?

Caleb signed to Ant, 'Let me do the talking.' Got a short nod in return.

'Let's stick to English,' Gideon said.

'I was telling him you're not going to do anything violent.'

'I'm not?'

'No.' Not yet, anyway. Gideon might not be the kind of man who barged in, fists flying, but he was standing like someone who could whip out a knife and fillet a couple of interlopers without breaking a sweat.

'Just came for a chat. Wanted to know why you didn't want the clinic on the island.'

Gideon took his time answering. 'Heritage concerns.'

Was there another word that looked like 'heritage'? Sewerage? Armitage?

'What'd you say?'

'Heritage.' Gideon moved into the room, leaned against the wall. 'Building's an excellent example of Georgian-style postcolonial architecture. Should be preserved for the public.'

Interesting, but not quite the information he was after. 'What do you know about a dead man with an alt-right tatt on his arm? SS bolts.'

A crack of a smile. 'That you shouldn't talk in front of Joyce Kaplan.'

Cardigan Joyce, spreading the news around the island like he'd suspected.

'What do you know about –?'

'My turn,' Gideon said. 'What were you looking for in here?'

'A rifle.'

'So you haven't found the sniper.' Falling intonation, as though disappointed.

'Do you know who it is?'

'No.'

'But you suspect someone.'

Gideon turned to Ant, who was still gripping the milk carton. 'Want to drink that before you go?'

'No thanks, I'm a bit lactose intolerant.'

A long, unblinking look.

Ant shoved the milk onto the counter and left, Caleb right behind him.

35.

They didn't stop until they reached the hayshed. Ant leaned against a post, clutching his side but bright-eyed and animated. Adrenaline obviously still coursing. 'So, that was terrifying. Guess we should've had a lookout. Hindsight, huh? Still, reckon we handled it well, all things considered.'

Caleb gave it a second. 'Lactose intolerant?'

'Mate, I was worried about shitting myself, couldn't risk the extra pressure.' He glanced back at the perched hut. 'Why would anyone live like that? Miles from anyone and anything.'

'He's broken. Too many sharp edges to be around people.'

Ant studied him. 'You can be surprisingly poetic for a boofhead. Gives me hope. So what's the verdict? I know you had him down as the arm retrievalist, but I can totally see him as the sniper.'

Caleb could too: the kind of stillness you'd need to lay in wait for prey. The air of someone used to giving orders, too. Crime syndicates weren't usually democracies; a strong likelihood the sniper was running this one. Someone controlling and in control, a loner. But Gideon seemed depressed rather than focused – that house and his manner, his evident drinking problem. Even his question about the sniper had been delivered with a weary air.

'Undecided,' he told Ant. 'But I can't see a sniper drinking that much.'

'True. Maybe that's why he objected to the clinic. Constant reminder of his own failings.'

Caleb opened the car, body-blocked Ant from getting in the driver's side. No way was he letting Ant drive while amped up on adrenaline.

While Ant rolled a cigarette in the passenger seat, Caleb texted another incriminating message to Sammi. Asked for an expedited deep background check of Gideon – and leniency in her billing. Her reply came quickly: a thumbs-up alongside a laughing emoji. At this rate the case was going to cost more than Ant's treatment.

Beside him, Ant was feeling in his pockets, peering at the dashboard, unlit rollie in his mouth. 'Where's the car lighter?' He flipped open the glove box, stopped. A dull blush crept up his face.

Oh fuck – the naloxone. Should have hidden the OD antidote in the first-aid kit. And coming just after that diatribe in the caravan, like he was actively trying to undermine Ant's shored-up foundations.

'It's old,' Caleb told him. 'Got it after – It's been there ages.'

Ant nodded. Closed the glove box, cheeks still burning.

Caleb tried again. 'Not doubting this rehab.'

'It's fine. You bought it after I OD'd, I get it.' Not quite meeting Caleb's eyes as he signed. 'Seen a few ODs over the years. Sticks with you. So where now? Tail Arlo?'

'He's pretty volatile. Let's wait until Sammi gets back with the info on Gideon.'

'Reckon I'll turn in early, then. My ribs are killing me.' Tucking the cigarette back in the pouch, he faced the windscreen.

Prolonging the conversation would probably make things worse, but avoiding it hadn't worked so far.

'Sorry I was such an arsehole,' Caleb said.

'You'll have to be more specific.'

'In the caravan. And before that. Leaving you to go it alone all those years.' Ant didn't react, his face blank. Caleb kept going. 'My failings, not yours. Takes real strength to do what you're doing.'

Ant turned abruptly to the window. Long seconds just sitting, the car rocking slightly in the wind. Eventually he wiped his face with his hands, gave a nod. 'Thanks.'

They drove without more discussion. A comfortable stillness, no need to fill it with speech or sign.

When they reached the clinic, the high wrought-iron gates were closed, fastened by a chain and padlock. Never seen them shut before.

'That normal?' Caleb asked.

'Since the break-in, yeah. Got a key.'

Locke trying to keep his patients safe, or trying to hide? Impossible to tell. Just had to hope the doctor was as smart as he seemed and wouldn't risk harming anyone on his own property.

A blast of cold air as Ant opened the door. He stopped to remove the borrowed jacket.

'Keep it,' Caleb told him.

'Mate. All offence intended, but I'd rather freeze to death.' He got out and unlocked the gates. Walked through them, an ease to his movements.

Caleb returned to the caravan. An early night for him too, with the quarry's CCTV to keep him occupied until a prearranged call with Kat later. The rest of the tape would almost certainly be as bad as the few seconds he'd seen, but cases had hinged on far less than unwatched surveillance video. The sun hadn't set yet, but he closed the curtains and tidied his ransacked belongings. Stuck a bowl of tinned minestrone in the ancient microwave, trying not to think about Gideon going through the same motions in that empty hut. Too easy to see an alternate version of himself in that picture.

As he ate, he fast-forwarded through the murky footage, stopping at each bright flare of passing headlights; a slow process, the road busier than he'd expected. No way of knowing which car was Taylor's, or who'd been chasing him. He moved on to the daylight hours, the morning of Taylor's murder. Overkill, but you never knew when you'd see something unexpected.

Like a familiar Hyundai hatchback driving past the quarry, Etty at the wheel.

He lowered his spoon. The car slowed, pulled into Cardigan Joyce's driveway, disappeared from view. How did Etty know Joyce? As far as he knew she'd only been on the island a few times; her weekly visits to Ant. Still, small place, maybe Etty had heard about the goat's cheese, popped in to buy some. After a ten-minute gap, she reappeared, the rear of her hatchback stacked with white boxes. No boxes there on her way in.

Suspicion stirred like sludge. Etty working some scheme with Joyce? Or, much more likely, Etty and Joyce working for Locke. Joyce's nervousness at her scrubbed-clean house that day; Etty's plea for Caleb to take over the clinic payments, her insistence that Locke was the best doctor for Ant.

Driven by directionless urgency, he got to his feet. Think it through. A single trip to a farmhouse didn't mean anything. And Etty's affection for Ant was patently real. But two seemingly contradictory things could be true at the same time. Love and betrayal; care and selfishness. Frankie had taught him that.

He flung open the door, headed towards the shop. Arlo was in the forecourt manoeuvring a diesel barrel to the bowser. He straightened as he saw Caleb, stood with his arms wide. OK, intermittent service on the pier it was. Caleb pivoted hard right. Crossed the empty quayside to the long pier, strode up the weathered boards to the end, the low sun in his eyes.

One bar on his phone, hopefully enough to get internet. His

email account first, the page slow to load, endlessly unrolling. Finally managed to grab Etty's email address from it. Over to her server. No phone verification needed for her account. Terrible security, excellent news; couldn't run hacking software with internet this slow. He tried the standard passwords, getting desperate by the time he'd done reverse birthdate, family names, the childhood dog she'd mentioned a couple of times. Of course – the chickens. He typed quickly: *EltonJohn*. And was in.

A search on Locke and the clinic netted a string of invoices and receipts, the dates and amounts right for Ant's stay. Nothing worrying in her recently sent or received emails, just a constant bolstering flow to Ant, subject lines like: *love you*, *believe in you*, *only two days!*

Login details for her bank were saved under Accounts, every email update easily searchable. Why were people so trusting? The bank's website was even slower to load, each data point floating across the water of the bay. Finally in. Etty's finances were in worse shape than she'd let on: no savings and a hefty personal loan she wouldn't be able to service. But no unexplained income, and the payments to the clinic matching the receipts. Not impossible she had another secret bank account, but five years of emails didn't hint at one.

Caleb lowered the phone, breathed in the salt air, the last of the sunlight warm on his face. Thank God for that. Hard to imagine Ant surviving a blow like that at the moment, or their own relationship surviving its revelation. Good to have been proven wrong.

36.

The caravan was still the next morning. No pushing restless wind, blue sky visible through a gap in the curtains. A feeling of not having slept, limbs weighted. Some old nightmares revisited, a few new ones tangled in the mess. Ramsden's sightless eyes and bloodstained shirt. Kat – no, not going to think about the horrors of that one.

Her texts were all positive and reassuring, variations of Etty's supportive emails to Ant: *I'm fine. Love you too.* But she'd looked wrung-out in their call last night. Good phone service at the end of the pier by then, the sharp image showing how drawn she was. Two days since Ramsden's murder and it didn't look as though she'd slept the entire time.

He showered in the caravan's grim plastic cupboard and rechecked messages. Still no word from Sammi on Gideon's real name, but a text from Jarrah. Hopefully not with news of another dick pick. Or an opinion about Kat.

—*Coach quit this morning*

A major blow to the Numbats' future. Hard to see anyone else stepping into the role, unless Caleb could find the culprit. Strong odds the team would quietly fold over the summer break, next year's season begin without them. Once that happened, the club would be very hard to resurrect. And he had no idea how to prevent it, or how to face Mick.

He went to grab breakfast, was halfway across the clearing

before noticing his car. Parked at the edge of the quayside where he usually left it, driver's door and boot ajar. He went over. The few things he'd left inside were scattered across the seats, floor mats lifted, Taylor's birdwatching book and binoculars on the ground. Risky, searching the car out here in the open where anyone could have seen them. That whiff of desperation growing stronger.

After shoving everything back in the glove box, he retrieved Taylor's book. The indented writing at the back – hadn't studied it in daylight. He flipped to it. No additional words revealed, just the 'son' that may or may not be from 'Katsonis'. Or was that first mark a 5? Angling it to the light. Jesus, it was. Not *SON*, but *50N*. Leaving him exactly nowhere with Katsonis; the cop possibly dirty, possibly clean. Which meant there was no need to admit to Ant that he'd managed to misread two numbers as letters.

Numbers.

One of those too-rare light-bulb moments. He pulled out his phone, found the images of the printed pages Lara had burnt. There it was, in the middle of what Ant thought was a shipping number: *50N*. Finally getting somewhere. Confirmation Lara had found and destroyed the blackmail documents, and that the conspiracy involved some kind of trafficking. A chance Lara would remember some detail from the papers, an address or name. And might admit it to Ant if he asked. High-risk proposition: Ant and Lara discussing blackmail documents, a powder keg of possible indiscretions.

A decision to be made after coffee. Or what passed for it around here.

Max, the scruffy-headed ferryman, was coming through the door when Caleb reached the steps. Tucking into a meat pie like a man who didn't have to pilot a ferry through late-morning swells. Caleb paused. Etty had come across on the ferry just a few days ago, one of the operator's dreaded carless passengers; Max might remember her because of that, despite his facial recognition issues. Due diligence to ask a couple of questions, nothing more. The kind of diligence that might let him sleep at night and look Ant in the eye this morning.

He met Max on the veranda, started going through the usual introductions.

'Yeah, got you now – Caleb the non-spewer. Get to recognise the regulars.'

'Great. The other day a woman came over here on foot. I drove back with her. Small, short brown hair, around thirty. Any chance you remember her?'

'Etty? Sure. Non-spewer, too.' Unique classification system, but it seemed to work for the man.

'You ever seen her with the doctor who works on the island? Late fifties, grey hair?' He thought about it. 'Or a young guy with a tatt on his forearm? Like double lightning bolts.'

Max shrugged. 'Think she's always alone.' Lifting his pie in farewell, he started down the steps.

Great news. Things definitely looking up. A feeling of eyes on him. Across the road, the two oversized men from the quarry were standing outside a house, drinking takeaway coffee. Staring at him. Oh good, they'd been joined by Arlo. Nice to see him making friends.

The ferryman had turned, was coming back up the steps. '. . . interested in that white van? Who drives it?'

Good point, should have followed that up. 'Yeah.' He nodded towards Arlo, still giving him the greasy from across the road. 'Arlo over there use it much? Guy in the black beanie.'

'Oh. Yeah, I guess.'

Obviously not the person Max had been thinking of. 'Someone else?'

'Yeah, a woman came across this morning, reminded me of your question. Seen her a bit. Wears a fuck-awful cardigan.'

'Goats? Staring eyes?'

'That's the one. Been wondering how she got their eyes to follow you like that – well, more wondering why.'

Cardigan Joyce driving the van. Filled with boxes under a blue tarp? Could put the stream of night-time traffic near her house into an interesting perspective.

And Etty had been visiting her. Dampened suspicions flickered back to life. If Max had needed an ugly cardigan to ID a local like Joyce, how had he remembered Etty so easily? Remembered her name.

The yellow jeep was pulling into the forecourt, Ant at the wheel. He waved at Caleb, smiling.

Caleb quickly turned to Max. 'Etty – she come over a lot?'

'Be three or four times a week, I guess.'

'What, every week?'

'Yeah. Better get going, recognise ya later.' He ambled away.

According to Ant, Etty only visited him once a week. A mutual agreement for a healthy relationship. Oh fuck.

Ant was out of the jeep, heading towards him, fresh-faced, possibly whistling. Yellow T-shirt under his aviator jacket today, a large winking cartoon sun on the front.

Couldn't tell him. Couldn't not tell him.

'Come here,' Caleb signed. Moved away from the shop and watchful eyes, headed for the caravan.

Ant kept pace. 'And good morning to you too. I've been thinking about our mate Arlo over there. I reckon we should stake out the jetty in Res Bay, wait for him to come across.' He went on, outlining ways to keep hidden while managing toilet breaks.

Caleb stopped outside the caravan, his back to the sea. 'I watched the security tape last night.'

'He announced with a dramatic pause.' Face bright, leaning forward in an exaggerated pose of rapt attention. 'So, what? You saw who was after Taylor? Solved the case?'

'No, but the camera picks up the end of Joyce's driveway. Etty visited her, left with a lot of boxes in her car.'

'Huh, so my girl likes a walk on the unpasteurised side.' He grinned. 'Little rebel.'

'A *lot* of boxes.'

Still smiling, Ant put a hand up. 'Stop right there, Mr Paranoid. Etty's not involved in anything dodgy.'

'She's been coming to the island three or four times a week. Not just your visiting day. Did you know that?'

Ant's forehead creased. He shook his head. 'Stop.'

'She's broke. Asked me for –'

'Stop.'

'– money. A lot of money.'

Hard-eyed fury in Ant's face. 'Don't ruin my happiness with your twisted fucking mind. Get the fuck away from me. Stay away.' He stormed back towards the jeep.

Caleb followed, speaking out loud so Ant couldn't avoid his words. 'Locke's got a bad history with women. His last girlfriend was a patient. Rich. Killed herself and left him everything. I'm sorry, I really am. Etty's obviously fond of you, but she's up to something. She's been sneaking around –'

Ant swung back, fist already moving. Caleb instinctively blocked. Solid punch, pain radiating along his arm. He shielded his head as Ant kept coming, red-faced and yelling. Uncontrolled blows to arms, shoulders, chest, gradually weakening.

Finally Ant staggered away. 'You miserable prick. Can't help yourself, can you?' Hands shaking as he stabbed out each sign. 'You have to drag everyone down with you. Your poor kid, having you as a father. Poor Kat.' He strode away.

37.

In the early afternoon Caleb risked going for a run. Couldn't stay still any longer. Sprinting hard across the beach behind the caravan, water snatching at his ankles. A day spent watching the quayside through the window, waiting for the white van to make a trip into Resurrection Bay. Waiting for Ant, for Etty, for some faint idea of what to do next. Had to be able to make it right. Slot the final pieces into place and present it all to Ant, hope he'd accept enough of the truth to stay safe.

'You have to drag everyone down with you.'

Seagulls stalked across the sand as he passed, staring at him with red eyes. A scattering of bottle tops and plastic tags strewn at the high-water mark, detritus from the storm still washing up. At the far end of the beach, an elderly man was dropping rubbish into a plastic bag – a heroic action, trying to clean up that. It'd keep washing up forever, damage done, unfixable.

They'd never fought before. Not as adults, not like that, hatred behind Ant's blows.

'Your poor kid, having you as a father. Poor Kat.'

A burst of speed, arms and legs pumping, pushing past comfort. Enough. He pulled up, chest heaving. No more waiting around for something to happen. Catch the next ferry, check out the brothel Arlo had parked near. Some risk if the place was linked to the murders, but Secret Angel was a legitimate business with customers and employees; unlikely anyone would harm him on the premises.

Seagulls up ahead suddenly swarmed into the air. Flapping in messy circles, beaks open in protest. A ripple down his spine. The birds settled again, didn't stir as he walked towards them. Nothing except sand, the sharp marks of the gulls' beaks and feet.

He scanned the area, jogged slowly back to the quay.

———————

Leaving his car near the caravan, he caught the ferry over on foot. New black beanie from the shop pulled low on his forehead like Arlo's, a matching black scarf around his neck. Not much of a disguise, but enough for a casual glance at a distance. Hopefully as close as he'd get to any cops.

He crossed Bay Road a block from the police station, had a good look while he did it. Four news vans pulled up outside the building, a few locals lingering on the street opposite, drawn by the bright lights and stiff-haired presenters. Probably more around the corner. One live-cross happening now, the other news teams standing around talking casually. No big discoveries on Ramsden's death, then. Or none that had been leaked to the media.

Caleb kept going, trying to walk like a man with nothing to fear.

Secret Angel Gentlemen's Club looked like an upmarket hotel for insomniacs. Plush carpet and banquettes, flocked wallpaper. Colours and lighting muted. The only decent wattage was by the reception desk, positioned for the security camera subtly mounted behind it. There'd been another outside the front door. It took Caleb a fair while to get the receptionist to call through to the owner, but they eventually bonded over her need for fifty bucks, and his desire to give it to her. He went to wait on the velvet banquette, checked his phone as it vibrated: Maria. A surge of adrenaline.

Caleb, the police have been here asking for you. They have been here three times. The two today left a number for you to call. Constables Willis and Farrero. Could you please attend to it?

His heart settled a little. Not local cops: extras brought in for the task force. Probably dozens of them in town by now, knocking on doors. A request to ring felt like they were following up on his attempted meeting with Ramsden, not about to arrest him for murder. But no good could come from cops hassling Kat's family. Best-case scenario, there were a lot of very anxious people; worst, the cops led the wrong person to Kat. Have to meet with them, try to deflect with some story. Might buy him a day or two. Breathless sensation, the walls closing in. He let Maria know he'd deal with it, didn't get a reply.

A discreet door opened in the wall opposite him, and a woman strode out: Jeanie Wilson, the proprietor. Short and tanned, wearing a navy pantsuit and tailored cream blouse that was uncannily like one of Maria's outfits. The unyielding gaze of his mother-in-law too, but the resemblance stopped there. Jeanie Wilson had been nipped, tucked, dyed and suctioned to achieve an excellent impression of a human woman in her late-somethings.

As he introduced himself she examined his business card, a dull murmur coming from her swollen lips. Deep weariness: lip-reading in dim light was hard enough, but those lip-fillers made it impossible. 'Could we speak somewhere else?'

The lips parted briefly, maybe a 'why'.

'Business related.' He waited, then added, 'Discreet business.'

Another impenetrable mouth-movement before she turned for the internal door. Invitation or dismissal? He chanced following, caught up as she strode through the door into a brightly lit room. Like being in a different movie, the plush surrounds abruptly giving way to plain plaster walls, a heavily built man watching a bank of monitors. Jeanie walked briskly through the room and into an office at the back. Functional and plain, a couple of finger paintings taped to the wall behind the desk, along with a sticker supporting the Mighty Fighting Numbats.

Jeanie caught his swift examination. 'Disappointed?' Much better enunciation than in the foyer for some reason.

He relaxed – no need to conduct the conversation via text. 'Impressed,' he said.

Her mouth twitched, possibly a smile. She settled herself behind the blond-wood desk, waited for him to take the seat in front of it before speaking. 'There's a security camera on you. If you're here to extort, threaten or steal, Brett out there will come in and hurt you quite badly.' The calm tone of a dental nurse holding a large needle. 'That clear?'

'Crystal.' Remarkably so. That improved diction had to be a deliberate effort. 'Who told you about me?'

'I'm sorry?'

'You know who I am. That I'm deaf.'

'I didn't need anyone to tell me that, darling. You clearly had no idea what I was saying in the foyer. I've had a few hearing-impaired clients over the years, I can usually spot it. Lucky for you. It's the only reason I let you back here.'

'Thought I'd be a pushover?'

'Oh, honey, that chip on your shoulder's got to be heavy. But no, I knew Brett would be able to smack you over the head without you realising.' She interlaced her fingers, the plump diamond on her ring finger glinting. 'Before we go any further, I have to tell you that I won't discuss clients. Not with you, not with the wives, not with the cops.'

'This client might be involved in a murder.'

'Sounds like a job for the police.'

She wasn't wrong. He found the stock photo of the lightning tattoo on his phone, showed it to her. 'This familiar?'

Face a blank slate. 'No.'

'What about the name Arlo Reid?'

'No.'

He swiped to the photo he'd managed to sneak of Arlo outside the shop. Three-quarter profile, beanie pulled low. The slightest of flickers in Jeanie's eyes. Recognition? Attempt to blink? Like trying to decipher a badly photocopied page. 'Bald under that beanie,' he said. 'Witnesses say he visited here.'

'He was hanging around for a while, but I don't know him.'

'Business partner? Supplier? Purchaser?'

'Honey, I don't know how I can make this any clearer, but I don't know the man. He kept parking around here, sitting in his van. It was upsetting the girls, so I got Brett to have a chat with him. He parks further away now.'

'So you won't mind if I mention Secret Angel to the cops, say I think you're involved in sex trafficking? Maybe give all those journos in town a tip-off?'

'Go ahead, my books are clean.' A taloned nail tapped the desk. 'Publicity could be good, too. Make sure you mention we're upmarket.'

If she was rattled, she was really getting her money's worth out of that botox. One last attempt. 'Fair enough. I'll just speak to your workers, see what they know.'

'I like your spirit, hon, but I think you know that's not going to happen.' She turned to the computer, began typing.

Papers on her desk fluttered as the door opened. The guard was next to him, arms folded but looking ready to swing.

Caleb stood, but didn't leave. A security-conscious person like Jeanie would definitely have kept an eye out for Arlo once he was on her radar.

'One last question. You said Arlo parks his van further away now – where?'

She waved a hand. 'All around.'

'Specifically?'

'The hospital, the park up the road, the shops, the mechanic's.'

Three mechanics in town. The one owned by pie-eating Greg? The van not following Caleb that day but waiting for him?

'Which mechanic's?'

The guard put leaden hands on his shoulders. Shoved him towards the door.

Caleb nodded and left.

38.

He got to the mechanic's right on five, caught Greg closing up. Some multitasking involved, wiping down tools with an oily rag in between bites of a snot block. He straightened as Caleb came in, gave the pastry flakes on his overalls a cursory brush with the rag, leaving a few more grease stains. 'Don't tell me your shit box has broken down again.'

Go in hard, a frontal assault. 'Tell me about Arlo's van.'

'Don't reckon I know it. You finally getting a new vehicle? Bout bloody time.'

'White Toyota, *Fuck a Greenie* sticker on it?'

Greg paused, mid-bite. 'Oh, mate, no. I've seen that hanging around. Piece of shit, don't buy that. I don't want to be lumped with another one of your tragedies. Bad for my rep.'

Clueless. Both him and Greg. He went through the motions anyway, showed the mechanic the tattoo. 'Know anyone with a tatt like this?'

Greg chomped on the vanilla slice as he examined the screen, spoke around the yellow goop. 'Just Robbo, I reckon.'

Caleb went to ask the next question, had to put the brakes on, do a mental U-turn. Robbo the young footy player? Hurt in that car smash? A man he'd in no way connected to the sniper or the island.

'Robbo from the Numbats?'

'Yeah.' Greg sucked his teeth. 'Something like that, anyway. Got a few.'

Suspicion catching every thought. Not impossible that Greg was involved and blowing smoke at him. 'So Robbo's teammates would recognise it, too?'

'Some of them, I guess. But it's a racist sign, you know. Usually keeps his arms covered. Embarrassed, I reckon, got 'em when he was younger.' Greg nodded to the wall beside them, a Numbat fundraising calendar hanging from a bent nail.

A candid shot of the full team on a hot day, all wearing shorts; some players bare-chested, Robbo in a long-sleeved top. Too small to make out any detail. Caleb lifted the calendar from the wall, flipped through it until he found a larger photo. Robbo going for a mark, arms extended, reaching for the footy. Black tattoo showing above the hem of his pulled-back sleeve: SS bolts. Mick had commented on Robbo only getting on well with his white teammates – should have paid more attention to that.

Two men with white supremacist tattoos: one dead on the island, one in a near-fatal accident on the mainland. Couldn't be a coincidence. Some kind of Neo-Nazi group running the Res Bay end of things? The man killed due to infighting? But there were no organised groups like that in the Bay; he kept a very close eye on that type of thing because of Kat. More so now, with the baby on the way.

Greg shoved the last of the pastry in his mouth. 'This a Numbatgate thing?' he sprayed. 'Solved it?'

'No.' This was a long way from numbats and ridiculous photos.

'Better hurry up,' Greg said. 'Me fellow council members are getting antsy about the late rent on the oval.'

Really? 'Talking about selling the oval?'

'What, from underneath the Numbats? Be a suicide mission.

Don't worry, I've got the boys' backs. Never vote for something like that.'

Even if Greg did do the dirty on his beloved Numbats, the theory still fell at the first hurdle: an entire council agreeing to sell for a very meagre kickback. But the guy had bought land through Jarrah, should push that button, see if it made him jumpy.

'You have anything to do with Jarrah?'

'Sure. Top bloke. Great captain.'

'Business-wise.'

'Yeah. You looking to buy? Can recommend him as a real estate agent. Gave me a great deal on some land I bought out at River Views. He'll cut his commission for a Numbat supporter, no worries.'

He left Greg opening a packaged egg sandwich, didn't get any further than the rear laneway. Tired, body aching where Ant's blows had landed. No idea what to do, or even what to think.

Robbo had to be mates with the murdered man or members of the same, very discreet, Neo-Nazi group. Couldn't approach him directly at the hospital, impossible to keep a visit like that quiet. Particularly with the ever-present Arlo, now squarely back in the frame. But the cops could. Those two officers who'd been hassling Maria? Not locals, so probably not involved in the conspiracy. Meet with them, tip them off about Robbo. Not a brilliant plan, not even a mediocre one, but relatively safe. No notice, text from his house, go out the back way if they came with reinforcements. After that, he was out of ideas.

———

Mrs Naylor was out in her garden, soaking up the last of the sun again. So, definitely not a vampire. She was tending to her roses, whacking around a fair bit of fertiliser too, the smell noticeable as he ducked into his other neighbour's yard – safety precautions, not hiding from an elderly woman for the second time in a week. He jumped the side fence, cut across his front lawn. Quick check over his shoulder as he got to the front door. Oh, shit. She'd spotted him, was shuffling towards her gate, waving. Nope, not today.

The key jammed in the lock. Hadn't fixed the damn thing. He jiggled it, trying to get it to turn. Stronger smell here, rotten egg, like a gas leak. Couldn't be. Cylinders out the back, valves safely shut since Ant left.

The lock finally clicked, door swinging open. No. Gas.

He turned. Sprinted away.

Slamming pain.

Falling, flying through bright white burning air.

Down.

39.

The cops came while he was waiting for the X-ray. Or was it a CAT scan? Somewhere in the hospital anyway, sitting on a trolley in a large grey waiting room, skull wrapped in something that felt suspiciously like barbed wire. Bandage, according to the nurse. The two detectives paused as they exited the elevator, reading the direction board in the corridor. Possibly bent Katsonis, and his underling, Chabon. Possibly also bent. Fast work, them getting here. Only half an hour or so since he'd arrived. Maybe. Time seemed slippery; didn't even remember the trip in the ambulance. Reasonably unscathed though, all things considered. Bit of a bang on the head and some grazes, few splinters of glass in his back. OK, more than a few, the nurse picking them out for ages, but no reason for Kat to look so upset. Not good for her to be stressed. Where was Kat? She'd been here a minute ago. With Mick.

Caleb turned to the orderly at the foot of his trolley. 'Where's my wife? She OK?'

'Upstairs. She'll be there when you get back.' Bored patience in his expression, as though he'd answered the question before. Young guy, pink uniform a bad match for his razor-burn. Be better off in one of the bile-green uniforms some of the other orderlies in the room were wearing. Green uniform – something niggling him about that, but it kept sliding out of his brain like grease. Congealed grease, chunks in it. His stomach heaved.

The detectives were beside him. Katsonis standing back,

watching with his dead-fish eyes. Lean face as unreadable as usual. Dick-first Chabon spoke to the orderly who went to step away.

'Better get a vomit bowl,' Caleb told the young man.

The orderly glanced around as though expecting one to appear, then made a fast track across the room, pink uniform shimmering under the strobing lights. Bad colour, that uniform. The niggling thought slid back, that was it – Arlo and green uniforms. When he'd tussled with Arlo at the van, there'd been an orderly in a green uniform. Maybe not a casual passer-by, but a helper. A creeping feeling he'd misjudged Arlo's actions.

Chabon was talking to him. '... dead, Mr Zelic?'

Shit. Who was dead? Mrs Naylor? No, a vague memory of her leaning over him as he lay bleeding on the path, yelling at him about 'ALL THE MESS.'

Caleb squinted at the detective. 'Me?'

'Yes. Who. Wants. You. Dead. Mr Zelic?'

'Sure it was deliberate? I smelt gas.'

'Let's make this easy, shall we? We'll ask the questions, you answer them.'

Easy for them, maybe; not so easy for him with the lights fluttering like that. No aids, either. The only sound, a constant, high-pitched whine. He patted his pockets, remembered he was wearing a hospital gown. Maybe he should have an interpreter here. Yes, sensible decision. Personal growth even with all the drilling and hammering in his head. Have to tell Kat, cheer her up. Not good for her to be so stressed.

'I need a terp, can you get one?'

'Tarps can wait until later, Mr Zelic.'

Tarp? What tarp? The one in the van? No, why would they be talking about that? Must mean the house. Jesus, how bad was it? Not that bad, surely, or he wouldn't be alive. Only metres from the door when it had blown. Probably need a few new windows, though; the nurse had picked glass from his back for ages. Upset Kat.

Been right about the house being safe from snipers. Only a C minus for that; forgot there were other ways of being murdered.

Chabon was waving a hand in front of his face.

Caleb blinked a few times, managed to focus. 'What?'

'Why did you ask ... ?'

'What?'

Mouth tight, Chabon went to repeat himself, but Katsonis pulled a bound notepad from his breast pocket, wrote unhurriedly. Turned the neat writing to Caleb: *Why did you ask for an urgent meeting with Sergeant Ramsden before he was killed?*

What was the worst that could happen if he trusted them and was wrong? Ramsden worst. Shattered body, blood and bone all over the door worst. Not his body – Ant's, Kat's.

Come up with a convincing lie. 'Doing some work for the footy club. The numbat suit stole someone.' No, wrong way around. 'Someone stole the numbat suit.'

Katsonis stared at him with sheened eyes. 'Why. Not. Just. Tell. The. Officer. Manning. The. Front. Desk?'

Good question. Should shut up now, wait for a terp, a lawyer, a vomit bowl. And there, like an angel, was the orderly, pink uniform strobing.

'What's the green uniform?' Caleb asked him.

'What?'

'Bile-green uniform.' Shouldn't have said 'bile'. Big mistake. He swallowed. 'Which hospital department?'

'Oncology.'

Cancer: one of the search topics Ant had found on the shop computer that first day. Chase the thought before it left again. He reached for his phone ... hospital gown, no phone.

Chabon was waving again.

'Need to ask this man a medical question,' Caleb told him, without turning. 'Private medical question.' He kept facing the orderly until the detectives backed off a few metres. 'Do me a favour? Google the words "oncology" and "bovis". B.O.V.I.S.'

The young man's gaze darted to the cops, but he pulled out his phone, typed quickly. 'Causes cancer, treats cancer – treats bladder cancer.'

Cancer. Got that whole argument between Skye and Arlo wrong. Got the hair-trigger, angry Arlo wrong. Not visiting brothels and smuggling sex workers; sick and hiding it, Skye trying to dig the information out of him. Broken one of the central rules, let personal dislike cloud his judgement. Almost as bad as letting his fondness for Etty cloud his judgement. History of that, trusting the wrong people.

The detectives were back. Chabon crowding the trolley, already speaking.

No, too tired. Too many thoughts banging around his skull. 'Come back later,' he said. 'Tired.' Let his eyes close.

Someone shook his shoulder. His stomach came loose, slithered into his mouth. He bolted upright. As he heaved over the side towards the cops, the orderly darted forward with the basin. A little too late.

40.

Three days later, Mick drove them to see the house: a quick detour on the way to dropping Caleb at the ferry, Kat at a new hideout. Another favour to add to the long list. Mick had organised everything the past few days: food, clothes, transport. Even their accommodation, a compound-like house belonging to an old prison mate. Just as well, because Caleb had been fuck-all use to anyone. Lying in a darkened room with a cold compress over his eyes, trying to ignore the screeching in his ears.

Kat stirred and sat up as they turned into Waratah Street. Only a fifteen-minute trip but she'd been dozing against him for most of it, head heavy on his shoulder. He suspected she hadn't been getting much sleep, always awake whenever he'd resurfaced, either staring unfocused at the television or pretending to read. Never sketching. He'd stopped telling her to leave once she'd laid out her argument – she could stay on the Mish with a weaponless 62-year-old grandmother, or with him, three armed men and a razor-wire fence. Never forgive himself for her matter-of-fact reasoning. Hoped he wouldn't.

'OK?' he asked.

'Refreshed despite your bony shoulder.' Her almost-convincing smile wavered as Mick slowed. Nearly at the house, the roofline just visible above the hoarding erected across the yard. 'Sure you want to do this now?'

'Yeah.' Always better to confront things directly. Face it, get over it, move on.

His breath caught as they drove through the open gate. A gaping wound in the centre of the house. Blackened and hollowed, windows blown out. It had burned fiercely for a brick building; a draughtier place would have fared better. Ivan Zelic's high standards bringing them all down again.

Kat reached for his hand, fingers icy.

After Mick parked on the lawn, he turned to face them. 'Take ya time looken around. Katy looks like she could do with another nap. I'll shut the gate, keep out the riffraff.'

Caleb got out, paused as the movement jarred his head. Moderate concussion, the doctors had said. Hate to think what a severe one felt like. Thoughts were still slipping in and out of focus, but he was ready to get back to the island. Had to be. Killers circling, cops hassling Kat's family, trying to find him. Ant ignoring all emails. Ignoring Etty too, according to her supposedly distraught texts. So, some good news there.

The house was worse up close. Charred joists, walls, furniture. The few remaining mementos from their childhood buried in a slurry of wet ash and charcoal. An acrid smell seared his throat, making his eyes water.

Most of the damage was from the fire, but the blast had ripped through the entrance hall. The heart of the explosion. Probably a simple incendiary device, little battery pack, its spark igniting the gas when he'd opened the door. If the lock hadn't stuck, if he'd waited a second longer, Kat would be a widow, their child fatherless. Blood drained from his head – or she could have been there with him; Kat dead, baby dead. God, he had to fix this, had to stop it.

A few slow breaths, then he turned for the car, started as someone popped up in front of him. Mrs Naylor. Where the hell had she come from, a storm drain? Worse than Lara for unexpected appearances.

Over by the gate, Mick was looking sheepish. He moved an open hand across his face; Koori sign, not Auslan: shame job.

Mrs Naylor was already in full swing, complaining about the mess like she had after the explosion, every distorted word drilling into his skull. The Naylor Conundrum: risk prolonging the conversation by turning down his aids, or risk bleeding eardrums by leaving them turned up? Go for incomprehension today.

'... said he'd clean it up. HE SAID HE'D CLEAN IT UP.'

He? Caleb paused with his hand halfway to his aids, lowered it. 'Who said they'd clean it?'

'THE TERMITE MAN. He broke your back door. He said he was coming back but he never did.'

She'd seen one of the killers. Maybe not the sniper, not with a messy attack like this, but one of the accomplices. At last, a break. 'What did he look like?'

'I told the police. I said, I TOLD THE POLICE. Rude man. How would I know? He was wearing a cap and overalls. I said, A CAP AND OVERALLS.'

He sorted through her words: the cop rude, the killer wearing overalls and a cap.

'How old was he?' He paused, added, 'Termite man, not the cop.'

'Young.'

Could mean anyone under seventy. 'Young like me? Like Mick?'

'Young.'

He pulled out his phone, showed her the photos of the few male islanders he'd managed to snap, along with Locke's online headshot, Mrs Naylor barely looking, shaking her head at them all. 'He was wearing overalls.'

As though they'd made the man invisible. 'When was he here?'

'Quarter past three. Your father would be devastated. He built this place, you know. You ...'

Three p.m. So Caleb's visits to the brothel and the mechanic's hadn't sparked the attack, seemingly just the killers' hunt for the blackmail evidence. An attempt to destroy it by blowing up a house? The wildest, most panicked move possible.

Why the constant escalation? Didn't make sense. They should be feeling safer, not more threatened, the blackmail long over. Or maybe it wasn't. Light-fingered Lara could have taken up where Taylor had left off. Quite a stretch: steal some documents and suddenly become an expert blackmailer, able to organise money drops or offshore accounts, avoid detection from ruthless killers. But it was time to dig into her background. If he could. Hadn't had any luck yet. Hard to research a common surname like – Shit, it'd fallen out of his brain. Simpson? Samuels? Stewart? Looking at his notes just this morning, the words shimmering on the computer Mick's mate had lent him. Got it – Sullivan. He'd seen that name somewhere else, hadn't he? Or maybe it'd been weeks ago, years ago; something written in a book.

He tuned back in to Mrs Naylor, who'd apparently run out of things to say about his father. She was peering at the car. 'Is that Kathryn? I must tell her –'

'She's sleeping,' he said quickly. He guided the old woman towards Mick at the gate, some desperate mustering needed to stop her making a break for Kat.

Mick rescued him, stepping forward with a boy-scout expression firmly in place. 'Better walk you to your door, Mrs Naylor. Dangerous area these days.'

Impossible to repay his debts to the man.

Kat was huddled in the back seat, fake leopard-skin coat

buttoned to her throat. Borrowed like the rest of her clothes; two sizes too large but pulled tight across her stomach. Daylight revealed the dullness of her skin and eyes, slight hollows in her cheeks. She'd lost weight. Not good. So far from being good. Six weeks until the baby was due, and she was sitting in the middle of a bombsite. Only some comfort to be gained from the fact her new safe house was closer to the hospital, Maria joining her for the duration.

'How are you feeling?' she asked. 'It's worse than I expected.'

'Fine. We might be able to save the back part. What d'you think? Rebuild, or just bulldoze it, start afresh?'

'We don't have to decide anything right now. Give yourself time to grieve.'

'I want to get things moving, get the demolishers in. So, bulldoze it? I'll email them from the ferry.'

Her gaze darted away. 'I don't know. I can't think straight, neither of us can. And we need to talk about a lot more than the house when this is all over.'

He sat still. Nothing good had ever come from a sentence like that; a conversation to be avoided for all eternity. Or had immediately. 'Talk about what?'

'This isn't the time or place.'

No, Kat didn't avoid things, she faced them head-on, honestly, openly. He lifted his hands, made himself form the question. 'Is this about Jarrah?'

'What? No.'

Of course it wasn't; he knew that. But unable to let it go. 'I know he's –'

'Jesus Christ, Cal. Look at where we are. That could have been you. It could have been me! Our child! Jarrah isn't the problem, *you* are.'

A punch to the throat. 'I know.'

She wiped the tears from her eyes. 'I know you do. Sorry. This is why I didn't want to have this conversation now. We're both feeling too fragile.' Twisting to face him properly, awkward in the small space. 'I love you, I want us to live together, be a family.'

The relief didn't come; there was more.

'But I don't know how we can. Not at the moment. Something very fundamental has to change first. I've wanted this forever. Half my life, ever since we met. But all I can think is that one day you're going to get yourself killed. Or me, or our child. *When*, not if. Because this keeps happening. You run into things full pelt, all the best intentions in the world, all the passion I love you for, but how can we bring a child into this? How can we live together when this keeps happening?'

And there it was. The hard, shiny truth plucked from his darkest fears: not that Kat would leave him, but that she should.

He sat with it, examined it from all sides. 'We can't,' he said. 'We shouldn't.'

She jerked back. 'What?'

'You're right, it's not working.'

'Not at the moment.' Signing with clear, deliberate movements. Her blue eyes fixed on his. 'I'm not saying never, I'm saying things need to change first.'

'We've had half our lives to work it out and we still haven't. I haven't. You don't want to live together, you're not happy, you're just caught. We're both caught. And it's not fair to bring a child into this mess.'

She stared at him without moving. The familiar curve of her face, the tilt of her head. Everything to him. Everything. But gone, let go.

He crossed heavy arms over his chest to sign, 'I love you.' Half lowered them, hands splayed: 'But it's over.'

Out of the car, closing the door gently behind him. Brief eye contact as he passed Mick at the fence, no words needed. He kept going. Through the gate and down the street, walking unsteadily from the wreckage.

41.

Caleb caught the last ferry to the island. Waited in the shadows until the vehicles had disembarked. Only two of them, a woman he didn't recognise in the *Fuck a Greenie* van, couple of kids crammed in the front seat, bales of hay in the back. And Arlo. Giving Caleb the odd stare but not attempting any confrontation, just sitting in his ute, the tray stacked precariously high with crates and barrels. Incredible – a whole sex-trafficking conspiracy created out of thin air because a sick man with a too-small vehicle had borrowed a larger one. Focused on the wrong person while the real culprits went about their business.

He took his time walking down the pier, head and back throbbing. Slight stumble on a warped board. Not drunk, not drunk enough, just a little unsteady. Third of a bottle of whisky, but every nerve ending still raw.

The road was empty, no one out walking their dogs or standing around staring at incomers. Doors and curtains all closed. Not a single person here he could trust, except a brother who didn't trust him. Everyone scared or complicit, secrets twisting around them like the island's roads. The sniper at the centre. Calm and calculating, picking up each thread and pulling it tight. Gideon or Locke?

Lights were on in the shop. No customers, only Skye restocking the shelves, fair hair brushed back, tea towel slung over her shoulder. He stood watching for a moment. Headed for the caravan, kept going past it towards the beach. Nearly a full moon, the breaking waves catching the light. Always liked beaches. Not land, not water, somewhere in between. A liminal space for a liminal man, Kat had said. He'd needed to look up the word, but had taken to it: the spaces between. Not hearing, not Deaf. Not in Kat's life, not out of it.

'*Jarrah's not the problem, you are.*'

He sat against the retaining wall, shadow stretching towards the water. Took a long swig. Not much of a whisky drinker, not much of a drinker at all, but he needed to do something. Anything. Couldn't run, couldn't sleep, couldn't be in his head.

Their child had been conceived on a beach like this. Just over there, on the other side of the bay. At least he had that. Hold on tight to that thought. Maybe not a husband but a father, part of a tiny, perfect family. Except he wouldn't be, really. There'd be no shared custody for years. Only an hour here and there, eventually a day, a weekend. Not enough time to share a life, a language.

'*Jarrah's not the problem, you are.*'

Punch something, break it, yell, scream.

A shadow joined his as someone approached. One of the killers, about to finish him off? Could only hope. Unsteady, he turned to look. Skye come to play games again. Wearing a dress now, instead of jeans, long puffer coat over the top.

She knelt facing him, knees almost against his thigh. A hint of summery perfume. 'Can you lip-read in this light?'

Taken his aids out. Hard without them, but he wasn't going to put them in, not in front of her. 'If you talk slowly.'

'Thought you'd left us.' Running a forefinger down his cheek. 'I like the stubble. Very rugged.'

He glanced over his shoulder to the shop, a hazy shape on the far side of the clearing.

Skye's gaze was on him when he turned back. 'Did you want to talk to Arlo? He's off playing with his mates.'

Still unsure about her. Trying to entertain herself, or distract him from something? Her husband, maybe. Could still be involved. Or Gideon, just over there at the pier, setting off in his tinnie, spotlight cutting through the darkness. Off for another box of vodka from town, another few cans of soup. Man with a life as empty as that; almost had to hope he was the sniper.

'Who was the tattooed man?' Caleb asked.

'I don't know. Let it go. It's got nothing to do with you and me.' She rested a hand on his thigh. Light touch. Brushed fingertips almost to his crotch. His body switched on; distant from him, separate.

'He was probably killed here,' he said. 'Washed up here.'

'Things wash up here all the time. You don't want to think about it too much. I don't.'

So different from Kat. Pale and angular, reckless, self-centred. Good to close the door and move on. The actions of a man finally, painfully, coming to terms with reality.

Her warm palm pressed against his cheek. 'Why are you so sad? You don't even know who he is.'

'Who killed him?'

'No one. Just forget about it.' She leaned in.

He kissed her. Different scent, different taste. Sweet mint, not honey, salt. Moving closer, mouths and hands urgent. Hard jab – a knee to his thigh. Kneeling, tugging at clothes, zips, clasps. Shock of cold air against heat, her hand grasping him. Different body beneath his fingertips, different lips on his.

A jolt, teeth clashing – wrong angle. Wrong woman. Wrong.

He broke away. 'I can't. Sorry.'

What the fuck was wrong with him?

Skye reeled, then shoved him hard, palms against his chest.

'You arsehole.' Whipping her clothes from the sand, she stood. 'I'm not good enough for you, is that it?'

He got to his feet, trying to balance and pull up his jeans, watch her face. 'It's not you –'

'Oh, fuck you. You're bloody right it's not me. I don't want your pity fuck anyway. Or whatever that was – interrogation fuck. I'm worth a hell of a lot more than that, mate.' She pulled her dress over her head. Stalked away, limbs white in the moonlight.

He dropped onto the sand. Relief; no relief. Couldn't have handled that worse. No idea how to be in the world without hurting people. How to be in the world without Kat. Be in the world. He lay back, bare skin against the cold sand, staring up at the star-bitten sky, the wind chilling his wet cheeks.

42.

The sat phone woke him the next morning, vibrating beneath his pillow. Kat; emergency. He lurched from tangled dreams, heart and head pounding. Snatched the phone from the mattress. Sammi getting back to him about Gideon's background check.

—*done. video call me*

A whiplash of relief, then breathlessness as the conversation at his gutted house unrolled in his mind. The reality of what he'd broken. Followed by the fumbling disaster with Skye last night.

He swung his legs around to sit on the edge of the bed. Heavy-limbed and aching. Couldn't even leave Kat without texting to let her know he'd returned to the island. Not that she'd replied. No idea how they would navigate things: the birth, the parenting, the future. He'd done the right thing. Just hadn't expected it to feel this hard, this wrong.

Deal with it later. Keep it together until this was over.

He texted Sammi.

—No internet. Text me

—*call when you can then*

Enjoying the power trip? Or had she found something she didn't want linked back to her? He couldn't use the computer in the shop – off-limits forever. Not cowardice – not *just* cowardice. Skye liked playing games, was rightfully furious with him; if she'd dropped any hints to Arlo about what had happened, things would get very ugly. Had to try the pier.

He chugged down painkillers and splashed water on his face in the tiny cubicle, averted his eyes from the mirror. His haggard face, four-day growth dark against sallow skin. Dressed, he hesitated over his aids. Had to do it. Pointless going around asking questions if he couldn't understand the answers. He looped the casings behind his ears, gently inserted the receivers: instant shrill. Fuck. Shrugging on his jacket, he went into the chill day. Should probably drive, care about the clear line of sight from the water tower to the pier. Not much use to Ant dead.

A raw wind bit through his clothes as he crossed the grass to the quayside. He angled his head away from it. A few people about, including Lara Sullivan, heading up the shop steps. Silver hair plaited today, bouncing against her back as she walked. Very nimble for a 72-year-old who supposedly had arthritis. Where had he seen her surname? Written in gold paint. Could see the letters, but not the location. Fog where his brain used to be.

He drove to the end of the pier; the ferry heading in, still a fair way off. Good signal, but Sammi didn't pick up straight away.

Gold lettering. *Sullivan* in gold lettering. On a shop window. Of course, the photo Taylor's son had shown him. The blackmailer posing with his parents in front of a store, *Taylor & Sullivan Drapery*. The pairing of those two names could be a fluke, but Caleb would bet anything it wasn't – Peter Taylor and Lara Sullivan knew each other. Family friends, cousins, mates. Business partners? With Lara setting the whole scheme in motion. Explained the speed of events. She'd been on the island for months, Taylor only days. She'd spotted the crime, told him about it. Played innocent while he turned up with binoculars and a birdwatching book, skulked around hunting for proof. Which meant Lara knew who the killers were. But how to get information from a liar, blackmailer and thief?

Sammi had answered, was gesturing to him. Not politely.

Black hair tied in the same neat ponytail, but no uniform today, a background of dismantled computers and hard drives. Wagging school.

'No school?'

An expression of deep weariness. She swiped through her phone, showed him a calendar: Saturday.

'Comes after Friday,' she mouthed clearly. 'Before Sunday.'

'Thanks. I'll make a note of it. What have you got?'

'Big job. Very hard.'

'I'm sure it'll be reflected in your bill.' Well reflected; he'd asked her to do a full search, including court records and bank accounts.

With a vigorous nod, she switched to a screenshot of a bank statement. Gideon Matthews' real surname was Blair. Modest savings of a few thousand dollars. Steady drip of money going to various shops in town, all on Bay Road near the police station. Good way for him to meet Constable Lloyd, pay whatever bribes were needed for the cop's part in the affair.

Gideon was getting regular income, too. Fortnightly payments from the Department of Veterans' Affairs – he'd been in the armed forces. A man who would at the very least have gone through basic training, know how to fire a rifle. Possibly much, much more.

Sammi's bright face was onscreen again.

'Thanks,' he said.

She raised a finger to stop him hanging up.

'More?'

Nodding, she brought up another screenshot, a typewritten page under a header from the Department of Defence. Good call on Sammi's part not to send him hacked information from the military. A summary of an official investigation, Gideon's name highlighted. Part of a unit involved in a war crime in Afghanistan four years ago. Civilians shot for no apparent reason. Six dead, including two children. Gideon investigated but not charged, four of his mates found guilty.

Not charged didn't mean innocent.

Gideon was a trained fighter and possible war criminal. One whose hilltop house overlooked wide swathes of the island. Seriously out of his depth with a man like that. Couldn't tail him, capture him, talk to him. Tell the homicide cops? Take a chance they were clean. Easy to see how that would play out: 'And how exactly are you involved with this man, Mr Zelic? Did you hire him or is he just a colleague?' Be on remand before he could draw breath.

Shuddering vibration as the ferry docked. Should move, a few vehicles queuing behind him now.

'Thanks,' he told Sammi, who'd reappeared on screen, seemed to be waiting for his attention. 'That's all I need.'

'Dangerous,' she mouthed.

Concerned for his safety. Touched by that, heart-warmed. 'Don't worry, I'll be careful.'

Her nose wrinkled. 'I. Meant. Pay. Me. First.' She hung up.

The ferry ramp had lowered, a lone vehicle waiting to disembark: white sedan, Ugly Cardigan Joyce at the wheel. Polystyrene boxes stacked beside her and on the back seat. White, like those the CCTV had captured Etty collecting.

A moment of doubt. If Gideon was behind everything, why had Joyce mentioned the man's name the other day? Sitting in that antiseptic kitchen, trying to get Caleb to leave. Desperation, maybe. Scared and trying to find a way out? Whatever it was, she knew something.

Her car was trundling down the ramp, heading past him to the shore. He waited until it reached the end of the boards. Made a shuffling manoeuvre, followed in her wake.

———————

By the time he reached her, Joyce was parked next to her house, car door open, a polystyrene box in her arms. She whirled around as he pulled up sharply behind her.

He stepped out into the grainy wind. 'What's in the box?'

'Nothing.' Backing towards her open car door.

'You can show me. Or you can show the cops.'

She thrust the box towards him.

'Put it down, then sit next to my car.' He waited until she was safely away. Kicked the lid off the box.

Stacked Tupperware containers in a bed of melting ice. Most of them empty; inside one, a few neatly wrapped wheels, each with a sticker of a laughing cartoon goat. He ripped open a wheel – cheese. Pulled it apart, tasting it. No drugs, no diamonds, no secret codes, just cheese. Same with the next two packets, and the next one.

Just a woman who ran a small business. He went to where she was sitting hunched by his car, staring miserably at him, a pile of disposable cloths beside her. The surrounding concrete was dark where she'd wiped away the fine dust from the quarry. All that scouring and bleaching – not covering up a crime, but responding to a pathological fear.

He helped her up. 'Sorry. I got the wrong end of things. I'll pay for damages.' He calculated the amount from his purchase the other day, gave her double.

'Well, I should think so.' She tucked the money in her pocket, found another disposable wipe to clean her cracked and reddened hands.

'Why all the secrecy?' he asked.

'It's on past your eyes.'

On past your eyes? Gone past your eyes? All bastards' eyes?

He gave up. 'Could you say that again? Slower.'

'It's raw milk, unpasteurised. Illegal to sell it. You won't tell the police, will you?'

Tell the cops he'd cracked a cheese-smuggling ring? Her secret was safe with him. 'No.'

Her pretence at indignation had taken on real life. '... ridiculous rules. Wonderful for the immune system. They love it at the farmers' markets. Two or three a week and I sell out.'

Two or three a week. Oh shit – Etty catching the ferry back and forth, her car stacked with boxes. Ant would never forgive him. Etty, either. On the bright side, they could hate him together. 'Etty's been selling it for you?'

'I didn't talk her into it, she suggested it! She wants money for that, that place.' A shudder. The same reaction the last time she'd spoken about the clinic, called it a 'disgusting place'.

'What's wrong with the clinic?'

She glanced at the road behind him, prompting him to look too. When he turned back she was frantically shaking her head. Scared, like he'd suspected, but she hadn't moved away.

Joyce the anonymous messenger? A woman who knew everything and everyone. Who was still out here talking to him when she could easily run into her house. Go gently, don't alarm her by letting on he knew.

The clinic's water tower was safely hidden behind the ridgeline of the quarry, but he shifted away from its imagined sightlines. Drew Joyce with him towards the house. He used her words. 'The clinic's disgusting, isn't it?'

'Yes! Yes. They should leave. You can't clean it.' Her raw hands rubbed at some imagined stain. 'I've tried here, but you can't.'

Deeply disturbed. How much did she know and how much was she imagining?

'Why can't you clean it?' he asked. 'Won't Locke let you?'

'Not Locke, the smoke. Everything's contaminated. You can't get rid of it.'

The incinerator? He pictured the towering redbrick chimney; the gaping furnace where fire had burned fiercely enough to turn silica into glass. Surely not – the whole island would know if that thing fired up. The whole island had known.

'Someone's using the incinerator?' he asked. Please let it not be bodies.

'Not anymore, Locke stopped them. But it's worse now. There's poison everywhere. In the soil and water. You can't clean it.'

Not bodies: poison, contamination.

'Toxic waste?' he said. 'They were burning toxic waste?'

'Yes! That's what I keep telling you. And now they're burying it –' She lurched.

A spray of warmth across his face.

Joyce swaying. Crumpling.

43.

Joyce sprawled on the ground. Head the wrong shape. Parts missing. Pink and white lumps spattered across the scrubbed concrete.

The world moving slowly. He turned away, ran down the endless driveway to the side of the house. Pressed against the peeling boards, the salt heat on his face chilling. Blood. Joyce's blood. Wiped it with his sleeve, scrubbing hard. As good as killed her. Like Ramsden. Stood in the yard talking about toxic waste while Gideon lined up the shot. Had to be firing from the quarry silo, the right side of her head gone.

Move now. Not safe here. Gideon would be repositioning himself, looking down the scope, finger on the trigger. Get in Joyce's car, just there.

Caleb walked the few steps to the sedan's open door. Joyce's keys and handbag on the seat, boxes of her precious cheese stacked all around. Engine on, seatbelt on. Checked the mirror. Only Joyce's splayed body, blood pooling on the concrete. An urge to clean it for her.

Drive. Have to go fast. Be a target as soon as he left the shelter of the house, driver's side exposed to the silo. He stomped on the accelerator. Straight down the long backyard, speeding towards the paddocks. A thud – bullet. Keep going, nearly at the fence.

The car jolted, skewed sideways, wheel pulling from his grasp. Tyre blown. He wrestled the wheel straight, slammed through the wire fence. Head smacking against the seat. Aching pain. Keep going, not safe yet. Hard left, goats scattering before him. Past the milking shed, bouncing over the dry grass. Out of sight, away from the silo.

When he was a long way from the quarry, he slowed. Drove parallel to the roadside fence until he found a gate, its sagging metal frame hooked open, inviting him through. He stopped on the verge, front tyres nudging the road.

Toxic waste. No industry on the island. Had to be some mainland factory producing small enough amounts to bring across. Or a hospital? Oh, for fuck's sake. Bovis. Arlo wasn't undergoing cancer treatment, he was helping Gideon dump it. Biohazards and radioactive waste, toxins. It'd be those diesel barrels. Driving them over in plain sight in that van. Using his ute when he had to; got aggro that day Caleb had seen him unloading it outside the shop, cardboard separating the different drums. So he'd been right about Arlo all along. Nice to be right occasionally.

But no idea what to do with the information. Eyes everywhere, vantage points everywhere. All the islanders potential accomplices. Except Locke, according to Joyce. He'd arrived on the island after the scheme was underway. Put a stop to Gideon and Arlo burning the waste in the incinerator. Not blameless, maybe a coward, but not actively involved. And there was a phone at the clinic. Ant could call every police station, reporter and news blogger in the area, get them over here in droves.

He turned right, away from the quarry. Heading for the back road to the clinic, rear wheel rim digging a channel in the dirt.

The clinic gates were locked when he finally arrived. Well over an hour to get here, Joyce's car struggling on the hills. He parked up against the metal bars, hit the horn. No movement except for the towering pines thrashing their limbs in the wind, the grounds empty as usual. Locke's old Jag was missing, only the jeep and nurse's car in the driveway. He checked the rear-view mirror, gave the horn another go. Sitting in full sight of the quayside – Gideon's spies surely watching for him, looking up the hill, wondering why Joyce's car was parked at the clinic. He thumped the horn again. Where the hell was everyone?

Finally. Lara cutting across the grass towards him in her baggy flannelette shirt and jeans. They'd be having a long chat once she let him in. More and more certain she'd continued with the blackmail scheme after Taylor's death. Set off the killers' frenzied attempts to find the evidence against them.

As she reached the gate, she shook her head, displayed empty hands to show she didn't have a key.

He opened the window, leaned out. 'Go and get one. It's an emergency.'

A jerk of surprise as she peered at him. Too far away to read, but she put a hand to her cheek, said something that looked like 'hurt'.

Asking about Joyce's blood. Some of it still on his face; could feel it. Crusted tight, itching his skin. 'It's not mine. Go and get the key, the –'

Her lips formed a familiar word. 'Anton's?'

Why would she think that? Dry-mouthed, he said, 'Why? Isn't he inside?'

'He went ... ago.'

Out of the car, to the gate. 'Where's Ant?'

'He went for a walk. What's happening?' She gestured to his face. 'Who was hurt?' Concern etched in the lines of her forehead. If he didn't know better, he'd think she was at a complete loss.

'Joyce,' he said. 'She told me about the hospital waste, and they killed her.' He was ready. Shot a hand through the bars as Lara went to run, caught her scrawny wrist. 'I know you're involved – I know you and Peter Taylor were blackmailing Arlo. And very soon he's going to know too. Because they're after me. So tell me where the fuck Ant is.'

'It's not my fault.' Twisting to free herself.

Shake the information from her, rattle her brains until the truth fell out. He made himself soften his grasp, his face. 'Of course not. I don't care about the blackmail, I just care about Ant. I know you do too. You're fond of him, aren't you?' Her story about regrets, him and Ant reminding her of her absent grandchildren. The best lies always contained a kernel of truth. 'He's like a grandson.'

She stilled, papery cheeks sagging. The first unguarded expression he'd seen. 'I think he went to get photos.'

Oh Jesus. Ant wandering around trying to collect evidence of a toxic waste dump.

'I didn't tell him,' Lara said. 'I tried to keep him out of it.'

'It's OK, no one's blaming you. Just tell me where the dump is.'

'I don't know! He just said something about birdwatching and left.'

How to get it out of her? Couldn't stand here much longer. Fast scan of the road and uncleared land to either side, the dense undergrowth.

Stabbing pain. Arm. He jerked back, grip automatically releasing, blood flowing down his wrist from his forearm. Long gash in his jacket sleeve. Silver flashed in Lara's right hand as she pocketed her flick-knife. And she was gone, running across the grass towards the back of the clinic.

He clutched his arm, blood oozing between his fingers. An entire island to search. Impossible, needed help. The nurse, Melissa. Practical and caring, an islander; she'd almost certainly know who to trust, be able to get together a search party. Back to the car, his fist raised to hit the horn. He lowered it. A local nurse with medical connections could easily be Arlo's link to the hospital.

OK, just had to do it alone. Be logical, think it through. Ant had walked, so he was somewhere he couldn't hide the jeep. Like a dead-end road. Lara's line about birdwatching was too bizarre not to be true. Wasn't it? Muttonbird Cove? No. He'd spent an entire day sitting in those dunes, swatting at mosquitos; would have noticed a dump. You'd need earth-moving equipment to bury those barrels, heavy machinery chewing up the sand, destroying the fragile burrows.

Earth-moving equipment. The quarry. On the way to Muttonbird Cove. No night shift, but all that night-time traffic caught on its CCTV cameras. And just down the road from Joyce's place, the wind casting invisible poisons onto her hosed-clean yard and spotless kitchen.

Thirty minutes from here on the winding roads, much shorter across country. He started for the trees, turned back to grab a bandage from the first-aid kit in the car. Not going to lay a bloody trail to Ant like a horror version of Hansel and Gretel. Good sign. Brain working well, not paralysed by dread. He set off through the bushland, binding his arm as he ran.

44.

He reached the wire fence at the top of the quarry's hollowed-out hill. Followed it along the ridgeline, searching for a way in. Couldn't see into the pit, but got glimpses of the tree-lined road beyond it, Joyce's yard in the distance. Dust would have settled on her body by now, clinging to the wet ruin of her skull. On the downward slope of the hill, a gap in the wire, long-handled boltcutters lying in the grass beside it. A headrush of relief: Ant. Those boltcutters he'd been on about when they'd discussed stealing the security tapes.

Through the hole to the lip of the quarry, crouching low, trying to ignore the thudding pulse in his temple. Silo to the right. Gideon probably wasn't still in it, lying in wait. A barren landscape, clear view to the office and large machinery shed. Ant had to be in one of them. Hiding or captive? Three parked cars, but the only movement an excavator filling a hole behind the shed, Arlo's black beanie just visible. Well hidden from the road. Nice big hole, deep enough to bury a lot of barrels.

Or a body.

A sledgehammer to his heart.

Up and running. Down the hillside, feet raising white plumes. He skidded, slid the last couple of metres, landed hard. Kept going, across the rocky expanse, dirt and grit blowing in his eyes.

The excavator had stopped, Arlo climbing down from it. Seen him? No, heading towards the office. Faster, feet pounding. And he was at the excavator. Down on his hands and knees, digging. Flash of red. Blood? Shirt? Clawing at the ground, grit under his nails, dust clogging mouth and nose. Metal. Rim of a red 44-gallon drum.

He sat back on his heels, trying to catch his breath. Just medical waste, that was all. No reason to think Ant's body was down there too, covered with gravel. None. Keep moving; shed first, then the office.

More barrels were stacked against the side of the hulking shed. Blue, not red, a generator beside them working away under a slanted roof: Arlo's legitimate business selling diesel. Smart move with the colour-coding.

Caleb went past the barrels to the end of the wall, stopped at the wide expanse of gravel that stretched to the roadside fence. Peered around the corner. Just past the open mouth of the shed, Arlo and the two surly quarrymen were standing with their backs to him. On alert, staring down the road towards Joyce's house. Red and blue lights just visible through the trees – the police had arrived. And not in on the scheme, if Arlo and his mates were nervous about their presence. Run to them for help? Wouldn't make it. Not with the high fence and electric gate, the men just metres away.

He edged around the corner, gaze on the trio as he backed slowly into the shed. Picking up his feet, making sure he didn't scuff.

They turned. All three heads whipping towards him.

Fuck. How?

Sat phone vibrating in his pocket. The noise Ant had complained about.

Already running, the men racing after him. Into the cavernous shed. Past looming machinery and blocks of stone. Glance behind him. Shit, Arlo right there. Other two close behind. Body slower than usual, limbs not quite connected. Make a noise, get the cops here – red *Explosives* sign up the back. But a locked cage, wouldn't have detonators. A weapon instead. He sprinted for a bench near the wall, the metal bar on top.

Full-body tackle. Down to the concrete, breath smacked from him. The weight on top of him already lifting. He rolled over, sat up. Both quarrymen drawing slowly in, Arlo on the ground, scrabbling towards him. Beanie half off, whites of his eyes showing. 'My wife ... cunt ... kill you.' A wild punch glanced off Caleb's shoulder, but both mates were coming in fast. Going to kill him. He knew too much for this to just be a bashing.

Arlo made a back-off gesture. 'He's fucken mine.'

Caleb struck. Hard blow between Arlo's legs. Twisted clear as the man doubled over. Hauled himself upright.

Blocked. Wall to his back, two quarrymen between him and the exit. They'd pulled back a few steps, ease in their stance, one with a chain wrapped around his fist. Waiting to pick him off if Arlo failed. Couldn't get past them.

In the shadows just behind them, slight movement. Ant. Crouched on top of a steel cage, getting ready to jump. No. They'd kill him.

Arlo was lurching to his feet. Caleb backed away, shaking his head, gaze on Arlo as he signed 'cop'. Quick pull of his hand over his wrist, like handcuffs. Prayed Ant had heard the police car going to Joyce's, that he'd understand, that he'd do it.

Nearly against the bench. Arlo up and moving, fury twisting his face. Caleb kept backing away, repeating the sign: hand over wrist, hand over wrist, trying to make it look like fear. Not difficult.

Ant shifted. Drawing back from the edge of the cage. Gone. Oh, thank fuck. Caleb turned, launched himself at the bench, the iron bar.

Sharp punch to the kidneys. He staggered, turned, fist swinging at air. Arlo shoved him against the bench. 'Fucker … kill you …'

Pain. Middle of his chest. Doubled over on the floor, dry retching. Get up, fight. Few more minutes until Ant was safely away. A boot rammed his side. Shockwave through ribs, gut, spine. Curled, knees to his chest. Lungs folding in. Breathless. No. Too much. Trying to crawl away, bloody saliva dripping from his mouth, wetting the powdered floor. Dragging himself behind a stack of stone. Slow roll onto his back.

Didn't get any further. Arlo beside him, leg drawn back for another kick. Aiming for his head.

Gushing heat. Light. Concrete shuddering beneath him.

No thought. No movement. White dust humming down from the bright sky. High ringing noise as it fell. Back at the house again, gas exploding. No, not the house, the quarry shed. Tumbled stone and machinery. Roof laid open above him, metal wall blown in like a punctured can.

Had to be Ant's work. Bit of overkill, but job well done, would certainly get the cops' attention. All three men out of action, too. Arlo sitting stunned, blood running down his broad face; the two big blokes down, one not looking great, iron beam across his back.

Good thing Caleb had been safely getting his ribs kicked in. Not hurt. Not badly hurt. Body not quite working yet, though. Might just lie here a little longer, bleed into the concrete. Limestone in concrete, tiny shells and bones from an ancient sea. Should tell Kat. Liminal man, seeping back into a liminal sea. Close his eyes for a while, seep. Sleep.

Ant was there, silhouetted against the sky, pulling at his arm. 'Piss off.'

Ant kept tugging. Signed with one hand, 'Come on, up. Rest of the explosives might go off.'

Explosives. Right. How had Ant set them off from outside the

shed? Without detonators? Questions for another time – Ant
yanking at his arm now.

He heaved himself up, sagging against Ant as they crossed the
yard. When they reached the road, a cop car was coming out of
Joyce's driveway, lights flashing. Ant held him upright, raised a
hand to flag them down.

45.

Caleb was dazed, zoning out for long seconds, by the time the two homicide detectives finished with him. Too many cops, too many questions, the tinnitus a constant wail.

He left them sitting in Joyce's sterile kitchen, walked slowly through the bleach-scented house. There'd be more questions tomorrow, probably for days to come, but the basics were done. His role change from suspect to witness helped by complete honesty and a negative result for gunshot residue. Helped a lot more by Constable Lloyd's on-brand aggressive response when his colleagues had gone to question him at his house. Hadn't caught all the details, but there'd been a flurry of whispered conversations, one of the uniformed cops using Joyce's landline to pass messages to the detectives. A stand-off involving weapons, Lloyd now in custody but not talking.

It was dark outside. A couple of crime-scene spotlights illuminated the yard. Wind-whipped trees casting wild shadows across the stained concrete where Joyce had fallen. His car was there, police tape blocking its exit. Impounded. Hadn't asked why, didn't need to know what the crime-scene examiners had found spattered on it. Only one uniformed cop at the gate, the rest probably still in the quarry or out hunting for Gideon. The man's house apparently empty, boat gone. Probably already setting up another identity in a far-flung place.

Ant waved to him from where he was sitting in the shelter of the low brick fence. Manky aviator jacket zipped tight, sheepskin collar up. Not the twitchy wreck he usually was around cops: leaning back while smoking a rollie, as though he'd been waiting a fair while, was having some downtime.

Caleb ripped out his aids as he crossed the grass: the metal-edged screech didn't ease. Lowered himself carefully beside Ant. 'How the hell'd you finish before me?'

'Pure of heart, shows in my face.' Signing lazily, the cigarette flaring between his fingers. 'Plus, I called Etty, who rang her parents, who rang a cousin who's a lawyer. Who I'll be paying off for years. Worth it, though. Things went a lot smoother once he got here.' He paused for a drag. 'We had a chat about the agg burg, too.'

'And?'

'Reckons I'll be fine as long as I finish rehab. Decade since my last offence, showing commitment to change and so on. Strong chance of a non-custodial sentence if I turn myself in. So I guess I'll be having another chat to the cops in a couple of weeks.'

'That's great.'

'I'll say, it's like I can breathe again. Reckon I'll retain him for all my burgs from now on.' He looked at Caleb. 'Little joke, lighten the mood.'

'Good one.' Ant facing up to things, making jokes about jail; something positive coming from all this. Could almost lie down on Joyce's raked grass and sleep with relief. Cosy here. He rested his head against the bricks. They'd have to get going soon to catch the evening ferry, but no rush yet.

'You right?' Ant asked. 'Look like shit.'

'Yeah.' Bruised and scraped and gouged, maybe some cracked ribs, but the shakes had been and gone, leaving him mostly numb. The stuff the ambos had given him after they'd patched him up was helping a lot, too. He'd rejected their offer of a ride to the

Bay's hospital, the thought of bright lights and people unbearable. Made do with washing the blood off his face and hands in Joyce's immaculate bathroom. Lot of blood.

Probably lucky to be alive. And not just because of Arlo's beating. Who knew you could set off explosives without detonators? Not Ant, apparently. Looking contrite when he'd explained things to the cops he'd flagged down – how his intention to create 'a small diversion' by chucking a lit cigarette into generator diesel had turned into a 'fucking chain reaction'. Fuel vapours igniting in all six barrels, the resultant heat detonating the explosives.

'Spectacular overreach with the diversion,' he told Ant.

Ant saluted with his cigarette. 'Fun, efficiency, safety.' Their father's ranking of priorities in reverse order. 'Hope you've noticed how restrained I'm being in not saying "I told you so" about the sat phone. Hope the damn thing's broken, too.'

Not even scratched. Kat's message had been waiting for him when he'd finally been able to check.

We need to talk

Shouldn't hurt this much. Had to be some way of stopping it.

'I fucked up about Etty,' he told Ant. 'She wasn't involved.' No need to go into the cheesy details right now. Or perhaps ever.

'Yeah, Locke convinced me to call her this morning. All good.'

That it could be so simple. A single conversation and your entire relationship set to rights. 'She's not angry?'

'Well, she did have a few choice words to say about my communication skills, but I blamed you, so that's OK. She fessed up about the fees, too. So I'm obviously in a state of intense embarrassment and gratitude. Pay you back out of my share of the house. Or the land, I guess.' His hands wavered. 'And, um, got to apologise for the other day. I was an arsehole. Complete bullshit, what I said.'

'Your poor kid, having you as a father. Poor Kat.'

'Usually is,' Caleb told him. 'The house – Etty told you about the explosion?'

'Yeah, but I'm choosing to process that later.'

A lot to process. Still didn't understand half of what had happened himself. No clue how the tattooed man or the Numbats player Robbo fitted into things. Maybe part of a much larger ring. The waste scheme would be a nice earner, but not huge. Not worth killing for. Then again, people had killed for far less.

Ant was stubbing out the cigarette butt. He studied it, then tucked it into the empty tobacco pouch, gave the packet a tap. 'Last one I'll ever smoke.' Contentment, not regret, in his face. 'Had a bet with Melissa I'd finish today.'

Shit, the nurse. Hadn't mentioned her to the cops. 'You talk to the cops about Melissa?'

'No, why?'

'She might've set the whole thing up. Connections at the hospital.'

'Nah, no worries there. Wasn't even on the island. Working for years in Tassie, moved back here for the job.'

An important detail it would've been good to know earlier. Pity he hadn't thought to ask.

The two homicide detectives were striding from the house. They cut towards the cop at the gate, Dick-first Chabon swinging his keys as he walked. Katsonis turned his flat stare towards Caleb and Ant as he passed, nodded.

Ant raised a hand.

'Mates now?' Caleb asked. Surely even Ant's charm hadn't warmed the detective. Hours in Katsonis's company, had only felt an aquatic chill.

'Besties. Said he'd tell me when Locke got back from his convention. They're off to talk to him.'

So Locke had been swanning around schmoozing while

275

Caleb and Ant had been fighting for their lives. Felt about right. Hopefully the detectives weren't relying on his statement to prosecute Arlo and the others. Hard to see Locke deviating from his silence-is-safest attitude. Why risk his reputation, possibly his career and clinic, by admitting he'd known who'd murdered his patient but had been too scared to say? Or too in their pockets.

Ant got to his feet, frowned down at Caleb. 'Email me tomorrow, yeah? Let me know you didn't die in your sleep.'

'Wait. You mean you're going with them? Staying at the clinic?'

'I've got two weeks to go.'

No. Seriously bad idea. Locke might not have been part of the whole mess, but he wasn't entirely innocent. From what Joyce had said, the doctor had known about the toxic waste since he'd bought the clinic, stopped Arlo burning it there. Had known a lot more than that.

Caleb struggled to his feet. 'You can't. Locke knew Arlo and Gideon were the killers. Suspected, at the very least. That last note, *I'm watching*, was them telling him not to get involved.'

'Yeah, maybe.' Looking at the driveway. The detectives had finished talking to the constable, were heading to the road. 'Better go.'

'Gideon shot you, for fuck's sake! Probably did it from the water tower. Locke was hurt that day. I'll bet anything he saw Gideon with the rifle, tried to stop him.'

Ant faced him, backlit by the spotlights, his untroubled expression clear. 'Yeah, none of that's good. Well, the bit about taking on an armed sniper's pretty impressive. But you can't blame the man for being scared.'

Could blame him for being a self-serving coward.

'What about his girlfriend killing herself? Leaving him all her money?'

'Asked him about that – well, stormed in demanding answers.

He told me about her. Did that calm talking thing he does, but kind of cracked, got teary. Said it was the biggest regret of his life not being able to help her. I felt like a right cunt. He set up the clinic in her memory.'

'And you believe him?'

'Yeah, I do.' Ant stood for a moment. 'Look, he's obviously flawed, but you have to trust me on this. I have to trust myself. Locke's helped me get some things straight. And I feel good, better than I have in a long time.' Sketching a wave, he set off towards the gate. He did look good: shoulders loose, head high.

'Ant.'

Wariness in his stance as he turned.

Caleb brushed an open hand from his opposite shoulder, as though sweeping away a leaf. Realised when he'd finished that Ant had probably never seen that sign before, wouldn't know what it meant.

A smile crept across Ant's face. 'Proud of you too. Catch you in a couple of weeks.' Still smiling, he headed for the road, the blazing headlights of the waiting car.

46.

A slow walk timed to reach the ferry just before it left. Its low outline was sketched in safety lights against the night sky, pitching back and forth as waves rocked the hull. Max was in the pilot's cabin, a new collection of family photos behind him. The ferryman with his smiling wife and kids at a picnic, a fencing match, an athletics day. Caleb averted his gaze. So he wouldn't have that; accept it and move on.

Max eyed him doubtfully as he accepted the fare. 'Sure you don't spew? Looken a bit rough there.'

'Yeah.' Had he eaten today? Probably should do something about that when he got home. Got to a motel.

He stood at the stubby prow as the ferry heaved its way through the water. Face numbed by salt spray, the shrilling in his ears growing louder. No other passengers.

Most of the islanders had been standing in the street when he'd passed, a couple of uniformed cops going door to door. Relief in people's faces, but they'd gathered in tight clusters, already reforming their barricades. Only Skye alone. Sitting on the veranda steps, long arms resting on her thighs. He'd moved swiftly past at her expressionless stare, found the caravan empty, his few belongings gone. Hadn't done the right thing by her. A clearer picture of her now: unhappy but unwilling to fight for the changes she wanted. Trying hard to ignore what Arlo was doing. But she'd obviously discovered something about the tattooed man; evading every question about him last night.

The cops had no idea how that murder or Robbo tied in, either. Caleb's suggestion there might be an alt-right group involved met with dubious looks. Too dangerous to leave a loose thread like that dangling. If they didn't follow it up, he'd need to have a chat with Robbo at the hospital.

Hospital. Actual thought making its way through the head smog. Medical waste was more than just cancer drugs and contaminated syringes – all that storm-brought rubbish the day they'd found the severed arm. Not just plastic but a yellow biohazard bag. Skye's strange answer last night when he'd asked who'd killed the tattooed man: *'No one.'*

He pulled out his phone, texted Mick.

—The footy player. Robbo. What surgery did he have?

Mick's reply came quickly.

—*this a Numbat thing? Thought the accident was OK?*

—Not Numbat. Police reconfirmed accident. What surgery?

—*Few things but the poor bastard had his left arm amputated*

Queasiness rolled through him like a wave. He lowered the phone. No second murder victim, no gang, just a racist footy player caught in a horror smash. Arlo must have lost a load in the storm, diesel and waste all washed overboard. The quarry owner's daughter had even commented on the late fuel delivery. What a dickhead; had the colour-coding on the barrels sorted but didn't know how to strap down a load on his ute.

Bright light up ahead. A spotlight. Shifting up and down as a boat skimmed the waves towards them. Not swinging wide but heading straight for the ferry. Fear twisted his guts – Gideon's boat had a front-mounted spot. Gideon, coming for him, seeking revenge.

No. That didn't make sense. A man like Gideon would've cut his losses, moved on. Small scheme like this, working with people like Arlo who couldn't even tie a hitch knot.

Oh Christ – the barrels. Had to be the lost cargo Max had mentioned on that rough trip over. Max. Aware of his every movement, the ferry docked during every shooting. The ferryman was the sniper, not Gideon. In the pilot's booth right now, watching as the tinnie drew closer, Gideon waving to get Caleb's attention.

As Caleb turned, Max strode from the cabin, black rifle in his hand. Raising it. Caleb was already moving for the side rail. Running. One foot on the bar, then over the edge.

Hard smack of cold. Swirling darkness. Kicking off his shoes, trying to swim up, sodden clothes weighting his limbs. At the surface, dragging in air. Heaving, inky water. Ferry gone, boat gone. Thought Gideon might have circled back to help. Broken man, trying to atone for his sins. Couldn't do it. Couldn't mend what you'd ruined, mend yourself, the people you loved.

A wave smacked his face. Coughing, trying to inhale. Charcoal cliff crashing down, pushing him under. Snatched a breath, water where air should have been. Weight crushing his head, chest, lungs. Couldn't see the surface. No up, no down, just black nothing. Sinking. Floating. Pain drifting away, the shriek slipping from his ears.

Calm down here.

no noise no pain

just

beautiful

silence

High above, a rippling light unrolled across the water, sweeping slowly back and forth as though searching for someone – Gideon coming to save him. Too late, too tired. Nothing waiting for him up there anyway: no Kat, no family, no home.

But soon. One small life very soon. Waiting for him. Needing him.

He kicked, swam up towards the surface.

47.

A nurse finally took pity and let him take his lunch to the community education centre. Promised to return later with his discharge papers. An overtly cheerful room like a primary school library, with orange chairs and colourful bunting, the mood somewhat dampened by large posters of diseased body parts. Not very conducive to eating, but journos had been popping into the ward like whack-a-moles all morning. No escaping them until Ant brought him clothes and money, his wallet, jeans, phones, hearing aids all ruined or somewhere on the ocean floor.

The media had been following him ever since Gideon hauled him onto the jetty last night, asking for sound bites while he'd lain shuddering on the boards, hypothermia rattling his bones. Bad timing, according to the homicide detectives this morning, the news crews all gathered to capture the aftermath of Max's arrest – Locke having finally summoned the courage to ID the ferryman as sniper.

Everyone in custody, everything over. Should be feeling relieved, but he just felt hollow. He'd borrowed a patient's phone last night to text Kat an all-clear, received an immediate 'Thank God. Where are you?' Hadn't answered yet, didn't know how to face her. He'd got it so wrong.

Ant finally strolled in a couple of hours later, carrying a plastic bag. Caught him dozing on the carpet. 'That hygienic?'

Probably not: the hospital gown didn't cover as much as it

should. He levered himself onto one of the orange chairs as he examined Ant's T-shirt. Three sizes too small, *I'm a Big Sister!* emblazoned across the front in silver glitter.

Had to ask. 'Why?'

Ant glanced down at the T-shirt, smoothed the shining letters. 'Only size the gift shop had.'

'You spewed?'

'Mate, everywhere. In Gideon's boat, too. First time I've seen him react to anything. The man can move. Decent bloke, though, had a good chat. Well, until I spewed on him. Got quiet after that.'

Decent bloke who may have been involved in a war crime, killed children. At minimum, hadn't reported his colleagues' actions. Plenty to regret in Caleb's own life, Ramsden and Joyce only the latest victims of his mistakes, but he'd never be complicit in something like that. A low bar to clear, but he'd fucking leap over it. Could be certain of that much, at least.

Ant dropped the plastic bag onto the chair beside Caleb. 'Nice new clothes for you. Etty's gone to get shoes and cash.' Still not questioning why Caleb had asked the nurse to ring him instead of Kat; some benefits to Ant having the boredom threshold of a toddler.

A new stage in their relationship, calling on Ant for help. Not as toe-curling as he'd imagined. Actually pretty good. Though with a few possible downsides. He eyed the bag of clothes, dug cautiously in it. Pulled out undies and a T-shirt, both plain black, the right size. Underestimated Ant, assumed he'd buy something stupid – which he had: a pair of fluoro green and yellow board shorts. Had to dress slowly, sit down after doing it. Nothing really wrong with him, just needed some rest.

Ant examined him. 'Excellent. There was a pair of trackies in your size, but I thought you'd prefer the boardies.'

'Fuck you very much.'

'Gotta look good for your media appearances. Speaking of which.' He pulled a rolled-up newspaper from his back pocket, flipped it onto Caleb's lap. 'You're front-page news in the local rag. Well, Max is. You get a mention in the last para – *local man Cameron Zelig suffered minor injuries in the gunman's attempted escape.*'

They'd done a rush job on the article. Most of the page taken up with a large photo of Max in handcuffs, his shaggy head lowered. His poor family would see that. Those sporty, smiling kids; the son he'd said was following in his footsteps, training for pentathlons. Not shot-put and javelin like Caleb had assumed, but modern pentathlons with shooting. Add it to the list of things he'd assumed about Max. That he was laid-back, not calculating, that the blank looks he'd given Caleb had been lack of recognition, not cold rage and hatred, fear.

'Ferry guy, hey,' Ant said. 'Didn't have a clue.'

'Me? No.' Well, plenty of clues, just no idea.

'I meant me. Everyone. Read the article. "Such a lovely man," say all the neighbours. "Not so much," says his ex-wife and two magistrates. Restraining orders and jail time, supervised contact only with the kids. Still trying to get custody of them, though.'

So a controlling man. Definitely should've seen that. All those photos of his kids, maybe not a sign of pride but possessiveness. Some insight into Max's overreaction to being blackmailed: more jail time would have lost him the rights to those possessions.

Ant had wandered over to study a gruesome anti-smoking poster of gangrenous toes. He examined Caleb's untouched lunch tray below it. 'Hey, can I eat that? Stomach's a bit empty.' Without waiting for an answer, he started in on a tub of green jelly. Signed between spoonfuls, 'Got a message for you from Lara.'

Lara. Barely given her a thought since she'd skewered him with that knife. 'Cops get her?' Wouldn't put it past her to ask him to be a character witness.

'Nah, long gone. Emailed to say she's off travelling. Wanted me to pass on her best regards, and that she hopes your arm isn't too sore. Signed it with a couple of kisses.'

'You're kidding?'

'Think the kisses are for me. Chicks love me.' He waved the spoon to someone behind Caleb.

Kat was coming through the door. Windswept and flushed, looking a little wary.

His throat constricted. He'd fucked up. Fucked up so badly.

'Hey, look,' Ant said, 'it's that gorgeous wife of yours who tells me that you've chucked a nutty and are avoiding her. What a coincidence she's here.' He went to greet Kat. A hug and a few murmured words, and he left, still clutching the jelly.

Caleb stood as Kat crossed to him. Paint-stained overalls, daubs of blue on her fingertips and tattooed feathers. She'd been back home for her clothes, working at the studio. The world righting itself slightly without him.

An uncertain gesture as she reached his side, her arms half-opened for an embrace. He let himself hold her. Draw in her salt honey scent, feel her warmth. Stood back. 'You OK?' he asked.

'I'll be a lot better once we've sorted this out. You and me, us, this is a work in progress. I know I freaked you out, but you didn't stick around to get the rest of it. We can make it work.' Her hands faltered as she added, 'If you want to?'

'Of course I do. But I don't know if we can.'

Relief lit her face. 'Why? Because you're doing some big macho thing, trying to save me? I don't get a say in it? I'm a grown-arse woman, about to be a mother. I love you, I even like you when you're not being so patronising. So let's work it out.' She settled on a chair, gazed at him until he sat beside her. 'Start by telling me what's happened. I know Constable Lloyd and that ferryman were arrested, but is it really all over?'

'Yes. Cops got Arlo and his offsiders too.'

'Which one's Arlo?'

'Runs the shop on the island.'

'Husband of the woman who likes good hair?'

He couldn't control the wince.

'Still scared she's going to come at you with the scissors?' Kat pulled back, smile fading as she searched his face. 'Something you need to tell me?'

Nothing but unbroken trust between them, even after all they'd been through. Kat would believe him if he said no. They could go on, build their future on a lie. But she deserved more than that. Their child deserved more.

'I don't know,' he said. 'Do you want to know?'

'What are we not quite talking about here? Got too flirty? Overstepped with the whole charm-the-truth-out-of-them technique?'

He shook his head.

'You *slept* with her?'

'We didn't quite – go through with it.'

She didn't move. Staring at him, her face stripped bare.

Even worse than he'd imagined.

'I'm about to have a baby, and you –' Tears flooded her eyes. She kept going, signing slowly, as though not quite sure she'd understood. 'I thought I knew you. All these years, I never once thought you'd deliberately hurt me.'

'No. Never.' He went to touch her arm, pulled back as she flinched.

Air gusted in as someone opened the door. The helpful nurse back with his discharge papers. Bright smile as she noticed Kat. She patted her own flat stomach, talking happily as she came towards them, clipboard in her hand.

Kat stood abruptly, moved past the chairs to the far end of the room. Stood facing a low bookshelf.

The nurse grimaced as she reached him. 'Bad news?'

No idea how to classify a disaster of his own making. Taking the clipboard from her, he rejected the offer of a cup of tea for Kat. Rejected it again. Managed to coax the nurse from the room.

Kat didn't move at his approach. Standing with her head bowed, shoulders heaving. Never hidden her tears from him before.

'I love you,' he said out loud. 'It wasn't about you. Or her. It was about me panicking and fucking up. But I realised as soon as we – I realised and stopped.'

She turned a tear-swollen face to him. Hands tight fists by her sides, she spoke out loud. 'You think whether or not your dick got wet is the betrayal? Was this happening the whole time you were on the island? Is that why you were so desperate to be there?'

'Jesus no. How could you think that?'

'Because I obviously don't know you at all.'

'No. Of course it wasn't. It was after we broke up.'

'No, after *you* broke up. Straight after you broke up. What was it, a couple of hours? You walk out on me when I'm terrified and pregnant. When I need you more than anything else in the world. And you go and fuck another –' Her face contorted. 'You wanted to destroy any chance of us being together, is that it? Good job – it worked.' She strode away from him. Across the room and out the door. No backwards glance as she disappeared around the corner.

Standing still, an afterimage of her in his eye. He'd done the worst he could, the best he could, just had to find a way of living with it.

But not now.

Slowly lowered himself to the floor. Back against the wall, bare feet outstretched, garish boardshorts clashing with the bruises on his legs. Ant would come and rescue him eventually. Just rest for a while, work out how to face the future tomorrow.

He closed his eyes.

EPILOGUE

He waited for a cool day to start on the swing set. Good to be outside, feel the sun on his skin, muscles working. The simple task of shovelling sand into a wheelbarrow satisfying. Too many hours spent sitting in the car or office. Might even get on to the front fence tomorrow, finally get rid of the wire panels that had been there since the demolishers left.

Last scoop done, he stuck the blade into the ground, waved to draw Mirii's eyes to him. Lying in the shade on a quilted rug; dark curls and eyes, edible cheeks. Six months old, been in his life forever.

'See,' he signed, 'the sand goes in the wheelbarrow, not your mouth.'

She gave him a wide gummy smile. The flare of joy still stunned him at times. A bright light to match her name – 'star' in Kamilaroi, one of the languages of her people. He got to have a few precious hours with her every day, the walk to Kat's timed to the second. And it was enough. Had to be.

He knelt beside her, rubbed her warm belly. Had to sign left-handed as she grabbed his right pinkie. 'If you eat all the sand you get a yucky tummy and the concrete won't work. Remember the ratio? One part cement, two sand, three aggregate.' He went through the sums again, holding up each finger. 'One, two, three. Because we want a sturdy swing set.'

Not just sturdy: indestructible. Metal frame with cross bracing, well anchored in the ground. It'd be the only solid structure on the block except for the sunroom and bathroom from the old house, the only parts salvageable. Home for now. Ant had helped make it habitable before leaving for his travels up north with Etty. Two weeks fitting beams and installing windows, a relaxed version of the work they'd done on the place as teenagers. Ant the most relaxed. Filled out and tanned, the threat of jail time long behind him.

Plans for the new place were done. A small house, perfect for a single man who would one day have his child stay over. Just hadn't quite been able to start it yet, the ghost image of an almost-life clouding his vision. Hard to move on from someone you saw every day. The raw hurt had left Kat's eyes, replaced by distance. Holding herself apart, every conversation via text or a polite handover on her parents' front step, her once open face closed and unreadable. Hopefully one day she'd forgive him enough to relax. He missed her friendship.

Movement by the wire fence. Mick was there, shaking his head as he tried to haul a panel out of place to squeeze through. Wearing sunglasses and a blue-and-black Numbat club T-shirt. The old guilt stirred. Footy season starting soon, the Numbats unlikely to be in it. The photos had stopped months ago, but there was no money to pay the club's debts or hire a coach.

Caleb wriggled his fingers at Mirii, then signed, 'Here comes Uncle Mick. You can tell him how Daddy won't let you eat the sand.'

She paddled her plump hands together, forefingers just meeting.

He stared, open mouthed. She'd signed 'Daddy'. Six months old and she understood him. His child was a genius. 'That's it! That's right! Daddy!' As Mick reached them, Caleb stood, asked out loud, 'Did you see that? She just signed "Daddy".' He turned back to Mirii, signed, 'Do it again. Daddy, Daddy, Daddy.'

Mirii kicked bare brown legs in excitement, arms pinned to her sides.

'She did.'

Mick lifted the sunglasses onto his stubbled scalp. 'Mate, I believe you, blackfellas are smart. How d'you reckon we've survived a coupla centuries' cultural cleansing.' He squinted around the freshly mown lawn, the holes dug for the swing set. 'Keepen yourself busy. Good man.'

Subtle reference to the day Kat had taken Mirii home from the hospital. The reality of it not being his home hitting hard; not quite able to hold it together when Mick had stopped by. Doing a lot better now, though. Long hours without the tinnitus, sometimes days. Might be running a bit much, hitting the whisky a bit hard, but he'd ease off as soon as he started sleeping again. And business was booming, the area showing an unexpected need for fraud investigators keen on driving long distances. Due in part to Tedesco handing out referrals like sweets, the detective almost weirdly relaxed in his newly wedded state.

Caleb had even managed to take Mirii to Alberto's a couple of times. Sign name instantly bestowed on her by the doting cook and gathered customers: twinkling finger flicks in the air to match her spoken name.

'Got some news to buoy ya sprits,' Mick said. 'Numbats are saved. Injection of cash from the council. Money for a new coach and stadium, whole new sporting precinct. Doesn't hurt to have a councillor on side, hey?'

The town was almost as broke as the club – how were they funding all that? Even with Greg the mechanic on the council, it was an impossible feat.

'How?'

'Selling the oval, moving out to cheaper land.'

Jarrah. He fucking knew it. Full-time nice bloke, part-time real estate agent. Ruined the club so he could pocket the commission.

'Jarrah handling the sale?'

'Nah, some Melbourne lot, big firm.'

Who then? How?

Mick lowered his sunglasses. 'Trainin' starts next week. See ya there.'

'To do what?'

'Wing, I reckon. You're pretty fast. Rover if you feel like havin' a biff.'

Join the Numbats? Caleb shook his head. 'Not really a team player.'

'Fit right in, then. Sundees at ten out at River Views. You can christen the new oval.' Mick waved to Mirii. Headed down the path.

River Views, the cheap housing development Jarrah had encouraged him to look at. Pity he hadn't; prices would have skyrocketed with news of the sporting complex. You'd make a fortune if you'd bought a lot of land out there when prices were low. Particularly if you had a persuasive vote on the council and access to inside knowledge about the Numbats. Greg the mechanic, finger in every pie and pastry down his front, set to make a killing on the real estate market. Might just have to let the footy club and council know about that.

'Let's go for a walk,' he told Mirii. 'Have a chat to some nice people about a naughty man.' He scooped her warm body against him, turned for the street.

Kat. Standing outside the fence.

His heart slipped. The first time she'd come here since that day they'd sat together in the rubble. First time since their break-up he'd seen her without people around and schedules to discuss. No pram or sling for Mirii, no bag of forgotten baby food. Just

Kat. Not the grinning seventeen-year-old he'd once known; much more. Standing motionless in a sleeveless red sundress, loose curls stirring around her face. Expression readable, even from a distance – wanting to talk.

No, he wasn't going to let himself hope. Just talk.

He swung Mirii higher, went to meet her.

ACKNOWLEDGEMENTS

I'm deeply grateful to everyone who helped along the way.

Medina Sumovic for her continued insight into Deaf culture, and Auslan. And for not laughing too hard at my first attempt at Ant's sign name.

My moodji, Gunditjmara elder, Jim Berg. For guidance with all things Koori(e) and, far more than that, for you and Sarah being such a special part of my life and family all these years.

To pedantic ghoul Kate Goldsworthy, whose editorial insight is second to none and almost makes me want to write another book. The Echo Publishing team, with special thanks to Tegan Morrison for her support and wise words, and Sandy Cull for her gorgeous cover design. Janette Currie who helped get me started, Sophie Viskich who spurred me on and Deviani Segal for the best-catered writer's retreat in history. I owe reformed barrister Jock Serong many chicken parmas for sharing his legal knowledge. Big thanks to Maria Katsonis and Lara Sullivan for their generous support of the Authors For Fireys auction. I'm truly appreciative of a grant from the Australia Council, which allowed me much-needed time to write.

Heartfelt thanks and grovelling apologies to Meg and Leni for having to endure me writing a book through one of the world's longest, strictest lockdowns. And last, but never least, to Campbell; for everything, always.

MORE FROM
PUSHKIN VERTIGO

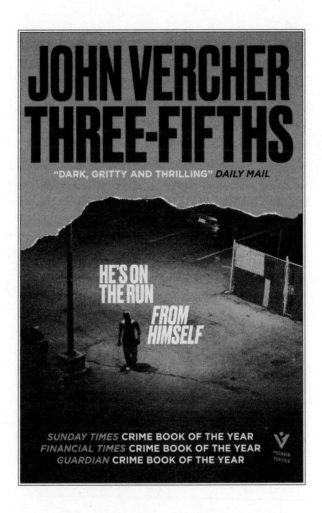

JOHN VERCHER
THREE-FIFTHS

"DARK, GRITTY AND THRILLING" *DAILY MAIL*

HE'S ON
THE RUN
FROM
HIMSELF

SUNDAY TIMES **CRIME BOOK OF THE YEAR**
FINANCIAL TIMES **CRIME BOOK OF THE YEAR**
GUARDIAN **CRIME BOOK OF THE YEAR**

PUSHKIN
VERTIGO

Set against the backdrop of the simmering
racial tension produced by the LA Riots and
the O.J. Simpson trial, comes this powerful
hardboiled noir of violence and obsession

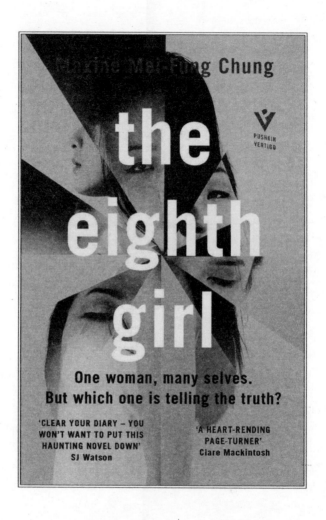

The literary suspense story of the mind
where nothing is as it seems